As she paid her fare again and crossed to the returning ferry, the boat whistle sounded. It tore through Frenchy's heart like the memory of Mercedes. She'd wrecked things all right. Driven Mercedes from her with her game of hearts . . .

And what if she stopped playing? A wave from a passing boat threw spray into Frenchy's face. Chilly and wet, she moved again to the front of the boat. As the boat neared it, the City grew bigger and bigger.

She stood at the bow, looking at the City with determination, her legs wide apart, her hands in fists at her sides. She felt as if she were going home, only not home to the Bronx. Home to a world of her own. Pam lived there: Pam and the Frenchy she was uncovering. Jessie and Mary lived there too. And Mercedes lived there. All of them, thought Frenchy, were doing okay out there on their own. When the ferry bumped the padded dock, Frenchy swayed, but didn't lose her balance. Humming a bossa nova, she went into the City again.

The Swashbuckler

a novel by **Lee Lynch**

The Naiad Press Inc.
1988

Printed in the United States of America
First Edition
Second Printing–June 1988
Cover design by Tee A. Corinne
Typeset by Sandi Stancil

Library of Congress Cataloging in Publication Data

Lynch, Lee, 1945–
   The Swashbuckler.

   I. Title.
PS3562.Y426S9 1985   813'.54   84-29611
ISBN 0-930044-66-5

DEDICATION

For every dyke who's stared down a straight;
for every dyke who's dared dress in drag;
for every dyke who's been proudly femme or proudly butch;
for every one of us who's survived the insults, the daily fears
    and humiliations, the beatings;
for every dyke who's dared to live her life

— and for every dyke who didn't survive —

I offer this book as tribute.

ACKNOWLEDGEMENTS

This book was inspired by the writing of Joan Nestle. Chapter One was written in response to her "Esther's Story" which appeared in *Common Lives/Lesbian Lives*, Number One, Fall, 1981. Chapter Two grew out of a weekend Deb Pascale and I spent talking lesbian literature in Provincetown with Carol Seajay, writer and editor of the *Feminist Bookstore Newsletter*. Chapter Ten was written for Tee Corinne, whose pioneering and courageous erotic art and writing have been as crucial to my development as they have been to all lesbian culture (*Yantras of Womanlove*, Naiad Press, 1982, et.al.).

The Swashbuckler could not have been written at all without Deb Pascale by my side these last thirteen years. I also thank for their encouragement and technical help: Katherine Forrest, Caroline Overman, Carol Feiden, Judy Sloan. And, for braving those very early years with me: Susan Kenler.

Chapter One originally appeared in *Sinister Wisdom*, No. 24, Fall, 1983 as "The Swashbuckler."

Chapter 1

The Swashbuckler
1960

Frenchy, jaw thrust forward, legs pumping to the beat of the rock and roll song in her head, shoulders dipping left and right with every step, emerged from the subway at 14th Street and disappeared into a cigar store. Moments later, flicking a speck of nothing from the shoulder of her black denim jacket, then rolling its collar up behind her neck, she set out through the blueness and bustle of a New York Saturday night.

She stripped the cellophane from her pack of Marlboros, hit the base of the pack against her fist and drew a cigarette out with her lips. Though the summer breeze was light, she stopped in a doorway, tapped the cigarette against her fist and used her Zippo. She lengthened the stride of her short, exaggeratedly bowed legs and found her rhythm again, diddy-bopping downtown.

Silently singing Brenda Lee's *I'm Sorry*, she eyed the people around her on the street as she settled more into her walk. She knew she angered straight people, provoking merciless taunts and threats, but it was her own natural walk. She would walk as she wanted on Saturday nights.

The hell with them all, she thought, straightening proudly, dragging deep on her cigarette. Yeah, she walked like a man, or better still, she walked like a butch, lighter and more graceful than a man. All 4'11" of her was in the tough, bouncing walk. It said who she was. When guys on the street menaced her, she just got cooler, throwing herself into it more, dipping and weaving and dancing down the street. Yeah, she was a bulldyke, and every Saturday night she loved being a bulldyke in a bulldyke's world.

A breeze ruffled her pompadour and she smoothed it back, walking down a line of stores lit from within as if by magic lamps, their goods gleaming. At one window she stopped to pull a long black comb from her rear pocket. When she was satisfied her jet black hair had slid neatly back into a d.a. she began walking further into Greenwich Village, surveying her turf, easing her way into the gay world. She sang a few lines from *Will You Still Love Me Tomorrow*, feeling good. She was twenty-one, good-looking, and wearing her best clothes: black denim jeans with the jacket, light blue button-down shirt, sharply pointed, black ankle-high boots. She felt the edge of her garrison belt buckle. Those knife-carrying butches were dumb, she thought. Even if it really was a femme weapon, her belt was nearly as sharp, and she couldn't be arrested in a raid for concealment. So far she had not had to use it, but she was ready if any of those old deisel dykes crossed her, tried to take a woman from her.

Frenchy entered the last block before Campy Corner, the drugstore where everyone hung out until nightfall came and darkness, or the cops, pushed them into the bars. Would she stay at the Corner tonight or visit a few places before she went to the Sea Colony Bar several blocks away? The grand excitement of Saturday night swept over her, tinged with the fear which accompanies a secret life. She slowed to savor it. Here in her own world she was handsome and funny. Women liked her, wanted to dance with her, wanted to make out with her. The other butches, those not too busy protecting their femmes, joked with her, talked baseball with her. It made six days of standing behind a checkout counter melt away. Her straight clothes, her meekness before the boss and shyness with the other girls — all were bearable because down here she was a prince, a sharp dancer, a big tipper.

She saw the Women's House of Detention on the corner of 5th and Greenwich. This was her landmark, and she felt as if she was at home. Inmates called from windows to their lovers on the street. The flower shop across 6th blazed with color which spilled onto the sidewalk. She filled her small chest with air smelling sweet from the perfumes of a thousand passing femmes. An orchestra of rock and roll musicians played in her head.

A few early fags stood against the drugstore window. They weren't hustlers; she'd seen them before in the bars. They just wanted to find boyfriends for the night to take them drinking and dancing, then home. Wallflowers, she thought. The only place I've ever seen guys be the wallflowers.

A butch and her femme came out of the drugstore and Frenchy nodded to the butch, avoiding the femme's eyes. They had seen each other a few times, Frenchy and the femme, and the femme wouldn't want to let on to her new girlfriend. Frenchy tried to remember her name. "Hey, Frenchy," she heard a bass voice call from the curb.

"Hey, Jessie, how you doing?"

"Okay. I'm doing okay."

"Where's Pat?"

Jessie shook her head. The big soft face seemed to sag with sadness. "We broke up, Frenchy. She found somebody else."

"Hell, Jess. And you were together a long time."

"We were going to go for Chinese dinner on our six month anniversary," Jessie said, her hands in her chino pockets. A light summer jacket was open over an unironed plaid men's sport shirt; her roughly cut brown hair was combed wetly back from her forehead in a wave. "I swear I thought this was it. I thought we had it made, me and Pat would last forever. But," she sighed, "I guess it's like that song, *It's All in the Game.*"

"Yeah, love is some game," Frenchy agreed. "I'm sorry it had to happen, Jess, but lookit, you and me can have a good time tonight, how about it? Want to go to the bars with me?"

"Sure. I was hoping I'd see you around. You're not meeting no one?"

"Maybe. It's hard to tell. I said I'd be down here, but I don't know if Donna's going to cooperate, you know what I mean? We haven't been getting along any too good."

"You ready to split up with this one too, Romeo?"

"I really love her a lot, Jess. I don't know. She wants to get a place together. Or stay at a hotel Saturday nights. You know I don't go for that."

"Still don't want to settle down? Boy, if I could just find a girl who would." Jessie sighed again, watching a group of women round the corner.

"I'd get itchy feet. No, I don't want that. And you know I'd like to spend the night with her, but I can't get away with it. If I gave in once she'd be expecting it every week."

"I know. You're not made like that. Better to keep it light."

Frenchy smiled, a large winning smile, and leaned back against the plate glass window, hooking her thumbs into her belt. She mused, "That's how I like it, Jess, light. A new girl every few weeks would suit me fine."

Jessie poked at her with her elbow, chuckling and nodding. "That's you, Frenchy."

"Where do you want to go tonight?" Frenchy asked.

"It's kind of early. How about PamPam's?"

"Yeah, I could use some coffee. I worked all day." They started walking across 6th Avenue.

"You still up at the A&P in the Bronx?"

"Sure thing," Frenchy said as she stopped outside the Women's House of Detention to run the comb through her hair again. "How about you? Still typing for that insurance company?"

"Yeah." Jessie made a face as she borrowed Frenchy's comb to prop up her wave and flatten the hair cut straight across her thick neck. "Still sitting all day typing forms. Wish I could get a job loading trucks or something. Alls I do is listen to the girls gossip. Talk about getting itchy, I can't take it much longer."

"I know what you mean. The other cashiers never shut up. There's a cute new girl, though, Marian. A little blonde. Wears these tight black sweaters. Winks at me," Frenchy confessed to Jessie. "Wish I could make her." She grinned lasciviously.

Jessie stretched her arm across Frenchy's shoulders. "Listen, if I didn't know you're called Frenchy from that long French names of yours, I'd say it fits you anyways.

You never think of nothing else, you know that?"

Frenchy's smile was smug as they entered PamPam's and looked for a booth. She stopped and narrowed her eyes as she looked around, half-posing, half-looking at the women scattered among the gay men. They found seats at the counter. "Sometimes I want to break my own rule."

"About mixing work and fun?"

"Yeah. She's really something else. Something special. I dream about her all day." She broke into a smile again.

"And you count money like that? With your head in the clouds?" The door opened and they looked stealthily in the mirror at the women who entered. "Nobody," whispered Jessie.

"Yeah, I've got to make the right change so's I can teach the little blonde. The boss gives her to me to teach because I'm the best he's got," Frenchy boasted. "And believe me, she needs all the help she can get." She laughed, pointing to her head. "She may be cute, but she's got confetti for brains."

"If she's that dumb, maybe she thinks you're a guy."

"Not the way I dress at work."

"So ask her out already. Since when are you shy?"

"I don't want to lose my job. And I don't want to fool with girls in my own neighborhood. You know that. But I sure am in love," Frenchy sighed, glancing at herself in the tarnished mirror behind the counter and pressing her pompadour higher. Suddenly she stopped, hand in the air. Her expression changed to an almost sultry look that narrowed one dark eye and lifted one side of her upper lip off her teeth. She made a clicking sound in the corner of her cheek and nudged Jessie. "Donna's here. And look at what she brought you."

Jessie looked into the mirror as Frenchy's current girlfriend walked in with another woman. They could have been twins — both with teased hair piled high on their heads, tight black pants, tiny white pointed sneakers. Donna wore a chartreuse angora sweater with a high neck, her friend a lavender cardigan buttoned low. "What a body," Jessie said admiringly to Frenchy as they swung their stools in unison and stepped off.

Donna quickly kissed Frenchy on the cheek, one eye on the man behind the counter who was ever vigilant of affection between queers in his place. Frenchy asked, "How you doing, chickie? Who's your friend?"

"What do *you* want to know for?" teased Donna, unsmiling, snapping her gum at Frenchy. "This here's Marie, my cousin. The one I was telling you about?"

"Yeah, from the Island, right, Marie?" Frenchy bowed slightly to her and winked.

Marie was at least 5'7" and looked down at Frenchy and Donna. "You didn't tell me how cute she was, Donny."

Donna laughed, finally. "I didn't want you to know. This one's mine," she said, sliding her arm possessively under Frenchy's.

"Okay, girls, that's enough," the counterman said. "Order or have your meeting outside, understand?"

"Sure, Charley," Frenchy sneered. "Anything you say." She shrugged to her friends. "Let's get out of here and go someplace nicer, huh, Marie?"

Marie dropped her eyelids half-shut and began to snap her fingers and sway. "Where's the dancing? I just turned twenty-one, you know."

"That's why I never brought her down here before, Frenchy. She was too young. And too scared to fake it."

"Well, I'm glad you finally got to twenty-one," Jessie interjected, butting with her blunt body into the closed group the three had made, an embarrassed smile on her face. "I've been waiting for you all my life."

"Oh, hey, Jess. Marie, this is my best friend, Jessie."

"Pleased to meet you," Marie said, then giggled.

"I'm really glad to meet you too, Marie," Jessie said with a glance at the open cardigan. She stepped back and took our her Marlboros. She offered them to Marie, then to Donna and Frenchy. Each took one, and they went outside.

On 6th Avenue Frenchy turned to light Marie's cigarette, but Jessie already had, so she lit Donna's and her own. Their eyes met and Donna cupped her hand around Frenchy's to shield the flame. She was just slightly taller than Frenchy and leaned very close to her. "Going to take me dancing, lover?"

A thrill went up Frenchy's arm from the touch and she inhaled the scent of Jean Naté. She stood there smiling a moment before she answered, savoring the girl and the people thronging around them, gay couples and tourists mixed. "Sure thing, babydoll," Frenchy answered, still touching Donna's hand and holding the unlit Zippo.

"You sure are looking handsome."

Frenchy allowed a smug expression to cross her face. "So are you, angel baby. Real pretty. I like that sweater," she said, touching it lightly on Donna's breast.

"Hey," Donna objected, pulling back. "You want us to get arrested?"

"I wouldn't mind a night locked up with you, beautiful," Frenchy smirked.

"In there, bigshot?" Donna asked, pointing over her shoulder with her thumb at the Woman's House of Detention. Its windows were empty now and the building looked heavy, looming over the intersection where they stood. "The house of D isn't my idea of a good time. How about it tonight, though? You got a place we can go?"

Frenchy smoothly took a drag on her cigarette. "No, I couldn't come up with any place."

"Did you try?" Donna asked sarcastically.

"Sure I did, babe."

"Well, *I did*," Donna said proudly, patting her hair back where the warm city breeze had pushed it. She raised her penciled eyebrows. "What do you say, lover?"

"Where is it?" Frenchy asked, coughing on her smoke, her poise shaken.

"Marie's got a friend with an apartment in the city. He's out of town. All we've got to do is make sure Marie's got a date. And it looks like you made sure of that when you brought Jess along."

Frenchy silently cursed Jessie for breaking up with her girl. "Donna," she began, leading the way along the sidewalk toward the bar, glancing back to make sure Jessie and Marie were following. "Donna, I can't tonight."

"How many times are you going to give me that?" Donna whispered angrily. "I finally got us a place, something you say you can't do. It doesn't cost any money. It's private and away from our neighborhoods and you're telling me you *can't*?"

"Donna, honey, you know I love you," Frenchy said, tossing away her cigarette and placing a hand on Donna's arm. "I just didn't know. How could I know you'd have a place tonight?"

"Sometimes I'd swear you've got another girl, Frenchy. I don't know why the hell I bother with you."

"I don't, Donna, you got to believe me." Frenchy's brow was creased and her eyes had the look of a trapped animal. "Come on, girl, you can believe me," she said, shaking Donna's arm.

"Stop it, Frenchy, don't make a scene. I brought Marie down here for a good time. She's never been with girls before. Except me, when we were kids."

"You two? That's a laugh. You're both femme!"

"Hey, we were only kids. It was a few years ago. We were experimenting. We both liked it, but we were scared to talk about it till a few months ago. Then when I told her

I'm gay she wanted to do it again. I told her how I'm femme and all. Besides, we're cousins. It wouldn't be right for us to do it together now we're older."

"No," Frenchy agreed thoughtfully, "it wouldn't be." She glanced around at Marie who smiled brilliantly toward her. Frenchy turned back and hitched up her jeans again, bowing her legs more and swaggering.

"You have your eye on her?" Donna asked suspiciously.

"No, angel. What are you so jumpy about? I'm just making sure Jess is showing her a good time." Frenchy was thinking about how sexy Donna's tall cousin was. She really ought to bring her out herself, not Jessie. There was something clumsy about Jessie. What did the femmes see in her? She was a great pal, but still, if it was the girl's first time out with a butch, someone more skilled ought to do it. Donna's fooling around with Marie didn't count, they hadn't known what they were doing. She needed an expert, somebody with a lot of experience. Somebody talented — like Frenchy. One of her girls had told her that. What was Donna complaining about, she wondered. She gave her a good time even if they couldn't stay together all night. She'd probably be ugly in the morning anyway, she thought, remembering her mother making breakfast all those years, her hair still in pincurls, no pencil on her eyebrows yet, her shapeless nightgown hanging sloppily on her body. No, she preferred her girls all spiffed up on a Saturday night, looking their best. She remembered to put more spring in her diddy-bop. Marie might be watching her.

"Hey, you coming in?" Donna asked, stopping.

"Sure, I was thinking."

"I thought I heard wood burning," Jessie quipped as she halted next to Donna and Frenchy.

Marie laughed and looked excitely at the door to the bar. "I've never been in a gay bar before."

"Don't worry, beautiful, we'll protect you, right, Jess?"

"I'll protect you from Frenchy, is more like it, ain't it, Donna?"

"Hey, I thought you were my friend." Frenchy playfully punched Jessie, and held the door for Donna.

She and Jessie paid the bouncer and the group walked the length of the bar. Frenchy half-wished she were sitting at the bar cruising all the women who went by. If she wasn't with Donna and wasn't Jessie's friend, she wouldn't have to keep her hands off Marie. I'm falling in love, she thought, then smiled over at Donna as they reached the back room.

They sat at the last empty table. Frenchy looked around the small room. She waved at a few women and nodded distrustfully to the man who sat with his arm around his bleached blonde girl friend. Potbellied and middle-aged, he was one of the owner's friends. Every week some man like him sat surveying the dykes. It made Frenchy mad. She could imagine what the men thought. More than once she'd been approached to accompany a straight couple home. The men acted like they had a right to be there, in her bar, just like out on the street they thought they had the right to humiliate her. "Pervert," she hissed low, wishing she didn't even have to dance in front of this week's grinning man.

"Okay, girls," the waitress said. "What'll it be? How you doing, Frenchy? Still got the shackles on Donna, huh? Let me know when you're free, Donna." She winked.

"You live around here?" Donna asked the waitress. Frenchy turned to stare at her.

"Over on the East side, hon. Got my own place. You come up any time at all." She turned to Frenchy. "Just kidding, lover. I wouldn't touch her."

Frenchy eyed the waitress' slicked back hair and the white turtleneck she wore under her black shirt. She was competition, Frenchy decided. "Give me a seven and seven," she ordered sullenly, throwing a five-dollar bill on the table.

"Jealous?" Donna asked.

"Let's dance," Frenchy said roughly, pulling Donna from the booth with her. Little Anthony and the Imperials sang *Tears on My Pillow*. She walked bowlegged onto the floor, holding Donna's hand and scowling at the waitress' back. She told Donna harshly, "I don't want you fooling around like that."

"Why not? It's a free country."

"Yeah, but you're my girl."

"Not hardly." Donna yanked herself away from Frenchy.

Frenchy pulled her back. "Keep your voice down." She looked around and deliberately took her jacket off, still moving to the music. She leaned off the dance floor to lay it neatly on the back of her chair, then returned to Donna and looked into her eyes. "You don't want to be my woman any more?" She neatly rolled her blue sleeves up toward the elbows and took Donna into her arms once more. "Don't you remember the good times we've been having?" She knew she sounded half-hearted, her uncertainty about wanting Donna in her voice. But if Donna was going to give her a hard time, better to get out now.

Another woman caught her eye. Her long blonde hair was in a flip and she was wearing a straight light green skirt and a silky white blouse, the collar wide open and flat against her throat. Such pretty blue eyes, Frenchy thought as she brought herself back to Donna.

"I want someone who'll hold me all night, Frenchy. Don't you understand that I want a girl who'll take me home?"

"You want a woman who'll *keep* you home. You want a husband," Frenchy accused.

Donna's dark eyes flashed anger and she pulled away. Frenchy grabbed at her arm, looking around to see if anyone had noticed. The other couples were either pressed against one another, dancing, sweatily erotic in the dim smoky light, or stared unseeingly at the dancers from their crowded tiny tables. "And what's wrong with wanting that?" Donna asked loudly. "I'm twenty-three. I want to settle down. I thought..." Her voice broke and she chewed her gum for a moment as she let Frenchy lead her into the dance again. *Tears on My Pillow*, Little Anthony sang. She raised her head and looked wistfully at Frenchy. "I thought you might want to settle down too. I mean, you have a steady job, but no place of your own. I thought maybe we could get together."

"I ain't the marrying kind," Frenchy said, remembering the dream she'd once had of having a woman to come home to.

She'd never quite figured out how to do it, how to hide her gayness and live with a lover; how to be a butch and look the way she needed to when she was with her femme, yet pass for straight otherwise. How to figure out the dozens of other details about a split life.

"No." She shook her head. "You were wrong. I'll never settle down. I like the gay life, the bars. I like having a good time."

"I'm tired of it!" Donna pushed Frenchy aside. She struggled through the crowd to her seat. Whispering something to Marie, she picked up her purse and walked around the dancing couples and out of the back room.

Frenchy watched her, sadness welling up. She was going to miss Donna, she thought as she finished rolling up her sleeves. She shrugged when she reached the table. "Easy come, easy go." She picked up her drink and swallowed it in three gulps, grinning down at Marie.

"You drink *fast*," Marie said, impressed. "Doesn't that get you drunk?"

"I can hold my liquor," Frenchy bragged, slipping her hands into her pockets, feeling the hot alcohol press down on her sadness. She shrugged again. "How are you two doing? You look like you're getting along like a house on fire."

Jessie blushed to the roots of her wave. Then she smiled toward Marie. "Want to dance?" Marie grinned across at her and gave her hand to Jessie. Frenchy could see their excitement about each other. "What happened to Donna?" Jessie asked Frenchy.

"It's over."

Jessie looked sad. "Tough break."

"Love 'em and leave 'em," Frenchy said, standing. "You two have a good dance. I'm going to see who's here."

"She always bounces back fast," Jessie explained to Marie.

Frenchy moved from table to table, greeting almost half the women in the back room. By the time Jessie and Marie had danced their third slow dance, to *Exodus*, bumping and grinding as close as the bar owners would allow, Frenchy was dancing too — with the blue-eyed woman. She held the woman loosely and they talked as they danced. Afterward they pushed their way to the table. "This is Edie," Frenchy said to Jessie and Marie.

"Hiya, Edie." Jessie smiled, shaking her head in wonder at Frenchy.

Soon after that the two couples separated for the night. Edie and Frenchy walked hand in hand along Greenwich Avenue past the male hustlers leaning against buildings.

"I better be getting home pretty soon," Frenchy sighed. The Village was difficult to leave. Even in darkness it seemed to glow, to light up the sky out of sheer Saturday night energy. The streets were still crowded, but now with young straight couples nervously visiting the bohemian coffee houses in their shiny shoes and pastel dresses. Beatniks shuffled beside their guitar cases to join other folk singers in their many gathering places. A few bars flashed neon signs, restaurants were still full.

They walked all the way to the East side to catch Edie's subway. Washington Square was quiet as they passed, though in one corner a classical guitarist played for some straight lovers. From Fifth Avenue on, New York University seemed to dominate the streets, silent and empty of its students. The streets narrowed, and warehouses began to appear.

"It seems awfully early to go home," Edie said as her station came into view.

"By the time I take you home and go back to the Bronx it'll be a lot later."

Edie's face brightened. "You're going to take me home?"

"At least as far as the subway goes. You think I'd let a beautiful woman like you walk the streets of the City alone at this time of night?"

"That's sweet of you. Somehow I imagined if I could ever meet a woman my first try tonight we'd go back to her place or I'd go home alone. I never thought of being escorted home."

"Queers are just like anybody else, baby. Got respect for a woman, treat them politely. Why," Frenchy drew herself up to her full height, "it wouldn't be gentlemanly of me to let you go all the way out to Queens alone." She was proud of the way she had skirted the issue of spending the night with Edie. "Just like I'd never ask a girl to — you know — go against her principles the first night."

"You're adorable." Edie laughed affectionately as they descended the subway stairs. "I just never imagined myself with someone like you," she said when Frenchy insisted on putting a token of her own in the turnstyle.

They walked past the blue and white tiling which lined the walls of the small station. "And I never imagined I'd have such a good time with a college girl. Or that a college girl would be interested in me," Frenchy said modestly.

"Why wouldn't I be interested? You're cute. And interesting. And sexy."

Frenchy leaned against a dark green iron column. "You think so?"

"I never dated a *boy* as good-looking as you. They don't go for my type: too studious."

Frenchy saw her reflection over Edie's shoulder in a mirror on a gum machine. She smiled and took Edie's hand. "I'm just glad I got to you on your first night downtown before someone else did. Were you nervous, coming down to the bars by yourself?"

Edie flushed. "I was," she said, her blue eyes seeming to search Frenchy's for sympathy and comfort. "But you rescued me," she said, laughing.

"How'd you know where to go?" Frenchy asked, moving slightly closer to her.

Edie stepped back a bit, as if afraid. Her warm laugh had turned to a nervous giggle. "My aunt is gay. She lives in the Midwest, but I wrote her a letter hoping she would know where I could go to see if I was gay. She said there used to be a place — The Sea Colony — and told me how to find it. She wished me luck." Her eyes twinkled with confidence again. "I guess her wish came true."

Frenchy had leaned closer, and Edie's eyes glittered. She seemed to have lost her breath while she spoke. Frenchy leaned up and kissed her, a fugitive kiss taken in fear that someone would come through the turnstile, but Edie relaxed into Frenchy's arms as if in relief. When they leaned back to look at one another Frenchy could tell Edie had found her answer. Edie grabbed her and returned the kiss, knocking Frenchy slightly off balance. "Hold it, hold it," Frenchy said gently, gaining control. "Somebody might come," she whispered against Edie's lips. She was a little taken aback by Edie's aggressiveness.

Edie didn't seem to care who came. "I've waited for a long time to be here, to be doing this," she said, tossing her hair back and straightening the white cardigan. "Isn't there somewhere we can go?"

Frenchy joyously sang more of *Will You Still Love Me Tomorrow* in her head. She looked toward the women's bathroom. Edie had too much class, she thought, to want to make out in a bathroom. But Edie had seen where she was looking and tugged at her until Frenchy led her inside. The floor was littered and the tiny room smelled strongly of disinfectant. They leaned against a grafitti-covered stall, kissing each other lightly, then more and more hungrily until Frenchy began to pass her hands across Edie's body and over her breasts, creating sparks on her silky blouse. Their breathing was so loud in the silence of the white tiled room that they barely heard their train in time to catch it. In an empty car they leaned on each other breathlessly, laughing and straightening their clothes. "You're pretty wonderful," Frenchy said, squeezing Edie's hand one last time as they pulled into 23rd Street and other passengers filed sleepily on.

They changed trains at Grand Central, staring into one another's eyes as they waited under the stairs, out of sight of the platform. Frenchy was glad she had broken up with Donna. The excitement had pretty much left that relationship, and she had almost forgotten how exhilarating it was to start a new affair. Especially when she was bringing someone out. Her heart pounded until it seemed as if her whole body must pulsate with it. Her hands were like ice, she shook inside. She was as excited as a kid going to a party, at moments so excited that a cold sweat broke out all over her body and she was almost overcome by a wave of nausea. This was living. This was the gay life. This was what made it all so worthwhile. It was a high better than any liquor could bring. The woman she was with became a thousand movie stars rolled into one — the most beautiful woman in the world. The subway became the most romantic of places, its trains rushing to exotic parts of the city, its passengers mysterious in their Saturday night finery, its promise of new destinations and new women. The Village truly was lined with magic lamps to lead her to all this.

Frenchy's life had become adventurous once more. She was swashbuckling. She stood tall in her black pointed boots and gazed romantically at Edie and felt herself melt in Edie's adoring, desiring gaze. When the train came they huddled on a double seat at the end of a car and Frenchy grinned at everybody who stared at them. She wasn't afraid of anything. She remembered once riding out to the end of the Flushing line with another woman and stopping at Willets Point; it had been big — and empty. She pulled Edie off the train there and led her to a high-backed wooden bench with seats on both sides. They went around to the side that faced the express tracks, empty this time of night.

"I love you, Edie," Frenchy breathed as they sat. "I don't want to leave you yet."

"Let's just sit here awhile."

Frenchy kissed Edie's hair and held her close. She could feel a wave of warmth rise through her body and began again to tremble. "Are you cold?" Edie asked.

"No," Frenchy answered in her deepest, huskiest voice. "I just want you so bad."

Reckless of being in the open, they began to kiss again. The summer air seemed to sit around them still as a wall and they could see stars, the moon over the track. The pillars and roof of the station hovered protectively over them and the wooden bench curved around them like an old grey hand.

Frenchy made love to Edie as if they were sitting on a living room couch, except that she went under her clothing instead of removing it. She was protective against possible discomforts for Edie to the point of painful discomfort for herself. When she touched Edie's breast she knew they would finish right there on the subway platform, college girl or no college girl. "Edie, Edie," Frenchy sighed as she spread her little hand across the flesh inside Edie's thigh.

"Frenchy," Edie said wondrously, digging her fingers into her shoulders. "I don't know why it took me so long to do this," she whispered.

"To come out?"

"Is that what you call it?" Edie asked between kisses.

"Yeah," Frenchy said, "and this is how you do it." Her hand reached under Edie's nylon panties. They were bikinis and she imagined them, black and sexy against the white of Edie's skin. Then she felt the matted pubic hairs, parted them with her fingertips, kneaded the soft flesh beneath and slipped to the cavity of the panties' crotch. She felt Edie's wetness where it had soaked through the nylon against her knuckles. She felt her own vagina tighten and loosen involuntarily and reached for Edie's softer parts as if to find release for herself.

"Ohh," Edie moaned, twisting against Frenchy's slowly stroking thumb. She let her legs fall more widely apart as her skirt rode up her legs. Frenchy parted her inner lips with her index and middle fingers and stroked her swelling clitoris. "Baby," Edie breathed, tightening. Frenchy began to kiss her face, tiny loving kisses all over, when the train she'd barely been aware of thrust a hot gust of wind against them and stopped behind their bench.

They held onto one another, not breathing, afraid someone would get off the train and come to their side of the bench. The train pulled out. Footsteps descended the steps at the end of the platform. They breathed in relief, looking at one another, falling onto each other's lips, desperate to retrieve their passion.

Although they went through the motions again, Frenchy

could tell their lovemaking had a pallid end for Edie. Disappointed, they waited for the next train, Frenchy still touching Edie with passion.

"Will you be at the bar next Saturday?" Frenchy asked, her mouth nibbling on Edie's neck.

"Oh, yes," Edie replied as if there had never been a question about it. "Will you?"

"There's no place I'd rather be if you're going to be there, sweetheart."

"There are plenty of other bars, Frenchy, I'm sure. And girls," Edie said, pulling away to pat her hair into place. "Now stop kissing me and let me fix myself. I might know someone on the train!"

Frenchy stepped back, grinning. "Sorry, angel baby. I just can't keep my hands off you."

"No kidding." Edie smiled back, combing her hair and renewing her lipstick. "Why don't you come pick me up next week?"

"Come all the way out here? I don't get out of work till four. Think of all the time we'd waste travelling when we could be together downtown."

"It was being together I thought was important."

"Sure, Edie. You're right," she said, already missing her walk downtown. "I'll pick you up. Tell me how to get to your house."

"I'll show you. Take me there tonight," Edie tempted.

Frenchy looked eagerly at Edie's hips, thrust forward with her hands splayed on them. She shook her head. "I can't. I just can't tonight."

"Why? Do you have another girlfriend waiting for you in the Bronx?"

"No, Edie, no way. I only got eyes for you, honest. I wouldn't two-time you. I just got to get home. It's late already." She shouted as Edie's train came in, "Tell me where you live!"

"Never mind. I'll see you at the bar. Call me. I'm in the book under my father's name: Aaron Marks. What's your number?" Edie cried as she stepped onto the train.

Frenchy hesitated. She didn't want to lose Edie, but she couldn't have her calling her house. "I don't have one," she shouted into the train's closing door.

The night had cooled. Frenchy pulled her jean jacket tighter across her chest and buttoned it. She crossed to the other platform, aware of the huge dark sky over her, over the whole city that was settling into the night. She whistled a bar of *In the Still of the Night.* At the edge of the platform she breathed deeply, lifting her chin, admiring the stars.

The magic had not yet left the night. Wasn't she, Frenchy, still out on a Saturday night? Wasn't she beloved of Edie who would soon be dreaming of her? Couldn't she go right back downtown and find another girl, give her just as much? She thought briefly of Donna at the waitress' apartment. She bet it wouldn't be as good as if Donna had stayed with her. Yes, Donna would miss her. She glanced up at the stars once more, hitched up her jeans and threw her cigarette to the platform where she ground it hard under her heel as the train stopped and opened its doors for her. The long ride to the Bronx began. It was with effort that she kept the spring in her diddy-bop as she changed trains.

By the Yankee Stadium stop Frenchy had unbuttoned her jean jacket and checked her collar for lipstick. She pulled a locket out from under her shirt and buttoned the shirt's top button, settling the necklace outside it. She rolled down the collar of her jacket and flattened it. At 167th Street she removed her pinky ring and ID bracelet. At 170th she slid her Marlboro box, almost empty, under the seat, glancing around to make sure no one noticed, then took out a stick of Juicy Fruit gum and stuffed it in her mouth. Her face changed as she chewed — from the bold arrogant look she had worn all night, to a wary expression. She clenched her jaw and looked, above the tightly buttoned collar and locket, almost old maidish, like a girl who'd never had a date and went to church regularly to pray for one.

At her stop Frenchy got off the train demurely, remembering the time she met her next door neighbors coming home from their evening at Radio City Music Hall. She walked up the subway steps, pulling the comb from her back pocket. The cigar shop on the corner was still open, selling Sunday papers, and she used its window to take the point out of her d.a. and to dismantle her pompadour. She whistled *I'm Sorry* softly as she wound small spitcurls in front of her ears. She walked past her building and glanced up, relieved that no one was at the window. How often she had wished the apartment was at the back. Behind the stairs on the first floor was a cubbyhole, a small hiding place she had discovered as a child, just low enough for her to reach. Her heart raced with the anxiety she always felt here, afraid someone might have discovered and taken her plain brown slipons. She removed them, and squeezed her black boots into their space, patting them goodbye for a week.

Then, Sunday paper in hand, she flattened her hair one last time, chewed her gum more vigorously before throwing it out, and gingerly ascended the stairs, key in hand. Each step creaked beneath her feet. The four-story walkup needed repairs; even the bannisters creaked. There was no way, it seemed, not to make noise. She opened her third floor door quietly. The little hallway was empty except for the light left burning for her. She slipped quickly out of her jean jacket and headed for her room. Then her mother called, in French, "Is that you, dear? You're very late tonight. I guess the girls wanted to play rummy all night this week, no?"

Frenchy stood frozen, remembering that she still smelled of Edie. "Yes, Maman, I'll be in to say goodnight in a jiffy. I need to use the little girl's room." She heard nothing more from her mother and slipped into her own room. She walked to her dresser.

The Frenchy in the mirror was plain, dull, sullen-looking. She had nothing of the attractiveness that brought girls to the other Frenchy's arms.

She hated that image in the mirror and the tiny woman in the other room who made her look like that. But how could she leave her widowed mother? And how could she be anything but what her mother expected when she lived with her?

"Dear. ." her mother called as Frenchy slipped off the remnants of her self.

Chapter 2

Frenchy Goes to Provincetown
Summer, 1963

Frenchy had seen no other dykes yet on this, her first trip to Provincetown, but Rob and his lover Gerald were having a great time cruising the gay men in neighboring cars. The three sat in the Thunderbird in stalled traffic, listening to rock and roll on the radio, Frenchy in the back seat peering surreptitiously through the darkness into the cars around them. The boys passed wine to her and Frenchy took a long draught.

"Ain't there nobody living around here?" she asked, shouting over the music. "There's no lights, no houses, no bars, nothing but cars sitting here in the middle of the night."

"It's the Mid-Cape Highway, honey," Gerald explained. "Everybody wants to live closer to the water. This isn't New York, you know, where we're all piled on top of each other."

"Gives me the creeps," Frenchy decided, "all this empty space."

The car rolled forward a few feet. "We'll be there in an hour," Rob reassured her. "Then you'll see all the lights and music and girls you ever dreamed of. It's better than the Village. And it's only ten o'clock. We'll have plenty of time to hit the night spots."

Looking dubious, Frenchy leaned back in the seat. Her jeans were wrinkled from sitting, and despite frequent combing, her pompadour was a mess from the wind. She lit a Marlboro, enjoying the click of her Zippo as she closed it. The line of traffic to the right moved slowly past and she heard Gerald belittle Rob for being in the wrong lane. They argued half-seriously for a while. Frenchy stretched her tiny body and ran her fingers through her d.a. as she continued to survey the moving populace around her. A convertible with six women in it came up beside them. Frenchy sat up. They all had long hair. One played a dull folk song on a guitar while the rest sang along. "Goddamned hootenanny," she muttered. Gerald yelled, "Hoot, hoot, hoot!" out the window. "Goddamned straights," she sneered, in dismissal of the women.

Despite the traffic out of New York City, the first part of the trip had been great, the three of them half-blottoed on a bottle of wine, gleefully riding very fast through the cool night and the suburbs of Connecticut, making silly jokes. Recently she'd been feeling restless, as if something was missing from her life. Except for some time she'd taken off to visit relatives with her mother, this was the first long weekend Frenchy had taken in seven years, since she started cashiering at the A&P right out of high school. Her mother had at first complained about being left alone all this weekend; but when Frenchy for once had not bent, Maman had begun to act as if Frenchy's excursion was all her own idea, insisting that *mon petit chou* take her little holiday with her card-playing friends. She'd even given Frenchy five dollars to spend with the girls.

The girls, Frenchy laughed to herself. If Maman only knew. They were hardly the cashiers Maman saw at the A&P. And the last thing Frenchy wanted to do with her girls was play cards. Once in a while, when she was particularly in love and felt the need to see her current femme between Saturdays, she told her mother she was going to the movies with the girls. But this made her nervous, just like the occasional "pajama parties" she claimed to be attending. In the past three years she had spent most of the night with maybe two girls. She felt that spending the whole night with femmes got them addicted to it, made them want to set up housekeeping. Frenchy had her mother to take care of. She couldn't be getting married. Besides, she liked her life the way it was. Always checking the crowds out for new faces, moving in whenever that felt comfortable. The only rules she followed, still, were to stay away from girls in her own neighborhood and never to step in on another butch's property. She couldn't see going home to Maman with a broken nose or razor scars, though that sort of fighting happened less and less among downtown dykes.

Edie was the only girl Frenchy had considered bringing to Provincetown with her. She'd graduated from college and now taught English in a Queens junior high school. She was a dynamite chick — caught, kind of like herself, between two worlds. Edie didn't know any gay girls among her co-workers. She lived in the one-family house in Queens her elderly parents left her when they died. Frenchy had been there once and it was as dark as her own place, full of the old folks' memories. And, like Frenchy, Edie kept her gay life separate from her life in Queens. While she hadn't found lesbians in her own crowd, she never felt quite comfortable with Frenchy's friends, either. Edie always feared they would be indiscreet, and the cursing, drinking, fighting and generally low-life women, as she called them, looked at Edie suspiciously, like she was slumming. So she and Frenchy met now and then on neutral ground somewhere and took in a movie or walked in a park. It was a nice change of pace for Frenchy, who could then brag downtown about the "teacher" she went with. And she always had someone to fall back on when she felt low.

Frenchy was coming down from the high of the wine. After working since 9:00 that morning and not eating dinner, she felt low enough to wish she'd brought comfortable, reliable old Edie with her.

A yellow sports car, two smiling dykes in it, went by on their right, half in the sand on the side of the road. Frenchy leaned far out the window to watch their progress down the road. "Wow," she commented.

"Those girls are just going to get stuck in the sand up the way," Rob said disapprovingly. "How they got this far is beyond me."

But Frenchy meanwhile had drifted into a reverie of the day when she'd have her own sports car and drive her own girl to Provincetown.

They moved slowly forward, then picked up speed. "I think we're out of the bottleneck, girls," Rob said, and they all cheered. They did not pass the sports car.

Once more Frenchy and the boys began to sing *A Hundred Bottles of Beer on the Wall* and to pass the wine back and forth across the seats.

Suddenly they were surrounded with beach cottages. Frenchy felt reassured by the presence of all those dwellings. "Is this Provincetown?"

"Not quite, hon. These are all straight places."

Frenchy had assumed they were. Weren't all homes straight? She couldn't imagine owning one. Or even owning a summer cottage like these. Perhaps, when she was much older, she would rent a place like this on Fire Island for a week, but for now she would stay in a room in the guest house where Gerald and Rob were taking her.

Soon they parked and took their bags into a neat white house filled with closets called rooms. She shared a bath with all the boys on the second floor. It was 11:30 and the house was deserted. She just had time to hang her shirts on the rack beside her bed and look once out the window into someone's back yard when the boys were back, ready to walk to the bars.

"Nice room," she told them as they joined the strollers on the street.

"We like it. All you need is a bed, right, Rob?"

Rob was eying a passing boy. "It's cheap for up here. That's what counts when you have car payments and parking fees back in the City."

The crowd became more obviously gay as the three approached the central district. Frenchy inhaled the salty air. It was good to smell the sea.

"The straights go home when the shops close," Gerald explained. "The streets are ours after midnight."

Frenchy felt more at home when she realized she'd been cruised a couple of times. Still, she was only mildly enthusiastic when the boys pointed her toward the Ace of Spades, the women's bar, and left her to fend for herself. She supposed she was very lucky to have gotten a ride up here with them, but right now she was tired, she didn't feel lucky at all, and she bypassed the bar to try and revive herself. Perhaps it had been a mistake to come.

It was almost midnight, but a few women were walking down the narrow road past one prim white house after

another toward downtown. Frenchy wished one of the tiny
little streets off the crowded main one was empty so that
she could comb her hair and work up her self-confidence a
little. None of the women looked welcoming. It was chilly
this late at night, and she was glad she'd brought her city
clothes instead of dressing for a hot beach weekend as the
boys had recommended. But then the women were all so
lightly dressed. Did she stand out too much in her black
jeans and jacket? The girls downtown always said they
could recognize her a mile off by her height, her walk,
and her "uniform."

Frenchy smiled at the thought of her popularity back
home and became nostalgic. If only she'd told her mother
she was going away for the weekend and stayed in the
city instead. Why hadn't she ever thought of that? Right
now she could be leaning on the bar or dancing with some
cute new chick from Jersey. Just the thought perked her
up, returned some of her confidence. "I'm a big city girl,"
she told herself. "Too big to let a hick town like this scare
me." She decided to check out the Ace of Spades to see if
it lived up to its reputation.

It was a real raunchy place. A butch in a man's sport
coat and shades came stumbling out, her femme support-
ing her at the elbow. The femme was not bad, Frenchy
thought, for her age. She was about forty and had a bee-
hive hairdo. Her makeup was heavy. The butch stopped
suddenly and turned on her. Frenchy couldn't make out
the words, only the threatening tone. The femme urged
her butch up the alley, but the butch wanted to say her
piece. As the femme turned to see if anyone was watching, the butch swung an arm, catching her fully on the
side of the face. The femme hardly looked surprised. She
staggered a little, settled her face quickly from pain to
hurt and began to cry. The butch softened immediately,
took the woman in her arms and comforted her. They walked

out of the alley entwined, the femme groping in her purse for tissues.

Frenchy felt sick. There were some parts of the life she hated, that made her question if it was still what she wanted. Gay girls had no business hitting other girls. Men did that. Her father had done that to her mother. Her brother's wife had confided to Frenchy that she'd been hit the first year they were married. Dykes weren't men, they should act better than men. She took a couple of deep breaths and swaggered the best she could toward the bar. Where else could she go? It was her world, the good and the bad. Two more couples came out, laughing and talking, their speech slurred, but their moods happy. One of the femmes, with soft-looking curly hair and lively eyes, looked Frenchy up and down, while the other met her eyes through light blue pointed eyeglass frames. Frenchy felt better as she handed over the cover charge, more confident that she could blend in here and meet some girls she would like.

The Ace of Spades was mobbed. Frenchy elbowed her way to the bar. Still a bit hungover from the wine, she ordered a scotch and water to wake herself up. As she leaned against the bar with her second drink, the first already cushioning the discomfort of being there, she tried to separate out individuals from the crowd. The jukebox blared Ben E. King. She was dizzy with tiredness and liquor by the end of that drink, but for lack of anything else to do, ordered another. By the end of the third she was practically drunk and had lost her cool. She had to make contact with a girl, she thought desperately. She didn't want to sleep alone in the tiny bed-filled room or go to the beach alone in the morning. She didn't travel alone.

As best she could, she stood up straight. In the bar mirror she smoothed her pompadour. As she moved into the crowd with yet another scotch, she realized she had to go to the bathroom. She looked at the long line and decided to remain uncomfortable. On the far side of the bar three women stood talking. Frenchy made her way toward them, trying to decide which was the woman alone and if she was femme. Another woman joined them and the two broke into couples. "See," she told herself, "you should never go to a new place alone. You just don't know the ropes." Looking around again, she spotted a tall woman by herself. "Come on, Frenchy," she chided herself, "you're not that desperate." The woman was at least five-eleven, with permed blonde hair that made her look even taller. A smile broke out on the woman's face as a pretty blonde appeared out of the crowd and hugged her. Frenchy was relieved; she suspected she *was* that desperate. She pushed on through the crowd, smiling at a couple of women who looked her way, but she got no response. By the time she got back to the bar she was chilled through with rejection, but she couldn't blame anyone. She looked awful tonight, had left all her charm in New York, and was sloppy drunk. She left then, weaving slightly up the alley and onto Commercial Street, worried she wouldn't find the house where she was staying, humming *Walk Like a Man* to herself.

Her head down so at least no one who saw her tonight could recognize her the rest of the weekend, Frenchy made her lonely way through the nearly deserted streets. Maybe she was tired of being on her own, of this constant hunt for girls. Or maybe it was the town: cute enough, but too small and not her style. Tomorrow she'd find a girl at the beach, take her out for a fancy dinner, and explore the town with her. There was *something* she liked about it, she thought as she breathed in the salty sea air and imagined being at the shore the next day.

She passed through the center of town. A police car moved slowly by. She wondered if there was a Women's House of Detention in Provincetown and quickened her pace.

Suddenly she felt a familiar and thoroughly unpleasant warmth in her loins. "Aw, shit," she said aloud. "Not this too." She jammed her fists into the pockets of her denim jacket and walked faster toward the guest house. It wasn't fair — every month to get this damned thing. There wasn't any sense to it. She was never going to have kids. It embarrassed the hell out of her to have to cram one of those fat sanitary napkins between her legs and catch the oozing red stuff like any woman would. She didn't deserve this, too, not up here at P-town. Now she wouldn't be able to swim, and if she did find a girl she'd have to hide the pads. It was humiliating to be a butch with the curse. She felt moisture start down her leg. Luckily, she had packed a pad just in case, and that would keep her till morning. But it meant getting up early, before the boys left for the beach, and finding some place to buy a box. Worst of all, wearing the blood-soaked thing till morning, till she found new ones. The whole painful and messy process was mortifying.

The small figure made her way up the street, striding on her short legs back and forth between two houses for a while as if uncertain which to enter, finally determining on one, and tiptoeing stealthily up the stairs. She closed the door slowly and quietly behind her as if, from habit, she feared to disturb someone sleeping inside.

* * * * *

The bright sky over Herring Cove Beach glared into Frenchy's over-sensitive eyes. Her hangover was bad. Her cramps were worse. All she had wanted to do when she woke that morning was stay in bed. The bloodstained jeans she'd managed to wash out the night before were hanging next to her, still damp. They were the only dyke pants she owned. She felt sorry for herself and her small wardrobe. Even if she had the money, her mother would notice if she bought too many butch clothes.

She staggered as she got out of Rob's car. Gerald was quick to jibe her. "Can't take the night life, girl?"

"You go ahead, guys, I've got to get used to all this light. Fire Island was never like this."

The boys laughed as they hurried off to sunbathe. Frenchy, slipping on her shades, wondered if she could catch a bus back to the City. As she leaned against the car, folding her arms and propping one leg up behind her in case anyone was looking, she visualized her neighborhood. Familiar, shaded by apartment buildings, full of cooking smells, the comfort of her mother waiting for her . . . the thought brought tears to her eyes. "What's the matter with you, Frenchy?" she asked herself. "Goddamn sissy."

She picked up the old beach blanket in which she'd wrapped a Coke, suntan lotion and two comic books, and slipped it under her arm. She wore an old pair of cut-off black jeans, a white sweatshirt and a new pair of white sneakers, bought for the trip. The sneakers filled with sand as she plunged onto the beach path.

Herring Cove was as famous as Fire Island for its gay beach, and all around her faggots and dykes converged. Unsteady from the hangover, squinting behind her sunglasses, she tried to check out the girls. When walking became too uncomfortable she stopped to slip off the sneakers. A few yards on, her feet began to burn. How did the other gays walk so comfortably? Tears rose again from the pain, but she wouldn't be so uncool as to stop and put her sneakers on again. They would just refill with sand anyway.

She reached a peak in the sand. As far as she could see, water stretched ahead of her, so incredibly blue she forgot her burning feet, her headache, her cramps, her desperation, her loneliness. She felt drawn to it, cleansed by it. The sun, tempered by the ocean breeze, was comforting, healing. Then she saw, everywhere between her and the water, gays — blankets and blankets of them. Twos and threes and groups. Women running into the water hand in hand, or lying close to one another. Men walking toward the other end of the beach together. Older couples sitting under beach umbrellas. Baby butches splashing water on their girls and dunking them.

She couldn't see Rob or Gerald anywhere. In all this sea of lesbians and gay men it seemed that she was the only one who was alone.

She looked back toward the water and it wasn't so pretty this time. But it was still somehow a source of strength. She squared her shoulders and started off across the burning sand toward the compelling wetness of the water. Striding, then, almost in comfort on the cool wet sand and small rocks along the shoreline, hitching up her shorts and plastering a devastating smile across her face, she was momentarily back in her element. As she passed good-looking women she gave them *the look* through her dark glasses. No one glanced up at her, but she felt better doing it. Sooner or later it would work. It always did.

The breezes off the water seemed to be dissipating some of her hangover. She angled up away from the water, looking for a sign of Rob and Gerald and for some place to put her blanket. She spotted a sleeping woman with short dark hair and a red bikini. The woman was alone.

Frenchy stopped, looking pointedly away from her. Slowly she drew a box of Marlboros from her pocket, tapped it on her hand, pulled a cigarette out and replaced the pack. The woman had not stirred. Frenchy found her Zippo and despite the breeze lit the cigarette in one try. This was more like it. Even though the woman lay sleeping and unaware, once more she felt better for going through the motions. Perhaps someone else had noticed her.

She spread her blanket a few feet from the sleeping

woman and settled back to smoke her cigarette. Despite the smoke searing through her hangover-raw throat, hot as the sand had been beneath her feet, and the dizzying effect it had on her aching head, she felt the sense of well-being — almost euphoria — that came with the ebbing of cramps. Here she was, Frenchy Tonneau, alone in P-town, on the make. She couldn't wait to tell the kids at the bar how much she liked the Cape.

Someone turned up a radio. *Big Girls Don't Cry*, it sang at Frenchy who agreed wholeheartedly. Cigarette finished, she sneaked a look at the still-sleeping woman and settled down to her comics, the sound of good music behind her, a nap, and maybe a try at that sleeping beauty later. Soon, she would put on the suntan lotion, but first she would let her tan get started. Like a lullabye, the Four Seasons still sang *Big Girls Don't Cry*, and Frenchy dozed off facing the woman, in a fantasy of dancing with her.

Frenchy's cramps returned to wake her. She knew, first, that she needed to change her pad. But it took a moment to realize that wouldn't be as easy as she thought. She rolled over onto her back. The left side of her face felt dry and withered. "Oh, no," she said, understanding what she'd done. She would be a mess, one whole side of her face burned lobster-red and the other side white. If she stayed on the beach, perhaps she could get some sun on the right side — but there was the problem of the bathroom. And finding the boys to get her back to town. In panic she remembered the sleeping woman and looked for her, thinking she might help — the hell with seducing her. But even her fantasy was gone. Many of the people nearby had left. The cramps were no better and she was afraid she'd double over from them. A building in the distance might be a bathroom, but if it wasn't she would have that much further to walk back to — to where? She might have to walk back to town. If only she had some water and an aspirin. All these women around. Surely some of them had the right supplies. But she couldn't, just *couldn't* ask a woman — a gay girl — for *that* kind of stuff. She'd die first.

She trudged through the burning sands, half-searching for Rob and Gerald, half-resigned to walking back to town. She made directly for the parking lot, her feet escaping none of the punishment she had spared them before. She had to get back to town, wherever it was. She'd worry about how she looked later. Now, of course, women were noticing her. Were they laughing at her half-red face? Had her period leaked through? She tried a new tactic and adopted a version of the walk she used in front of her mother and at work. The eyes drifted away as she passed. She was just another woman, not a butch on the make. She had sacrificed her image for anonymity, hoping she'd make so little impression they wouldn't associate her self later with her self now.

Once that had happened in the A&P. One of the girls from downtown stopped there to shop, not knowing it was where Frenchy worked. Without her butch style Frenchy blended right in and the girl stared at her, noting the resemblance, but not knowing her. "Do you have a sister?" she finally asked, as Frenchy checked her through the register.

Frenchy smiled a polite thin smile and lied, "Yes, do you know her?"

"I think so. You look a lot alike."

Frenchy nodded, the pallid little smile still on her face, and began to bag the order.

"Say hello to Frenchy for me," the girl had told her, and got a limp wave in return as Frenchy turned to the next customer.

Maybe it would work here, too, Frenchy thought as she left the lot and began to follow cars full of gay people toward town.

"Need a lift?" she heard a woman's voice ask. She was one of the two women from the yellow sportscar. "You can ride back here," she suggested, indicating a small space behind the seat.

"No, thanks." Frenchy waved, hiding the burnt side of her face, cursing her luck. What a chance. She could have ridden in a sportscar — which she'd never done before — and gotten to know those cool women. Maybe they could have had dinner together or met at the bar later. . . . But she couldn't stand for them to see her like this. Maybe she'd see them later and approach them. When it was dark. Then again, maybe she'd hide in her room the rest of the weekend hugging her cramps and her sunburn and her misery to herself, waiting for the boys to take her home. She accepted the next ride she was offered, from two faggots who seemed to sense how down she felt and took her right to her front door. She almost cried thanking them. Why was she being such a crybaby this weekend anyway? It didn't go with her reputation at all. Her damn period made her weepy.

Again she slowly mounted her steps defeated, exhausted and alone. She walked through the empty, narrow hallways to her room and looked at herself in the mirror. No one would ever like her in Provincetown looking as she did.

* * * * *

Frenchy spent many dreary hours at her window. She could see a narrow strip of the bay between two buildings. The view and several aspirins kept her going, but she didn't revive until twilight began to tease boat lights on in the bay. She decided to make the best of this rotten weekend and go out for dinner. She'd decided against taking a bus back to the City as it would use all her money, forcing her to go home once she got there. She couldn't face seeing her mother in their tiny apartment without something good happening in between. This trip was a reward to herself for being a good daughter, a dutiful employee, a discreet gay. So far she'd felt only punished. If this was what traveling would be like, she might as well stop planning to take more trips like this one when her mother's social security began in another few years.

She wandered down Commercial Street looking in the windows of all the jewelry and clothing shops, fascinated by the magic goods. If she ever did have the money, she'd come back here and do it up big. She passed a few gay couples on the street, but it seemed too early for most of them to be out. She was out of step again. Still, she forced herself to walk butch. If she met anyone from the City, she'd be embarrassed to be caught shuffling along weary and drained by her womanhood.

This was not the Frenchy she had packed to bring to Provincetown. This wasn't even one she knew. Tonight she felt thirteen again, like before she came out. She'd known there was something missing from her life then and had no idea where to look. She'd known she was different from other girls, but couldn't name her uniqueness. Then she'd learned who she really was and at least once a week, on Saturday nights downtown, she could be herself. She'd hung out at the underage joints until she got fake I.D. Then she began her career at the bars. The rest of the week her persona was a front she needed to protect her real self. Here in P-town she was someone in between, someone she had no time for in the City. But as long as she didn't meet anyone she knew, this Frenchy was okay. She could take care of herself, if not anyone else, and she looked funny, but about that she cared less and less.

One jewelry store was particularly appealing, with small garnet rings in the window. It was hard to find her small size in a pinky ring and she wanted one with her birthstone. Inside the store the salesgirl was so helpful Frenchy wondered if she could be gay, but she had long hair and was wearing a skirt. Frenchy decided the girl was straight. The rings were children's sizes and fit comfortably. She fought with herself over the expense. Then she figured a good pinky ring was a necessity, something she'd wear all her life to let girls know she was gay. She noticed this girl wore a pinky ring too, and studied her as she waited on another customer. It was just a coincidence, she decided; though in the paperback books, lesbians looked more like the salesgirl than the Village dykes. Maybe this was one of those uptown types — as Edie would be if she had money.

Maybe she might like to have dinner later, Frenchy mused as the girl returned. Embarrassed to be caught fantasizing about her, Frenchy decided to buy the most expensive ring. It was thick and gold, with a rectangular red stone the light caught in a way that made it sparkle. She handed over the money without taking off the ring, and slipped her old scratched signet ring into her pocket. She guessed the salesgirl was impressed, but decided to reconsider asking her to dinner. After all, maybe she'd come back at closing and find the girl's boyfriend waiting for her.

Buoyed by her purchase, aware of its expensive weight on her pinky, Frenchy hitched up her jeans and sauntered further down Commercial Street. She felt hungry. Suddenly she realized she had spent every extra cent on the ring. She wouldn't be taking anyone to dinner except herself — and cheaply, at that. At a take-out stand she ordered a hotdog, and sat with a view of the sidewalk to eat it. No one interesting passed, but darkness had fallen and she hoped her half-red face, though it burned like hell, was less conspicuous.

Should she even *go* to the bar? Had the sun burnt a warning onto her face that somehow she didn't belong in

P-town? The sight of the clean big blue sea that morning had stayed in her mind's eye; she wished all the cute girls could somehow break free of the bar and go down to the beach to dance at night. She touched her cool hand to her blazing cheek. Maybe she had a bit of fever from the sun, to be thinking like this. But it seemed kind of funny, to travel all the way to Provincetown, to all the beauty and open space, and go into a sordid little building to drink and smoke and be miserable. She could have stared at that water all day . . .

Letting her hand fall from her cheek, she noticed her new ring again. It made her happy. As a matter of fact, for all her misery she *was* happy. The air was different here. Even though Commercial Street was lined with shops and restaurants and bars like New York, the darkness was softer around it all, she could hear seabells ringing, foghorns beginning to mourn, gulls crying to one another.

Despite the soreness of her feet from the hot sand, she walked up the wharf to its end. She imagined going out on the fishing boats for days at a time — being apart from the land, buoyed up by nothing but water, with hardly anyone to talk to, just herself in her slobbiest smelliest clothes playing a harmonica out on the deck of a boat under the stars. The salt water would jump up and spray her. She'd work hard all day to haul in fish. It would be another kind of life, that was for sure. Grandpère had been a fisherman in Marseilles. Her mother remembered Grandmère pacing the sands waiting for him. Had she ever stood at the end of a wharf like this and wondered about the world?

Frenchy started toward the bar. She did not, after all, belong to the world of fishing boats. She'd found her place in the bars and knew best how to survive there. Maybe, though, someday she would have more money and could move to Staten Island or even Long Island. Wouldn't it be fine to settle there with some nice femme when she was older and didn't have to worry as much about her mother? Or if somehow her mother could live with them without knowing Frenchy and her femme were in love.

She was in the bar before she'd finished her daydream. She hadn't combed her hair, her shirt was half out of her pants, she needed to change her napkin. An extra was stuffed under her shirt, and she went to stand in line. No posing, no drink in hand, no cigarette. Somehow, tonight, she felt comfortable walking into a new bar and standing in the bathroom line. With her sunburned face and her weariness from cramps and being in a strange place, she felt like a washed-out, bedraggled fisherman home from the seas. Smiling, she leaned against the wall and looked at the woman behind her in line.

The woman turned and it was as if Frenchy were seeing the wide expanse of sea again from the beach. Like that morning, she again felt drawn, cleansed, comforted, healed. What was it about this face? It seemed to come from her past and hold her future. Confused thoughts of her grand-mère and the fishing boats in Marseilles, of the girls in the bars downtown, all swam in her head.

It must be the sun, she thought once she was in the bathroom. Still, she combed her hair, preening automatically for this woman. She tried to cover as much of the burnt side of her face as she could with her pompadour. She buttoned her jacket to cover the wrinkles of her shirt, then tugged at it to stretch out its creases. She ditched her crumpled pack of Marlboros, regretting the loss of the last two, even as she reasoned the sacrifice was worth it.

When she emerged from the bathroom her heart was beating fast. She smiled charmingly at the woman's averted face and diddy-bopped a path that opened magically before her across the dance floor.

Stupid of her to get caught up in all the sea-faring fantasies and let herself go as she had. The woman hadn't even noticed her. But Frenchy planned to change that. She ordered a Scotch again, promising herself not to get drunk tonight. Watching the woman come out of the bathroom, she took her Zippo and slid a Marlboro from its fresh box.

"Mercedes!" a voice next to Frenchy called. Mercedes walked across the room toward the voice.

Frenchy's eyes were riveted to Mercedes' face. Then Mercedes was next to her, but she moved onto the dance floor with her friend. She was a little taller than Frenchy and as slender, but in a more fragile way, as if her bones had been cast of finer stuff. Her hair was not as dark as Frenchy's, but still a rich brown, and not waved, but combed back stylishly. Her skin was a warm red-tan, as if she were flushed from excitement, and spread smooth and glossy on high cheekbones, ran freckled over a wide nose, and blended into small, full lips of a deeper red. Her eyes were brown and full of dancing lights. A red shirt added color to her face. She wore black pointed boots and blue denims, a box of Marlboros sticking out of a pocket. Frenchy watched her dance, fascinated.

And not just fascinated. Puzzled. She couldn't figure out if the woman was butch or femme. She was too pretty to be butch, but the clothes, walk, stance and cigarettes all looked butch. There was an outside chance she was femme. Frenchy was counting on that chance. She felt damned good considering her state since she'd gotten to Provincetown. Best of all, the woman, once she joined a group after dancing, didn't seem to have one special girl among her friends. Hell, thought Frenchy, I'll even take this one kiki.

"Buy you a drink?" Frenchy asked a while later, following Mercedes, alone at last, to the bar.

Mercedes, in an impassive appraisal, took Frenchy in. "Why not?" she answered.

"Good. My first time up here," Frenchy told her, nervous for once. "I don't know anybody. You from New York?"

"Yeah," Mercedes answered after Frenchy had ordered their drinks.

"Where?"

"Uptown."

"Not as up as me, I bet. I'm from the Bronx."

Mercedes seemed hesitant to reveal her neighborhood, as if afraid it might scare Frenchy off. "A hundred eleventh," she admitted finally.

"You ever go to the bars downtown?"

"No," Mercedes answered. "A lot of times I'm not welcome downtown." Her dark, bitter eyes met Frenchy's.

For the first time Frenchy was able to hear, under Mercedes' heavy New York accent, a slight Spanish inflection, as of someone who'd been in the States a very long time. "I understand," she said. "I sure wish it wasn't that way."

Mercedes shrugged. "Someday I'll get out of El Barrio and you'll *have* to get used to me."

"That'll be a pleasure," Frenchy said before realizing Mercedes might think she was coming on to her. She still wasn't sure what the woman was. "I mean, to stop keeping you out."

"You ever been uptown?"

"I don't know where to go uptown, but I hear there's a lot of action up there."

"A hundred twenty-fifth is good. A couple of places. Not so safe, though, for white chicks."

"Name me a place that's safe for queers."

"Provincetown?"

"I'm too new to know. How about you?"

"I was here once last year. Nobody bothered us."

"You here with friends?"

Mercedes narrowed her eyes as if to say she knew what Frenchy was getting at. Turning from her and leaning on the bar she said sadly, "A few kids from the bars. I haven't had a steady femme for a while. I have trouble with them, you know?"

Despite feeling as if Mercedes had stomped her heart, Frenchy answered, "You better believe it."

Mercedes brightened a little now that they had something in common. "You got girl trouble?"

Frenchy's heart was trying to mend itself with irrational hope. She turned shyly away to speak. "I never went with nobody long. I got one girl, a teacher, we been seeing each other on and off three years. My other femmes, they just come and go." Afraid Mercedes would think they left her, Frenchy explained, "I get itchy."

"I know what you mean," Mercedes said, smiling at Frenchy for the first time. "But sometimes, you know, when I'm down" — her smile faded — "sometimes don't you wish maybe one girl would come along you'd want to stick with?"

Their eyes met. Frenchy felt a warmth fill her chest and a tingle of anxiety flutter in her stomach. "Yeah," she said gruffly.

By all the rules Frenchy knew, the conversation should have ended there. They'd established that they couldn't have a relationship. Frenchy tried very hard to say the right words, to tell Mercedes so long, be seeing you, see you around . . .

But she was riveted to that smile when it reappeared and found herself grinning back like a dumb kid. Again she felt like she was looking at the vast cool waters off Herring Cove, like someone had pulled open the curtains of her heart. Something within Mercedes seemed to touch something within herself. And not because she was so good-looking. It was something else, something she'd got a spark of once in a while with different girls and then lost when they got too close, too demanding. Something she'd felt with Terry, her first girl, when she was thirteen — an incredible, intense excitement that made nothing else matter.

Maybe this Mercedes could change her tune, because she, Frenchy, couldn't be attracted to a butch. The woman was either kiki or had missed her calling.

"Want to go out on the beach?" Mercedes asked.

"Sure, why not?" said Frenchy, averting her eyes and hiding her pleasure. "You want a beer or something?"

"Can't take drinks out there. The place will get busted. Come on," Mercedes said in such a familiar way Frenchy was afraid she'd reach for her hand.

Frenchy followed the small woman through the crowd, wondering what had happened to her cool. She was far from drunk, yet she didn't care when they hit the sand and the wind took the waves out of her hair, didn't care that her boots were getting wet as they walked along the water's edge. She didn't withhold her most dazzling smiles from this butch who wouldn't appreciate them and would probably be offended by them. All she knew, once they had returned to the bar, was that it hurt to let her go, this Mercedes.

"My friends will wonder where I went," Mercedes explained. "Sometimes, when I take off on them, they got to put me together again when they find me." She laughed sadly. Then she smiled and looked Frenchy in the eye. "I want to thank you. I was feeling low. I liked talking to you." She was nervous now, skittish, as if afraid to spend too much time with Frenchy. And she left reluctantly as if she had to force herself to go.

Frenchy worried about her then. Mercedes had told her during their walk how depressed she was. How coming here was her friends' idea to get her out of the city. How they'd even had to lock her up awhile when Maria, her first femme, went back to her boyfriend. Ever since then, off and on, she still got a little crazy. Frenchy wanted to offer her own life to Mercedes, to tell her how steady and predictable it was, to share it with her until she healed — as a friend. And Mercedes seemed drawn to her, too. The bay breezes had lifted Frenchy's hair from her face at one point and Mercedes had put her hand to the sunburned skin, wincing in pain for her. "Poor face," she had said in Spanish, then translated.

Frenchy relived that gentle touch as she ordered another drink. Maybe the uptown butches touched each other like that more easily. Just a few minutes, she thought — though they'd been together well over an hour — just a few minutes is all it takes to fall in love. "Isn't that a line from a song?" she asked herself.

She downed one Scotch after another and watched Mercedes do the same. If only Mercedes wasn't butch, she lamented. If only she wasn't still so hurt by that one girl she'd mentioned over and over and instead ready for a new love.

She had no interest in any of the other girls, forgot how bad she looked, didn't want to leave until Mercedes did. She saw Mercedes cry at her table (she couldn't be a real butch to do that) and watched her friends comfort her. She was really tempted to ask her to stay in her room for the night — as friends. But she knew she wanted her for a lover. She couldn't do that to Mercedes under the guise of friendship. And knew Mercedes couldn't accept her as anything but a friend. *One Fine Day* was playing over and over on the jukebox. She listened to the words: someday the guy would want the singer. She wanted to shout, sing from the rooftops, somehow tell Mercedes how she felt about her.

Toward closing Frenchy lost her sense of time. Now and then she'd light a Marlboro when one burned still in her full ashtray. She'd turn away so Mercedes wouldn't see her staring and realize she'd forgotten she was not in New

York. One of those times, as she turned back, she just caught Mercedes' friends helping her walk out the door. Frenchy staggered after them.

In the clear chilly night air she tried to shake the dizziness from her head and concentrated on walking a straight line. Usually she didn't drink as she had this weekend. Didn't even really like liquor or how it dulled what she felt. It was just something you had to do in the life. A gesture you made in response to any situation: introductions, depression, trouble. A car came slowly down the street toward her and she moved out of its way. One of Mercedes' friends was driving. Frenchy lurched at the open back window of the car. "Mercedes," she cried. "Mercedes!" She didn't care what they thought of her.

"She's sick, honey," a woman called out of the car. "We need to get her home!"

"Mercedes," Frenchy whispered, puzzled, as the taillights got smaller and smaller. She turned herself around with effort and headed toward the guest house, hesitating now and then, as if she had some unfinished business to attend to, as if something in the air was calling and calling to her.

* * * * *

Sunday came, Frenchy's last full day in Provincetown. It was raining, but she was too hungover to be bothered by it. "It figures," she told herself as she rolled over to sleep more. She'd been too drunk to undress and she was painfully uncomfortable and sticky between her legs, but she couldn't get up, not right away.

Later, after more sleep, she lay comforted by the muted drumming of rain on the roof, something she never heard in the apartment building at home. She'd awakened seeing Mercedes' face before her, and smiled. It felt good, the way she loved Mercedes, even if she couldn't have her. Sometimes she worried about how she went from woman to woman, simply seeking the high of love, of romance, but it was different this time. The high was there, but so too was something more diffuse, something which felt as warm and steady as she imagined this Cape Cod rain. There was a little of the feeling she had for Jessie, a little of the way she felt about her close friend Marian at the store. It was a little confusing, to suddenly feel this way about a woman she'd just met. Jessie and Marian had been her friends for years. And it gave her hope, as if by mixing the love she was used to with this new deeper thing, they were fated to be together, she and Mercedes. As if, given time and patience, it would all work out. And meanwhile she glowed with pleasure in anticipation of seeing Mercedes at the bar that same night.

She sat up suddenly, and felt as if she'd bashed her head against a beam. What if Mercedes went home today, what if she wasn't staying over until Monday?

She ran to the bathroom. It was noon and all the faggots had left for brunch. She had a temporarily helpful bath and scrubbed at the new spots on her pants, grateful the black denim mostly hid them. She dressed quickly and went out. Between her hangover and her compulsion to see Mercedes, she didn't give a thought to her sunburn, or to the rain which would keep her from evening it. She had to be able to see Mercedes again in New York.

She had no idea where even to look for her. Could she be having breakfast before leaving? She walked Commercial Street all day, stopping here and there for coffee, new cigarettes. She'd never thought to bring a raincoat to the Cape, so her clothes were wet, her hair was limp. By seven that evening she was able to swallow a cheeseburger and afterward set off for the bar, squishing as she went. She'd met Rob and Gerald once and extracted a promise that they would send the short beautiful woman dressed in red and black to the Ace of Spades as soon as they saw her.

As she sat at the bar Frenchy combed back her wet hair and tried to light a damp cigarette from her pack. The woman next to her offered a dry one and Frenchy gratefully took it.

"Looks like you need a hot toddy," said the woman.

"That would go down nice about now."

"I'm Jenny."

"I'm Frenchy."

"Frenchy?"

"Yeah, my name's too long and foreign, so people call me Frenchy."

"Okay, Frenchy, then. Are you from New York?"

"Yeah. How about you?"

"Ohio."

"Really?" Frenchy asked, wide-eyed.

"Is that exciting?" Jenny asked, laughing. She was tall and red-haired with an open plain face and manner like Jessie's.

"I never thought about gay girls living in Ohio before. It sounds like such a straight place. Why do you stay there?"

"My hometown is there, Frenchy. We're not all big city girls, you know."

"Yeah, but is there any life there?"

"Just about enough for me. I couldn't keep up with your pace. There's a small group of us, all living in small towns within about a hundred-mile radius. We get together for dinner a lot, visit each other weekends."

"How do you find each other?"

"I don't know, really. We just do. There's Daughters of Bilitis in Marion, the nearest city to me. I've met a couple of girls there."

"What a funny way to live," Frenchy marveled. She realized she was just talking to this nice woman, not trying to get her into bed. She must be butch.

"You up here for long?" Jenny asked.

"Just till tomorrow. But it seems like forever."

"How come? I've only got two weeks and they're flying by, it seems."

"What can I tell you? Everything that could go wrong did. You're *not* looking at the real Frenchy, you know. I don't always go around looking like a drowned rat."

"I could tell by the way you combed your hair. And combed your hair." Jenny laughed again.

Instead of becoming embarrassed, Frenchy joined her. "Buy you a drink?" she asked.

"I don't drink, but thanks. Maybe a Coke when I need it," Jenny said, lifting a half-finished glass.

"You don't drink?" Frenchy looked shocked.

"I say a lot of astounding things, don't I?" Jenny chuckled.

"Hey, I really don't know anybody who doesn't drink. At least that goes to a bar and doesn't. How come?"

"I hate hangovers. And once I start drinking I can't stop. Then I hit people." Jenny smiled warmly at Frenchy. "It's not healthy — for me or anyone around me. When I lost my last girl over hitting her I decided to lay off."

"I never thought about not drinking. How do people treat you in bars? Do they look at you funny?"

"You mean like you are?"

Frenchy joined in the laughter. She wished Mercedes would come in to be warmed by this fiery woman. Soon they were joined by a woman Jenny had met the night before at dinner: Pam. Frenchy could have sworn this heavy woman in a long skirt and many necklaces was in that carful of folksinging women that had passed them in the traffic jam on the way up. Pam was an artist who lived in the Village but never went to the bars. Too smoky, too much cruising and drinking, though she liked a little wine now and then. She accepted the glass Frenchy offered to buy her, though she'd only come to the Ace to meet Jenny.

"But what do you *do* if you don't go to bars? How do you meet women?"

Pam tossed back her long black hair. "My last affair was with an artist's model I found so incredibly beautiful I couldn't keep my hands off her. I was .open about being a lesbian and she told me she was too."

"You mean you couldn't tell?"

"Honey, she was sixty-five and looked like somebody's grandmother," Pam said, laughing. "No, you couldn't tell. Not till you started drawing the part of her that was all wet because you were a lesbian admiring it."

Frenchy was still blushing when Jenny and Pam left to shop at the bookstore. She had declined to accompany them because she was embarrassed by Pam's frank talk and she still held hope of seeing Mercedes.

"Sweetheart," the bartender said after they'd left, "you said you're waiting for Mercedes?"

"Yeah, you know her?"

"Cute little Spanish chick?"

"That's her."

"They took her home."

Frenchy didn't attempt to hide her disappointment. "I wouldn't get mixed up with her if I was you."

Frenchy's disappointment turned quickly to anger.

"Don't get rattled, I'm just telling you. She freaked out on them. They're all staying in the place where I rent, and last night when I got home they were carting her out to the car. She took somebody's sleeping pills and they got her to a doctor who pumped her out. He wanted to put her in the hospital, but by then she was awake and screaming about getting back to the city to take care of her daughter."

"Daughter?"

"Yeah. The grandmother was taking care of her, an eight year old."

"But she's queer as I am. How could she get pregnant?"

"Let me see if I remember this right. This Mercedes took a girl away from the girl's boyfriend. Then the boyfriend raped Mercedes to get back at her. She turns up pregnant and has to talk about what happened. But the femme believes the boyfriend who claims Mercedes was two-timing her. So Mercedes is minus a girl, has the kid, tries to act like a normal mother for a few years, then goes bonkers and comes out again."

Frenchy was silent.

"You still looking for her?"

Frenchy looked up quickly. "Of course." She brooded for a minute. "You meet somebody and really like them for whatever reason, but you don't talk to them enough, don't tell them all you wanted to, kind of hold off from them. Then you hear something like this and you wonder if you could've done something. If you went just one inch closer maybe she would have opened up to you and felt better and not hurt herself. Maybe you talking to her just made her feel worse, like she'd never be able to make new friends with everything she had to keep inside."

"You can't take it personal," the bartender advised. "Like you said, if it's someone you just met . . ."

"You can still hope you would of done something, made a difference . . ."

"Have a drink. On the bar. Cheer up. I'm sorry I told you."

"That's okay. It's better I know. Maybe someday I'll see her again and it'll be different. But I'll take a rain check on the drink. I think I'll go home and get dry before I catch pneumonia. When it rains up here it really gets chilly." She began to walk away, but stopped. "Listen, I may never get the chance to get up here again. Do me a favor?"

"Sure."

"You ever see her around, tell her Frenchy said hi. Okay? Frenchy. And tell her I'm looking for her downtown. Just give the bouncer my name if she has trouble getting in."

"Frenchy. Downtown. You're looking for her."

"Thanks, pal."

* * * * *

Frenchy and the boys drove out of Provincetown Monday afternoon. The three had spent a couple of more hours on the beach and Frenchy was beginning to look, and feel, less lopsided. In another day her right side would turn as brown as her left.

She'd done a lot of thinking the night before in her tiny room, gazing toward the water from her window. That morning, while the boys ran in and out of the water, relishing the last of their freedom, she knew something had changed inside her, but she couldn't figure out what it was. She went over and over her Provincetown adventures until it became clear that three events stood out most in her mind. Her first view of the broad, clear expanse of sea, so soothing, so exciting, so moving, whose smell alone still made her feel different, better. Then the women in the bar Sunday night who had just talked to her and didn't go off to dance with other women or treat her like a prospective bed partner. It had been like talking to people at the store, in her neighborhood, except that she could be herself and talk about things that mattered to her. And then Mercedes. Damn, if that woman didn't pull on her more than any girl she'd ever had. Was it her sadness, how much she needed someone? Frenchy had never wanted to be encumbered with a femme's problems — if they got to be a nuisance drinking or crying too much then it was over, she wasn't interested anymore. She had never wanted to help a girl like she did this one.

She asked Rob and Gerald, "Guys, do you ever go up to Harlem?"

"Once in a while, babe. Why?"

"Like to go with you sometime is all."

"Sure. We'll let you know. You're fun to party with."

"Thanks," Frenchy said, leaning back, not feeling as complimented as she would have even on Friday. Maybe she shouldn't go looking for Mercedes with a partying crowd. Maybe this was something she had to do alone. Maybe the rusty French her mother had taught her would help her talk to Spanish women.

They crossed the bridge which connected the Cape to the mainland, and slowed for traffic. The air filled with car fumes and they were surrounded by asphalt and buildings. Frenchy clung to her vision of the sea as she breathed the poor air. *Release Me,* sang Little Esther Phillips on the radio. Frenchy sang along.

Chapter 3

Mercedes' Story
1965

Listen, I move here, I move there. Always, the crazies, they come to me, they get me. New York, Newark, Hartford, Bridgeport. I tried them all. Always the same: a big apartment high up in an old house, cracked windows, stove so old you can't get it clean, ripped cheap furniture, and cousins. I got so many cousins I bet I could move to a new city every year of my life.

Avila — that's my mother's people. Velez — that's my father's. All the aunts and uncles followed my mother and father from Puerto Rico thirty years ago. They all welcome me, try to get me to talk Spanish while I tell them they better learn English. If the crazies come, they take care of me and Lydia, my daughter.

Until they hear I'm still seeing girls. Then they throw me out, or drive me out with their worrying about me and Lydia. That's when I go back to my real family, the queers in the town. The black girls who have no one but each other for family, the gay boys all the time partying, the Puerto Rican girls who get beat up if they go home — and, like me, they're always trying to go home. And the white girls so poor they hang around with us.

Then I'm okay for a while. Maybe I'm in love. Maybe I just got Lydia back from my mother in New York by promising to stay with family in the new city, promising to stay away from girls. (I half mean it.) I don't mind either way, taking Lydia or leaving her with my mother, who takes good care of her, loves her — so I don't have to worry about her. But I love to have her with me too. She's the only good thing that's come out of the mess of my life. But I don't know. I worry maybe my mother is right: maybe I'm not a fit mother. But those times, when I'm starting out again in a new city, with a job packing or sewing — or the welfare if I got Lydia — with a place to stay, and sharing food with friends or family or a lover, I'm okay. But always one night I drink too much and there's cops pushing and pulling on me, or I wake up in the emergency room from too many pills. Sometimes I get beat up or I beat on my girl and I take off. Nothing ever ends good for me, you know? It's like I can be happy, safe, only so long, then things go bad. If somebody doesn't do it to me, then I do it to myself.

So this time, this time I'm telling you about, I got out of Elmhurst General in Queens after thirty days observation by being a good girl, taking my pills, staying away from the chicks on my floor who were worth my time. You should have seen this one girl, man was I good to stay away from her. She said she was gay, but, you know, they all say that when they're locked up with you. I could've had her, but this time, I don't know what happened, I wanted to get out of there. I didn't want to give up like I usually do and have to get pushed into getting better. I guess I got kind of mad at myself.

I'd drunk myself blind again 'cause I saw Maria, my ex, with her kids, shopping with the food stamps. She didn't see me, but when I saw the stamps I knew. Her husband took off. After all we been through. Him breaking her and me up, doing what he did to me, getting me pregnant. I'm sorry. I still can't talk about it much, but believe me, I left *scars* on him. And he left me with my own kid and Maria with three more little kids to take care of. I bet it makes him feel like a big damn man to know we both got his kids.

So I saw her that day, I hadn't been around the old neighborhood in a while, and I wanted so bad to talk to her, ask her did she want me back now, couldn't we make a home together. It was too hard. I started thinking about all the problems: what if he came back, what if I couldn't stand living with her kids by him, what if we couldn't live together except just on welfare, forgetting all our dreams when we first came out together... The Supremes sang it for me: *You Keep Me Hanging On.*

I never did ask what happened to land me at Elmhurst — just decided that was enough of that. I couldn't tear myself up over Maria and him all my life. We couldn't have what we had wanted. I had to leave that dream go, like a balloon in the park when you're a kid and you forget you're holding it for a second and when you look up it's traveling to the sky where you'll never be able to go: lost, it's gone, you're so little and so low and all you can do is roar out your hurt till your mother slaps you and you forget the balloon, the beautiful balloon, because then you're mad at your mother. So that night I drank to shut up my roar but it must have come out somehow . . .

For the first time in years I can think about what I had with Maria and say, "It's gone," without the crazies jumping all over me. I guess the tranquilizers help, but I've been on them so long I can't tell any more. I want it to be over now, that's all, I want to do something with my life.

The song that was playing that night goes on and on in my head now: *Stop in the Name of Love.* Those Supremes have it. They sing my music. Lydia and me, we dance to them all the time at home, and I always play them at the bars. Now, though, I mostly go downtown to the bars. When I came out of the hospital I decided to stay in the city, not try any place new, partly because I had a new part of the city to go to. I met this other butch, Frenchy, way back, up at Provincetown where I went exactly twice when one of the black chicks I hung out with was dealing and bought a car. Man, it was something else up there. The beaches looked almost as good as P.R. Not that I'd know, I never even visited there, but one of the girls said so. Someday, you know, I'm going to live on a beach and just lie there listening to the waves slap the sand like a band with a good beat and forget all of this, all this craziness I've been through.

So anyway, this second trip I meet this Frenchy and there's just something about her, something that makes me want to talk to her. I'm afraid at first she wants to make it with me and I try to warn her off, because, you know, we're both butch. But she doesn't make a move, so we just talk and I always keep her at the back of my head with the waves and the beaches — and sometimes when it's really bad, but I haven't gone over the edge yet, I remember her and wonder what her life is like, not being Puerto Rican, or even New Yorican, but otherwise living the same life as me.

So a few years later I see her uptown and she invites me, again, to hit the bars downtown with her. Me and my friends, sometimes we have trouble getting in those places. They tell us they're full up or some bullshit, then we see white girls going in after we leave. Pretty soon you don't go back after you've been told enough you don't belong. Like me going back to my family all the time. But Frenchy, she really seems to want to be friends and after I check her out to make sure she *just* wants to be friends I say okay.

I've been hanging out downtown awhile now. Frenchy's a little older, like me, and not so smooth as she used to be, not so sure she wants things always to be the way they are, she tells me. Not so much the butterfly with the girls. I met her one girl, Edie, who she's been seeing off and on years and years now. I'm not sure they're going together any more. I guess Edie's some kind of teacher, not Frenchy's type at all, but they seem to like each other okay. Then there's Frenchy's best pal Jessie, who's been with her own girl two years now. They want to move out to College Point, Queens together near the water. Nice, if you can. And all these little white chicks Frenchy knows — I haven't gone with any of them yet. Mostly Frenchy and me we sit and talk and watch the action, because we're closing in on thirty and we're running out of steam. But I'm happy too, just sitting there talking to Frenchy.

How do I feel being down there? That's what Edie asked me one night. "It must be different from uptown," she says.

"Yeah," I say, lighting a cigarette for her, hoping Frenchy won't mind. "It's not that I don't love my people," I tell her, "I do. That's one of the problems. Much as I like you guys, and sometimes feel like I fit in here better than uptown, in other ways I'd rather be dancing to a Latin beat with a girl just off the plane from P.R. I feel good up there, more at home."

"But you do fit in here."

"I know, but don't you understand, it's just a size too small down here. I have a little trouble breathing."

"Nobody's going to lock you in the House of D for coming in here," Frenchy says, bringing drinks to our table. I'm drinking coke so far this night, afraid of what the booze does to me.

"Not as long as I'm with you," I answer her, looking at this tiny friend of mine with her pompadour and the clothes I always see her in: black jeans and jacket, light blue shirt, a comb sticking out of her back pocket. She's Frenchy Tonneau (I can't pronounce her first name — she's named after her French grandmother), and she knows she's good-looking. She's even shorter than me, which is going some because I'm only 5'1". We're the same age, but it seems like she won't let anything touch her inside, you know, and I always let everyone and everything touch me and leave their mark. I respect her cool, the way she never gets involved, but I don't know as I'd like to be like that for myself. So far, what I've been through doesn't show on my face any more than her shutting herself up inside shows on hers. When I catch us in a bar mirror together I'd swear we're sisters except my skin's darker and my hair a little lighter. Also my face, it looks more like a girl's than hers. She has these sharp tough features. Mine are little and "cute," people say.

"Take a picture," she says to me, "it lasts longer," and I blush from staring at her. Sometimes it's like I'm a little in love with my friend Frenchy, but I know that can't be, because I'm butch too. Sometimes I catch her looking at me that way too — but maybe I'm not used to having such a tight friend.

"Maybe now they know me they'd let me in alone,"

I say, "but they wouldn't let me in with the other kids from uptown."

"They don't let *me* into the bars uptown without somebody *they* know." Frenchy always defends her turf.

"That's in case you're a cop, not just because you're white."

"Same difference."

"No, way, man," I say, a little angry because she never understands this. "The white people always come busting into our bars and hurting us. We come down here looking for a good time."

"Not all white people are cops."

"*No* Puerto Rican people are."

"That ain't my fault."

"Maybe, maybe not, but you could at least try and understand how I feel. I mean, honkeys have always been my enemy. It's always them who don't give me the job or who arrest me or who try to take away Lydia. When that happens enough to all of us, we get scared to see a white person come around some place we're not used to them being."

Frenchy looks up from her drink. "Okay. I can understand that. And it's the same when the bouncer down here sees a bunch of strangers coming onto our turf."

"No, it's not the same. You don't bounce out a group of strange white girls from out of town, but you do if they're Puerto Ricans from uptown. And we have reasons to be scared of white strangers because we been hurt by them. Why are you afraid of a group of dark-skinned girls?"

"I guess we must of been hurt somewhere along the line too."

"When? That's what I'm trying to figure out. You always been over us."

Edie breaks in. "I'm just beginning to talk about this

with a friend from school," she says, "and I don't have any answers. But I think it has to do with the unknown. Not wanting to let people who aren't like us near us."

"But which group feels like that, hers or mine?" Frenchy wants to know.

"Both groups, I think," Edie answers. "But the darker skinned races have the additional fear of knowing what white people, the people different from themselves, have done to them."

Frenchy gets up. "Well, it shouldn't be like that." It's like she's clearing it up once and for all. She winks at me. "All this thinking is making my head swim. I'm going to see who else is here." And she walks off through the crowded bar, stopping at almost every other table to say hello. She knows everybody down here, and I mean everybody.

Edie and me talked small talk for a while, then somebody came over and asked her to dance. I sat alone a couple of songs. My Supremes were singing *You Can't Hurry Love*, and I sat there feeling restless and out of place in this white bar, hoping not to find love here because it would complicate my life. Hoping not to find love for a while anyway till I straightened out my head. Love was always cropping up where I didn't expect it and throwing me for a loop. This time, I hoped, I'd get a handle on it before it got a handle on me.

Frenchy sat down, startling me from my thoughts. "How about let's go check out this other place just opened on Sixteenth Street?" she said, a little shyly for Frenchy. "See what the action's like over there?"

She never asked me to go any place alone with her before. "What about Edie?"

"I didn't come with her. I told her we're going."

That's nice, I thought, a little mad. Telling Edie I'd go before asking me. That gave me a nudge to ask what I'd been wanting to know. "You two not going together any more?"

"No. Not for a while now. We didn't break up or nothing, but we didn't have it for each other no more. She's got a new girl anyways."

"Somebody I met?"

"No, somebody she works with. I never met her neither. Not our type, I guess," Frenchy added, winking and pointing to her head. "Brains," she explained.

"Oh," I said, surprised at Edie. I was just getting to trust her, too. At the same time I felt a little mad at Frenchy again. I mean, I know I'm not brilliant, but I read a lot, and I talk better than her. Which isn't hard. She works at "talking tough." So how does she know a brain *wouldn't* be my type? But it was easier to feel mad at Edie than at Frenchy. "Sure," I say, not minding walking out on Edie now. "Let's go."

* * * * *

Me and Frenchy walk along Greenwich Avenue which at midnight is bright and still filling up with faggots hunting for one another. They pose between the lighted plate glass windows of the shops, one leg propped against the wall, arms across their chests, their bodies like ads for the night. What always gets me about them when they're cruising like this is how serious they look. No smiles, no emotion at all, like girls in a fashion magazine. But I guess that works for them — the lineup's always changing.

Sixth Avenue is a little darker, and feels far away from the music and crowds we just left. It's more a daytime street with bakeries and food stores. As a matter of fact, Frenchy tells me how she dreams of coming downtown to work at the Sixth Avenue A&P. I realize I'm really enjoying our walk. Frenchy's got this old diddy-bop way of walking like the hoody guys at school used to do. Her shoulders dip back and forth like she's snapping her fingers to music only she can hear, stopping once in awhile to run the comb through her slicked-back hair. Makes me feel not alone because I walk butch too, my hands in fists, long fast steps, like I mean business. In my neighborhood, the kids on the street call me names, the guys laugh at me because they know right away from my walk I'm a queer. It's what tipped Maria's boyfriend off to us. So it's good not to walk next to somebody like me.

We talked about it. Frenchy never tried to walk the way she does on purpose either. It's always been the way we walk. And they've always laughed at us. Sometimes I feel this glow thinking about how Frenchy and me are alike.

So we finish our butch parade outside a very dark doorway on 16th, go down some stairs and I know we're in the right place because there's a bouncer at the door. Frenchy pays for the both of us. I'm not insulted, I told her I had no cash for another cover. Inside it's packed, a big room with a bar off to one side and colored lights turning around on the ceiling. One of those new type places just coming into style because of all the drugs the kids are using. That's one thing I won't do. A little dope, maybe, once in a while when my head can take it, but no smack, no hallucinating drugs. Just the lights inside make me feel kind of shaky, never mind taking something to make every place look like this.

It's mostly girls and some of them are dressed like hippies. I see it's a whole new kind of crowd here. I smell pot from one corner. It's funny to see some of the kids with headbands and jewelry. Don't they know if the bouncer knew how much Indian I am she probably wouldn't let me in? I see long hair a lot, too. And long hair dancing with long hair. We got to the bar and I say to Frenchy how different this is from where we just were. She's staring at them too. "You can't tell who's butch and who's femme," she says.

"It looks like we're going out of style," I joke back. But the music's pretty much the same as at our bar — after all, the same syndicate controls all the jukeboxes in the gay bars. We sit and listen to it, watching and drinking. Even I have a drink now because I'm nervous being here and being alone with Frenchy. We can't talk much because there are these huge speakers around the walls. I'm just starting to feel high from the drink, looking around for a chick to ask to dance — not wanting to leave Frenchy's side, though. Frenchy gets real close to my ear and asks me to dance.

Out of nowhere she asks me to dance. I feel real funny, scared, but not in a way I mind. Kind of like it feels just before a chick touches her lips to me down there. Like she could do anything she wanted just then and I wouldn't do a thing to stop her. But glad to have her there, glad to let her take me over like I took her over. As long as she knows it's only like that in bed. I'm not stone butch, you know. I like it too.

So all this goes through my head as Frenchy's asking. We're some place we've never been before, maybe never will be again, neither of us knows anybody, and it's dark except for one of those weird strobe lights. I'm feeling even shakier from the drink and the lights and now Frenchy knocks me all the way off balance. Her boots put her on a level with my eyes and I look at her face all lit up shiny from the strobe one second, dark the next. Asking me with her face to dance and nothing else, then blinking off into mysterious darkness with sex written all over my memory of her face when the light was there. Then the strobe flashes over her again and the sex is gone, it's just Frenchy. I keep staring at her, knowing inside me I'm seeing every gay girl

I've ever been with — the sex side of them flashing into the friend side. I see all of a sudden that every butch is a femme; every femme is a butch. I know the lips of my friend could get me hotter than the lips of any femme in the room. I remember how it looks like femmes and butches went out of style in this bar. I think, as I slip into Frenchy's arms, maybe I'm going out of style too.

I feel dizzy. I didn't know I was feeling like this about Frenchy before, I swear. We're on the dance floor, then, arms around each other and barely moving. The Supremes are singing *Stop in the Name of Love.* "Stop," I laugh into Frenchy's ear, quietly. This isn't supposed to happen till later. And then you need a slow song. You get so you're hardly moving, just grinding crotches. But we aren't that far gone. The strobing finally stops, but the song goes on. I'm glad I only had the one drink, with the tranquilizers in me and the lights. Rose and blue colored lights bounce off a globe hanging over the dance floor, a thousand tiny mirrors break the light up to the beat of the music, little rose fragments flying over the dancers, the floor, Frenchy's face. I pull back to look at her. The music is throbbing with a slow heavy bass. Frenchy's normally closed handsome face is naked now. She wants me. Jesus, she wants me. And all of a sudden I know how badly I wanted her all along.

We touch cheeks. I tingle, starting with my cheek, into my arm, my hand at Frenchy's waist. We touch breasts, and warm, lush shivers run all inside me; run into my shoulders, down my stomach, between my legs. My breath stops with my mouth open, unable to take in air. I press the whole side of my face to hers. She draws back and even though my eyes are closed I know she's going to kiss me.

I left my mouth open, just taking her kiss. I couldn't think. When her small warm tongue touched me I sucked it in further, dug my fingers into the small of her back and drank Frenchy in. I felt her breath in my mouth. I pressed our bodies together. She ground against me and everything between my hips melted while our mouths stayed together, lightly, open.

If we weren't both wearing heavy denim I don't know what would have happened. All this went on during that one song, but it seemed like forever. There was nothing, nothing in the world but Frenchy and me. As the music peaked the lights did too, and it was like we were in a world of rose and blue lights somebody just let go of so that they were wandering wild. Frenchy had led me deeper and deeper into this love-making, but as the music stopped I knew I wanted to lead her, too.

So far I knew I was acting like an easy femme. It felt okay, but I didn't want it to be like that between Frenchy and me. So I kissed her, struggling to reach her like she'd reached me. Wanting her to feel weak, to be giving in to me as I took my turn giving love to her.

She felt like an iron bar. I kept kissing her, pouring all of me into her lips, waiting for her to respond. She responded all right. She started pulling away from me.

After a couple of tries I let her go and just stared at her. Here I let myself go in her arms, trusted her, my friend, my equal, and she wouldn't do the same for me. "Don't pull no stone business on me, baby," I warned her. "Not after that. I'm no damn femme either."

I guess it was my pride. And my temper. She couldn't do this to me. If I couldn't touch her she'd see me as femme. I wanted her to know who I really was and to see I could move her like she moved me. Or else I wasn't interested. I'd rather just be friends where we knew our ground and treated each other the same. I was strong. A good dancer. Good-looking. Knew how to talk to a girl, how to please her. All that was me, not just the woman who fell apart at Frenchy's kiss. She couldn't ignore all that. She couldn't do this to me. Coming downtown I was turning my back on everything else I once was because I felt trapped up there in the Barrio by the old ways. But now, what could I do, as much as she meant to me I had to push her farther away from me. Frenchy was double-crossing me. She had no business doing that, no right to mess with my head, my reputation, my way out.

When she reached out for me I swung at her. The crazies were on me. I could feel them grab all the muscles in my body, tensing them up. Like all the little reflections spinning around and around, they were running wild in my head. I knew I should take a pill, but I let the crazies take me over. I'd let them do what they wanted to me. I wished I'd never been stupid enough to trust this white chick. I'd use them against her, I'd kill her.

I started to go for her again, but something stopped me. The dancers around us were still dancing, almost as if they understood our scene and were covering us so we could do our thing. Frenchy was standing there rubbing her cheek where I connected with her. All of a sudden I felt sorry for the friend I'd hurt. I thought, I didn't *want* to hurt her. But I couldn't comfort her the way I knew how. I could only hit her again or leave. There was only one way I knew to treat a girl I felt like that about, and she didn't want to be treated that way. Tears were coming into my eyes and I was damned if I was going to let her see me cry. That I could cry like any girl was none of her damned business.

"Damn you!" I shouted, but my voice was high and whiny.

"Mercedes, I love you!" she shouts back.

"Don't you understand? You got to let me love you too!"

If she would have tried then, if she only would have come to my arms then, we could have worked the rest out later. But she marches up to me like in the movies, like some dumb cowboy buying a whore.

"Let's talk," she says, trying to turn me to the door.

"Go talk to yourself, *man*," I hiss at her.

Then I realized that's how she made me feel. Like a girl with a man. Like being raped again. She had all the aces and wouldn't give me none. I turned and ran out the door.

Outside I kept running. I was humiliated and let down and ashamed of myself. Acting like a damn femme. Trusting a white girl like one of my own. Wondering how long she'd planned this. Asking, why, why did she do it, why did I give in? How did I get to feel like that about her without knowing it? Did I really want to make it with a butch like Frenchy? As long as the questions ran through my head I kept running.

I turned downtown. By 13th Street I was out of breath and had to slow. I hadn't thought of Frenchy following me, but I turned to check. I felt calmer. But I didn't want to think about her. The Women's House of Detention was in front of me now and I remembered how bad it felt to be in there. It made me feel even meaner thinking about that place. I headed for the bar. Maybe Frenchy'd got to me, but the rest of the white girls hadn't. Maybe I'd find a girl tonight who knew the difference between butch and femme. Who'd respect me.

The first person I saw inside was Edie. Since Frenchy took off with me and left her behind, I figured Edie was fair game.

"Hi, darlin'," I said, sitting at her table.

"I didn't expect you back."

How much of her plan had Frenchy told her, I wondered. "We just did a little bar hopping. Can I get you a refill?"

"Just some seltzer, Mercedes. I've got to go soon."

I knew I shouldn't drink either, but I was still thinking about Frenchy and what she did to me, so I ordered one. The way they watered them down I figured it wouldn't matter.

"So what's been happening?" I asked Edie.

"Not much," she said, smiling, as Jessie and her girl Mary came over to sit with us. It was usually nice to see them, they were so much in love, but tonight it hurt. "I've just been visiting with people I haven't seen in a while. I don't come down here much."

"It doesn't seem like your kind of place, hanging out with a bunch of dropouts like us."

"I don't think of you like that," Edie said, looking hurt.

I felt guilty. "Sorry, sorry. I do, is all."

Mary and Jessie had been making out, but now they were listening. "When you get to know people," Mary said, "they're all the same underneath the school and the jobs and the color of their skins." She looked proud of knowing this. "That's what I've noticed anyway." Mary was nice, I thought, but like Jessie, not too smart. And speaking of not too smart, Jessie bought me another drink. I drank it.

I heard a Supremes song go on then and it shook me up. "Want to dance?" I asked Edie.

"That's the best offer I've had all night." She smiled, and I believed her. She's one of those girls who always seems to mean what she says. I couldn't help but like her.

"Hmm," I said as I took Edie in my arms.

"Like this song?"

"I like everything The Supremes do. They sing about my life. Mostly, though, I'm feeling the liquor. Makes me warm inside. Makes me feel strong like bull." I said this jokingly, with a Russian accent.

"I understand. But the next day, doesn't it make you feel weak like baby?" She laughed.

"I'll worry about tomorrow tomorrow. Who knows where I'll be? I could be dead. Maybe better off that way."

"You don't mean that."

"Sure I do," I answered her, smiling, and hearing the Supremes singing *Where Did Our Love Go?* "You can't get ahead in this world if you're a Spic and a gay. Your own people don't want you because you're queer. The white girls walk all over you. You end up living in dives in Harlem with kids as bad off as you. You know you'll never get out."

Sometimes I can't stand the way white people look at me when I tell them what it's like to be inside my skin. All sympathetic like they want to put a bandaid on you. A "flesh-colored" bandaid. Edie, though, she looked me straight in the eye. "Where do you want to get out to?"

I laughed. "Now that's a hard question. Maybe I just want a choice."

She nodded seriously. "I understand."

The music ended and Jessie was coming back to our table with another round. "We got here late, got to catch up," she explained. Mary scowled at her.

I was drinking this one slowly, because the other drinks were mixing with the tranquilizers always in my bloodstream and were starting to knock me over the head, when Frenchy walked in. She looked surprised to see me. I decided to pretend everything was okay and flashed a grin at her. But I felt my lips twist underneath in pain.

"Get bored there, mano?" I asked, leaning heavily on the mano so she'd get a whiff of how I was feeling.

"Strange scene," she said, combing her damn hair.

I wanted her to be holding me again in the worst way and at the same time wanted to hit myself for feeling like that after what she'd done to me. Frenchy acted like I'd taken some of the starch out of her, but mostly she was her cocky old self. After all, she'd had me. She was king of the roost again. I was hers — so she thought — almost as much as Edie was hers, and Jessie was her best pal. She'd even gone with Mary awhile a few years back. This was her turf.

She went off to the bar and brought back a round. I drank it to spite her. I wanted to bring on the crazies again. I wanted them to take me over so I could get her, never mind me sitting here playing nice to the little *man*. I went and stood at the bar. I asked myself, did I really want to do this? Then my brain shut off. It does that sometimes so I can take care of myself. Too much thinking makes me feel weird. I didn't have to figure anything out anymore. Whatever happened happened.

I pushed back to the table, another drink in my hand. I felt ugly mean. I was angry, too, because I didn't have the bread to buy a round. All I had left was my subway fare home. But with all the money they liked to flash around, I wasn't going to let these white bastards know that. Sure they worked every week and were proud of it, liked to show it off. I wished I had it to show off.

I stumbled a little sitting down, but Frenchy knew not to try and steady me. She was finishing a quiet conversation with Edie and I figured she was telling her how easy I was, what a hot-blooded Latin. Oh, how could I have? I yelled inside myself, humiliated all over again. I shut it off, though, and toasted them. "Here's one for the road," I said.

"You splitting?" Frenchy asked, smoothing back her hair.

"What's it to you?"

"Wanted to talk to you is all."

I didn't say anything. What did she want me to say? I shook my head. Besides, I was feeling dizzy, I didn't want to talk. I was afraid I'd cry again. My eyes were half-closed from the booze and the pills. My body was slowing down. It felt good, but I still felt mean. If I hadn't felt so sluggish

I would've knocked the table over to get at Frenchy.

"You bastard," I heard myself saying, real low. "You fucking bastard fake white *man*. You been sucking around me a couple of months now." I talked louder, thickly: "You got what you want now? You got your little piece of Mercedes so you can feel like the big man around here? You knock me down to your size yet?" I think I said some more stuff in between, but I can't remember what. Just Frenchy sitting there kind of blurry, looking at me sad, like she was so damn hurt. "You're lucky they got me doped up or I'd kill you. That's why the man dopes me, so I won't kill any of his white girls." I had them all looking shocked. "Yeah, I hurt girls. I'm an outlaw: PR and gay. How you like that? I tried it uptown, I didn't make it. I tried it out of town, I didn't make it. Now I tried it downtown and I'm just about to flunk that too. Seems like nobody wants me to win. Not even me. Seems like I just get back on my feet and somebody comes by to knock me down. Fuck all of you."

I found out later I put my head down then and passed out. Didn't do any damage this time. Just cursed them out and went to sleep. Good stuff, those tranquilizers. I didn't hurt any nice little white girls. They didn't have to lock me up, though I almost wanted them to. Sometimes it's easier.

* * * * *

I woke up on the subway halfway into Queens. Edie, Jessie and Mary half-dragged, half-pushed me that far. I remember asking if we'd passed the House of D yet and saying I'm sorry a lot. I was too exhausted to say more. Without really caring I wondered where we were going.

Edie's voice seemed to whisper in my ear. "We're going to my house, Mercedes. You can sleep there."

I knew I should be happy about that. Going home to

sleep with Edie. But I was in a heavy black fog I couldn't get out of. I guessed it was depression. The liquor and tranquilizers were sitting on my whole body, holding it down. Then I remembered, through a cloud, or like it happened long ago when I was a kid, that Frenchy, my friend Frenchy, had got to me real bad. The black fog moved back from me a little and I felt a warm glow. I wanted to be with her again. I wanted to dance again. I felt forgiving like a revelation from the Bible. Probably she didn't understand, I thought, didn't know why I got mad. "Frenchy?" I found myself asking out loud.

"She went home," Edie said. "She didn't think you'd want her around."

Even through my fog I knew for sure now Edie knew what had happened.

I risked falling off the earth by lifting my head to see Edie's face. It was full of concern. "I love you," I told her, meaning it. "And I love Frenchy." I let my head fall back to her shoulder. Then, to make sure everybody had it right, I said, as clear as I could, "But don't let that bastard near me again."

The noise of the train seemed to be a thousand voices singing, *Stop in the Name of Love*, over and over. When we got off the train the city seemed silent. I found I could walk pretty good, but I was still very weak. Edie told Jessie and Mary they could go back, that we could make it to the house alone. It seemed like a very long walk. There was a newsstand on a corner, but that was all the life I saw as we went into the trees and darkness. In my neighborhood, that time of night, there'd still be plenty of action. "Where's this," I asked, "Long Island?"

Edie laughed. "Not quite."

We walked up to a three-story house and I thought she'd live on the second or third floor. I wasn't looking forward to those stairs. "Let me stay here," I argued, but she pushed me inside. She was pretty strong for a femme. We didn't climb stairs. The whole house was hers. I couldn't believe it and kept staggering around to see different parts of it. Finally, she put me in a big double bed in a nice warm room on the first floor. I grabbed her wrist and tried to pull her in bed with me. I mean, I had to at least try, alone there in a house with a good-looking femme. My reputation was blown enough for one night. But Edie pulled away and disappeared.

At first I felt the darkness and the strangeness of the place as scary. Like Lydia does when we start out someplace new. But after a while, since I didn't have a mother to talk to me, I kind of talked to the house. Thanked it for giving me shelter. As if to the Madonna, I whispered into the comforting blackness. Shelter from everything, I thought sleepily. It was nice how the dark got mixed in with the cloud that still sat around me, pressing in on me until it went away a little. When the cloud was light enough, and I felt like I could breathe pretty good, I slept.

* * * * *

The next day Edie fed me and kept me in bed. I was kind of panicky about my tranquilizers, knowing what I would be like without them, so I called my friend Gladys, who had a car. I told her I was sick again, but somebody was taking care of me. Gladys was used to my calls and Edie said she'd meet her up at the newsstand.

When I said, "What's the matter, she's not good enough to come to your house?" Edie explained very cool how hard it was to find her house. Anyway, I apologized because, after all, didn't she take *me* in? I was a real louse, I guess, but I wasn't used to the kindness of strangers. Most times I'd be strapped down to a bed by now or still out with drugs. "Why'd you bring me here anyway?" I asked as we sat at her kitchen table around 7:00 that night. I wore an old bathrobe of hers and warmed my hands around a mug of coffee though it was plenty warm in there.

"I have plenty of space," Edie said easily.

I stared at her blonde head and her white face, suspicious again. She was too damn pretty. I mean, people say I'm pretty, but when did you ever hear a Rican winning the Miss America? "You could have dumped me at the hospital."

"You don't need a hospital, Mercedes," she said. "You need a home. I could offer you that."

"Oh." The feeling of revelation I had the night before — I couldn't remember what about — came back to me. "Oh," I said again, surprised how simple it all was. "Yeah. I guess I do need a home. A warm clean place where I belong," I said, looking up at her. "That might go a long way toward fixing me up. How'd you know?"

Edie poured me more coffee. "Different things you've said."

"How much did Frenchy tell you?"

"About you?"

"About me. About last night."

"About you, bits and pieces here and there over the last several months. About last night, just that she was coming on to you and you got offended."

That didn't sound too bad. But those were Edie's words, not Frenchy's. Edie said things nice. Still, maybe she didn't think I was an idiot. "She got me by surprise, you know. I didn't know how I felt. I'm butch," I explained. I wasn't planning to tell her anything, but it was coming out. She didn't say anything, just sat there looking interested and nodding.

"What do you think I should do, Edie?"

"I don't really understand about butches and femmes, Mercedes. I never have, really. I just fell in love with Frenchy Tonneau and learned to love by her rules. That was all I knew. Now, though, since she hasn't been as interested in me, I've met another woman, another teacher, who's more like me, and doesn't go in for roles."

"You mean you're both butch? Or both femme?"

Edie was smiling, and I noticed her teeth weren't so all-American. Some were discolored and one was chipped. That made me feel better.

"I guess we're a little bit of both. She's had more experience than I, so maybe she starts things more." She added with a sexy shy look, "But I can hold my own now."

I was smiling. "How come you weren't with her last night?"

"She sings in a gospel group. They perform a lot on Saturday nights. And of course she's often in church all day Sundays."

"A gospel group?" I asked, not able to cover my surprise. "You mean she's..."

Edie was grinning ear to ear and nodding. "Black," she finished for me. "You look as shocked as my neighbors."

"I'm sorry," I said, liking this surprising woman more and more. "I never figured you for the type." Then I got silly. "You mean I have a chance with you?"

She laughed, shaking her head and blushing. I thought, this chick is shy! "I'm sorry, I shouldn't ask you that. I was only teasing."

"I shouldn't be embarrassed," she said. "I'm just not used to being teased like this. Frenchy's always so serious. But there isn't a chance for you, I'm afraid. Esther takes up about all of me there is."

Was that woman ever in love. Just talking about this Esther made her glow. She looked like I'd felt when Frenchy was holding me the night before. "What's she like?" I asked, wondering if I might have met her.

Edie sighed. "She's short, like us, and not heavy, but a

little round — just enough." She was still grinning like she couldn't help herself. "She wears her hair in that new way — in an Afro? It looks like a halo around her head. She's not real dark, but not as light as you and she wears glasses. Her face is round and looks like an angel's, especially when she smiles. Her voice is as deep as, I don't know, as a woman's can get I guess, and when she mumbles I think she's growling."

"How'd you meet her?"

"That's the funny thing. All this time I was seeing Frenchy once in a blue moon and spending the rest of my time alone or running around with my teacher friends and thinking nobody knew about me. But Esther was watching me," she went on, all happy. "She's from South Carolina and got a scholarship to go to school up here. Afterward she took a job at my school teaching typing and, like me, English. She came to the department meetings, and I realize now because she was black, I thought she was on loan to English and really belonged in the trades department. She had her Masters in Literature, but the only way she could get a full-time job when she started was to take on the two subjects." She stopped and looked at me like she'd put on brakes. "I can tell you about Esther for hours."

"Tell me the important stuff," I said, catching her happiness and smiling. "How did you two get together?"

"It was simple. And very romantic. One day, maybe because I'd decided it was time for some changes in my life, including branching out from Frenchy, I noticed Esther. I was eating with my group in the teacher's lunchroom and I looked up to see this cherubic woman gazing at me over her sloppy joe with a look of such love and lust I thought she must be daydreaming about her boyfriend. She said later she was so used to me not looking at her that for weeks she hadn't bothered to hide how she felt. When our eyes met she didn't turn away. I definitely felt exactly what she was feeling and knew just what she wanted to do about it. The bell rang and I started taking my tray to the trash bin. She'd made me so nervous I dropped everything all over the floor and, of course, there she was helping me pick it all up, brushing me off tenderly, and asking if she could treat me to a pizza for lunch the next day, it would be less damaging to school property. She went on like that for a few minutes — she's very funny — and we were both late for our classes which turned out to be next door to each other."

She took a deep breath. "Of course I'd noticed that she taught her English classes next to me, but it hadn't registered. When I was too nervous to eat more than one slice of pizza the next day she took me out for dinner too, to make sure I got enough to eat *and* didn't break any china. We began to spend all our time between periods talking. I learned to listen to her voice and laughter through the wall. Oh, Mercedes, I can't tell you what she's done for me."

"You don't have to. I see it. When can I meet her?"

"She tries to get away from church early enough on Sundays to come over in the evening. I'm still hoping she'll make it."

I worried for a minute. "How will you explain me?"

Edie laughed that full happy laugh of hers. "I don't think she'll be jealous," she said looking at me wearing her bathrobe and slippers, my face pale and sickly, my hair uncombed.

"I must smell pretty bad too," I said, laughing with her. Then I got kind of weepy. "How come she doesn't live with you? I wouldn't pass up a chance like this for anything. Your house is so — I don't know . . . warm. Last night, going to sleep, it felt full of nice old ghosts who were all smiley and kind. You know?"

"I know exactly. They weren't like that when my parents

were living. Or for a while after that. As soon as I listened to one of them and acknowledged her good advice, they all seemed to come alive and be as helpful as all get out. You know, sometimes I can't help but wonder if they didn't create Esther for me, to bring me happiness."

I was as serious as she was. "Maybe not that, but I'm sure they told you to notice her when you didn't for so long."

"I hadn't thought of that. You're probably right. Have you ever known any ghosts?"

"When I was a kid there was this woman who ran a religious shop in my neighborhood. She told me a lot about ghosts so I wasn't afraid of them. An *espiritista*, my family called the old woman. She sold all this religious stuff, crosses and like that, but you could get other kinds of things. Things I promised her I'd never tell anybody about. She said I'd use them myself when I was ready, but, you know, I think I've forgotten all of them."

"That's too bad. Here I was hoping you could teach me a secret or two!"

"She had a crystal ball, too. She really did. All the old women would consult with her and if I was hanging around I got to watch the front of the shop. The old ladies, they would come out of the back room smiling or crying, talking to themselves, and I'd be real proud I worked for the woman who told the future."

"Did she ever tell yours?"

"Not from the ball. She said I was too young. I don't know if that meant she couldn't or wouldn't. She was probably afraid because my parents were so American, you know? They talked English at home and didn't want me to talk Spanish. They dressed to fit in downtown instead of where we lived. They didn't go to the neighborhood church. If my father hadn't died so soon I'd probably be living next door to you!"

"When did he die?"

"I was nine, ten. And I was the oldest. My mother had five of us, plus she used to work. But my father, he had three jobs, trying to save money to live in a little better place, to send us to college. Killed himself trying, I guess. My mother couldn't make it even though she started working two jobs. Just couldn't earn enough. We started to run through the savings. She started getting tired. Without my father's help she had to turn more and more to the rest of the family, the more old-fashioned people who followed us over. Pretty soon we were just another big poor Puerto Rican family. And worse off than some of them because my mother didn't have a boyfriend. She was waiting for another good husband with money and ambitions. What man like that would marry five kids?" I was shaking my head, remembering how hard it had been to go from being special and different to being laughed at because we were being brought down to our real size. "The neighborhood helped us, sure, but you could tell it was because now we weren't any better than them, there was nothing wrong with them after all. But I'm talking your head off," I apologized.

"No!" Edie said. "Go on. I'm interested. It's so much like my parents' story, only, as you can see, my father didn't die till he got where he wanted to be. Or at least close to it. And besides, I was an only child. It wasn't much different for Jews than for Puerto Ricans. Only instead of *espiritistas* we had rabbis, Talmudic scholars. The women would talk of *dybbuks*, our spirits, and other unearthly things, but it was the men who had all the religious say."

"I never understood why these same women who came to the shop also went to Church. Didn't they see the two didn't go together?"

Edie nodded. "Of course they did. They were afraid. The men said theirs was the right way to be religious. I wonder if any of our women had powers like your shop-keeper's and why they stopped using the powers if they did. Maybe, after World War II, they thought they had to give them up to be in America. Or maybe the Nazis killed off anyone like that first." She shook herself and stood. "Would you like some tea?"

"Yes, it tastes better than coffee today."

"I'm really enjoying talking to you," Edie said as she took cups down. "I can't talk to Frenchy like this. She's so superficial most of the time. Interested in clothes and who's going with whom and the movies she's seen. She never talks about herself, as if she didn't have a self. Never wants to hear much about me. Esther is much easier to talk to than Frenchy, even though our backgrounds are so different."

"Frenchy's gay," I said.

"Well, I *know* that."

"But, I mean, that's all of her: her past, her future." I wondered why I was defending the girl. "She can only go as deep as gay is. And because of how we live, that's not very deep."

"I'm not sure I understand," Edie said, sitting as if to listen better.

She's not really pretty, I thought. She had the kind of dark blonde hair you see on magazine covers, but her face was too full of real life to make it magazine pretty. Her nose wasn't big, but it was strong. It said, I'm a nose, not some cute little thing stuck on here. Her eyes weren't that big, but they were so deep you didn't notice their size. Her mouth was full, with plenty of surface for kissing. I smiled. This was a lot of woman for little Frenchy.

"I don't know if I can explain what I mean," I said. "I'm like Frenchy too, which is how *I* know what I mean. But so much else has gone on in my life I can't *just* be gay.

Frenchy doesn't let anything happen to her she can't control."

"Do you mean she's like a very religious person, but instead of converting other people to Orthodoxy or Jesus or Buddha, it's gayness?"

"Kind of. Only I don't know how much converting she does," I said, laughing. "She's either with straight people she's not out to, or gay people who already saw the light."

"She converted me."

"She bring you out?"

Edie blushed and nodded as she poured the water.

"I didn't know that."

"I more or less went looking, so it wasn't a difficult conversion." She smiled. "But her performance kept any doubt from creeping back."

We laughed and it felt good to laugh together. It felt good to be laughing, period. I hadn't felt so comfortable in a long, long time. And I wanted to hug Edie. Not make it with her, just hug her for giving me this. But she was fussing with the tea kettle so I just watched her in her cozy warm kitchen. "See, Frenchy's whole life is built around being gay," I went on. "All week she suffers through life with her mother so she can have a day or two of freedom at the end. So the gay part of her life, of herself, gets really big to her. Everything else in her life means whatever it does because she's gay. It's the end, not the way to get to the end. I know I'm not saying this too good."

"No, go on, I'm beginning to see what you mean. Like the person who wakes up with prayers, goes to *shul*, thinks of his friends as a *quorum*, follows the dietary laws, and on and on. She's self-conscious. Constantly aware of her 'religion.' But with the Jew, these are rituals in a life filled with marriage and work and kids. For Frenchy, the ritual *is* her life."

"So she's not all on the surface, Edie. She just talks about what means a lot to her."

"And if there were lesbian books and movies like straight people have, Frenchy would have a lot more to talk about." Edie stopped smiling. "Being a lesbian is almost as bad as being a Jew in Nazi Germany. You couldn't talk openly about it. You couldn't write about it. If you suffered, everybody ignored you. Or they put you in jail for it."

I shuddered. "I never thought about it like that. It's like being a Puerto Rican in the States, too," I said, thinking of my dead father and then of Frenchy. "You have to hide who you are to make a decent living."

"To survive."

"Frenchy will survive all right."

"Why do you say that?"

"I never met anybody so strong-willed. Except me. And she's got me beat." My mood began to sag. I remembered the sickening feeling of being humiliated. Yet there were the warm feelings I had talking about Frenchy.

"I worry about her, Mercedes. What's going to happen when she comes up against a situation where she has to give a little? Be flexible?"

"Wish I knew," I said. I felt tired again.

"Maybe we ought to finish this talk another day and get some sleep," Edie suggested.

I yawned. "What about Esther?"

"It's too late. I don't think she'll come now. We both have to get to work in the morning."

"Listen, get me up when you leave and I'll clear out."

"No," Edie said firmly. "I want you to stay longer. You need the rest. Your friend brought you enough clothes for a few days. I think this will do you good. Besides, I want you to meet Esther."

I started to say no, but she interrupted. "And I like your company. I'm lonely here by myself." Edie smiled at me. "To answer your earlier question, Esther doesn't live here because we're not ready for that."

"Okay." I smiled back, not wanting anything more than to stay under her wing, in her houseful of friendly ghosts.

* * * * *

The next few days I felt safe for the first time in years. I didn't have to leave the house to be with gay people and nobody in the house or within miles of me was out to hurt me.

Esther was just as nice as Edie said. I'd never hung out with a black girl who'd gone to college — a teacher — and it made me sad I didn't get to go because my father died. I knew I could be smart like Esther and Edie. I could be earning good money to bring Lydia up in a safe place in Queens. But I might not've had Lydia. Maybe it was better to have my daughter than a college education.

The times I tried to thank Edie, to tell her and Esther how good all this made me feel, they would say I could have it too, I could go back to school and be a teacher or something. That made me feel small again. How could I do that? Soon now I had to get it together again to get a job and support Lydia the best I could. After eight hours on a sewing machine, or packing fish in a cold room, you think I could stay awake in a classroom?

So as the days went on I got depressed again. The house began to seem lonely when Edie was at work. I started feeling left out of their love. Not that I should be included in, but I didn't have a girl of my own.

And I kept thinking about Frenchy. And what me and Edie said about her. Maybe she felt trapped in the life she was living and was restless to get out of it. She knew I was butch. It wasn't like her to break the rules she followed for so long. Yet she wanted me all the same. She knew I wasn't the type to turn femme, but maybe that was the only way she thought she could have me. And wasn't it? Maybe not, I thought. She did show me I was willing to be something besides butch all the time, but I've got to have a little respect too and be treated like myself, not like a femme, you know? There's nothing wrong with being treated like a femme unless you're not one. I mean, it'd be like dressing my personality up in drag, to all of a sudden get my cigarettes lighted and for me to do all the cooking. But that's not exactly what I mean either.

Take lighting cigarettes. I think it's really sexy to light a girl's cigarette. You touch her hand, she touches yours; you look in her eyes, she looks in yours. She breathes out the smoke in a certain sexy way from the side of her mouth because she's close to your face. You light your own cigarette to give yourself some time to breathe, to cool down and get back in control. By looking away, leaving the girl looking at you lighting your cigarette in this real butch flick of the match operation, she's now a little unsure of herself. She's digging you, but you're looking away from her, so she doesn't know if what she saw in your eyes was real or not, if it'll be there when you turn back, if she should turn away fast so you don't see her come-on look. You're wondering the same kinds of things, and thinking maybe you should say see ya and walk away. Or else you risk it and your eyes meet again and the lovelight's still shining and you're in love, at least for the night.

So all these little moves the girl made and you made, all the ones I left out here, they're all important. And who makes which move is important to me, right or wrong. *I* just happen to like the butch moves. You both get your cigarettes lighted, you both get to send signals, you both get to decide if you're going to risk it or not and you can both win if the risk pans out. But I don't even know *how* to do it like a femme. It must be a whole different feeling, giving a come-on look, getting your cigarettes lit. Probably feels just as good, just as turned-on, just as in control. But I like that little edge of being in charge, that make-believe feeling that it's up to me in a certain way, the bigger risk of knowing the first move is up to me.

So nobody's going to make me be femme.

But, I don't need for the other girl to be femme, either. I don't need to go through that particular operation. If two girls who are butch want to make it together, I don't see why they couldn't have a whole different way of doing it. Hell, maybe if butch and femme are going out of style, cigarettes will go out of style too and we'll all be a little healthier. I have no stake in keeping things the way they are.

Frenchy now, it's a lot more important to her. *Who* we do things with is, I think, as important to her as the *way* we do things. I think I put her on notice that if she wants me it can't be the way she's used to. I'll change for her, but she's got to change too. And I don't know if she can. So I'm knocking around this big empty house wishing and hoping.

And listen, except for these times of depression I was getting better. I felt better than I had in a long time. While I was staying at Edie's, my shrink at the outpatient clinic in Elmhurst put me on a lighter medication. The only thing was, I wanted a girl. But I only wanted damn Frenchy. I thought of asking the shrink what I should do, but you know how they are: he would've told me I was changing into more of a real woman by wanting a butch. Next step I'd be wanting a man. He didn't know shit about being gay.

I kept putting off leaving Edie's, figuring how I could live like this with Lydia. How a New Yorican poor unskilled dropout unwed mother bulldyke could live a little better and bring her child up better. What if there was two of us to bring her up, I kept thinking . . .

When I was little, the *espiritista* had looked at my hand and said, "Love comes to everyone, to some later than others. Life is hard for everyone — for some earlier, for some later. You've got to climb to the top of the mountain before you can see." It was beginning to make sense.

One day when I felt strong enough to go out and face the world, I bought myself some green cloth in a store on Roosevelt Avenue. Then I went to the vacant lot at the end of Edie's street and picked some wildflowers from the weeds. I didn't know what kind I needed, or what kind they were, but I figured some kind was better than no kind. I sewed the material into a little bag, filled it with weeds, and hung it all around my neck. The *espiritista* had taught me colors: green was for healing and I needed that bad. If the weeds didn't carry the right powers, the green might. And I hoped maybe somewhere in the years since I learned from the old woman, that knowledge had stayed safe in some corner of my head and I was picking the right weeds and colors and roads now. Even though I took a step backwards when Frenchy messed with my head, I was helping myself now. I wondered how strong I could get in another week. Longer than that I wouldn't stay with Edie. She was generous, but I wouldn't take advantage of her.

* * * * *

Two Fridays after I came to Edie's house, I had my clothes and pills piled in a grocery bag on the kitchen table. I sat fingering my herb bag, waiting for her to come home so I could thank her and say goodbye. And borrow a dollar to get home. She was later than usual, and if I had to I'd leave her a note, but I couldn't go through this again. Saying goodbye to this house was the hardest thing I'd done in a long time. Not only because I was sad, but because I'd made the decision myself and wanted to stick to it. I wasn't letting things happen to me anymore, I was planning them. Finally, I heard Edie's laugh. I'd have to give my speech to Esther too.

I watched them come in through the doorway together, laughing and bumping into each other with bags of groceries in their arms, two happy women; one so light-skinned her blue eyes were striking even across the kitchen, the other so dark I couldn't see her eyes behind her round, dark-rimmed glasses. I don't know if their love was catching or what, but I felt all warm about them. Now that I was with them and remembering how nice they were, what I was going to say hurt me even more.

Edie and Esther put their bags down on the table. Edie took both my hands in hers and made me sit down. "What's this?" she said, looking at my bag of clothes.

I said sadly, "I think it's time for me to go home."

"Home?" Esther growled. "Home, baby, is where you are at. What are you saying?" She likes to act up a lot and make faces. She hit her head and pretended it hurt. Then she walked around the kitchen like a drunk, finally falling in a heap at Edie's feet.

Edie put her fingers in Esther's hair. "That's what I wanted to talk to you about. Esther had an idea today which I have to admit has been half-forming in my mind since you came here."

"Go 'head, take all the credit, you sneaky white girl," Esther said.

"But it took wonder woman here to put it together for me," Edie added, pretending to tug Esther up to her feet by her hair.

I didn't know what was happening, but Esther was so funny I had to laugh.

Edie said, "I want to offer you my home. To share it with you as long as we can both be comfortable here."

I couldn't think of a thing to say.

Edie went on. "I don't want you to feel insulted. I'm not trying to solve your life for you. I know you can do that for yourself. But as I told you when you first came, I get lonely in this big old place, just me and the ghosts." Edie smiled. "The point is, Esther doesn't want to live with me. Not yet anyway. And I can live with that, even though I can't live without her. But I still have the loneliness problem. I've really enjoyed you living here. I'm anxious to try it permanently. There's enough room so that if Esther changes her mind she could move in too. We'd just have to put Lydia in your room or fix up the little sewing room for her."

"Lydia?" I asked.

"Well, yes. If I'm going to have a family, I want a big family. Just you and me can't fill up all this space."

"Hold it, I don't even know if I want to do this. But even if I do I'm not sure I'll be ready for Lydia. See, I was counting on staying with my mother who's still taking care of her. Trying to get on my feet, getting a part-time job. Maybe going back to school."

"You can sure do that as well here as in Harlem, girl," Esther said. "Better, as a matter of fact. You got connections here." She winked at me. When I looked like she was talking a foreign language at me, she went on. "I called the Board of Education today. They have all kinds of programs. Some of them you can earn money while you go to school or work half a day and earn the other half. My cousin Almeta worked her way through college cleaning houses. Don't look at me bad, girl. You make damn good money doing that, better than packing or even typing, not that you know how to do that either, you poor uneducated queer. And you know what she's doing now? With an Associate's in business administration? Administering a business, sending people out to clean houses. She just bought a house in Brooklyn."

"Listen, Mercedes," Edie said. "Don't think we're pushing this down your throat or that it's all planned out for you. But you don't have many resources. We do."

I needed time to think. Were they right? Should I go away and think at my mother's place? This was the chance of a lifetime. Even if she was only feeling guilty about being white and having more money than me, Edie was at least trying to do something good with that. And I didn't feel pushed or tied down. I wanted to say yes right then. For me. Lydia I'd have to think about later. If I wanted to move her again. If she could go to better schools out here. If she should live with queers. If I needed to be on my own without her for a while to be a better mother. If I should take her from the Puerto Rican ways I wanted her to know. The way I was brought up, you had to get past being Rican, you had to be American. But that's what I am. I didn't want her fighting herself all her life like I've been doing. Besides all those worries, I still had all the problems of the past few weeks. But in a safe place, I was thinking, by taking one step at a time, maybe I could solve them.

When I looked up, they were watching me. I looked at them, thinking about how many different kinds of love there are. My young love for Maria. The love I had for my family, my crazy huge family who would welcome me — to a point — wherever they were. How I loved little Lydia with her skinny growing body, her mind that soaked up everything, her love for me, such as I am. The way I felt about the uptown gay girls and boys, the way we hung out together and tried to help each other, and how little we had to give because it seemed like we were always at the end of our rope. The way I felt about Frenchy, like there was a knot tied between us that got stronger the harder we pulled away from each other. And my love for these two women who wanted to make a home for me, make my life easier, who thought I could give them something, too.

"Yeah," I said. "Yeah, sure. Let's try it." I was too embarrassed to thank Edie straight out. "It might help me," I admitted.

The two of them beamed and rushed at me, pulling me up into a bear hug.

"Hallelulah!" Esther said. "I thought I was going to have to *marry* Edie here. You have *solved* my problem!"

"You'll marry me yet!" Edie teased back.

"You've got a built-in best man right here," I told them.

"But you know what would make our lives complete?" Esther growled at me, looking around wisely. I hoped she wouldn't say anything about me marrying Frenchy.

"What?" Edie asked.

"I know this household is already pretty representative — a white girl, black girl, Spanish girl," Esther started. "Don't you think you could fall for an Asian dyke, Mercedes, so's we could open the Lesbian League of Nations here?"

Laughing at Esther's non-stop jokes, we began a celebration. But now and then, when we were laughing loudest, as the frozen chow mein was almost burning or the grape juice was pouring into wine glasses, I thought of Frenchy and my heart closed up just like a fist, to think of her sitting in her mother's apartment dreaming about her next night in the Village. How she'd look. How she'd act. Who she'd make out with. I couldn't get rid of this picture I had of her and her mother locked up together in the House of D.

I wanted her at Edie's house. At my house now. I almost started crying when I thought the words *my house*. But I didn't want her here before she belonged here. I wanted a whole Frenchy, not just the pieces she gave because she was afraid, or didn't understand, about giving more.

I went into the living room and put the Supremes on the record player. Edie and me danced around the room, like silly little kids. I felt great.

Chapter 4

She Wore Skirts, Didn't She?
Spring, 1966

The bus drove noisily up and down hills lined with small homes and large trellised gardens like calendar pictures of Italy. Small old people bent to measure the growth of the tomatoes that thrived on the College Point air, heavy with the smell of rubber. Frenchy felt like gagging each time the wind off the East River shifted towards her. Yet she stayed by the window, watching the many worlds the Q44 bus went through. She'd been tempted to walk the few blocks to the Bronx Zoo where she transferred to the Q44, but Jessie and Mary were expecting her. Riding over the grey river reminded her of Provincetown and she wondered if this was the way she'd gone that one time. She craned her neck to see the airplanes taking off from LaGuardia Airport. She changed to a bus that took her into crowded but unusually green College Point.

This had been Jessie's dream, Frenchy thought, sickened again by the rubber smell. To marry a girl and settle down someplace outside the City. Mary was from College Point. She worked in a factory there like her mother and father and her three sisters. Her brother had done better. He was a cop. They all knew Mary was queer and loved her anyway. Even the cop. That's how she and Jessie could swing an apartment together, because they'd moved in over Mary's sister and brother-in-law. Frenchy couldn't believe this would work out. Who ever heard of a family not minding if you were queer? And it was really pushing it to move in over them.

She reached her stop, across from College Point Park. Her friends lived just down the hill from the park. They went walking in it all the time, they said, even held hands sometimes when they could get off the sidewalks and be more alone. They loved to watch the water of the East River. To Frenchy it sounded like paradise. Not that she would ever give up her weekly walk into the Village.

She had a black sweatshirt on over her white button-down shirt. She hitched up her jeans, the blue ones she saved for special days like this when she was going to be with gay friends, not cruise or pick up girls. She stopped to comb back her hair. There wasn't even a store whose window she could use for a mirror out here in College Point. Her red pinky ring glinted in the sun and she smiled. It didn't matter how she looked today — Jessie and Mary were just pals now, she didn't have to impress them, they knew what she was really like. She strode on, remembering to tone down her bulldagger walk for the neighborhood. It was good she did; when she turned the corner onto Jessie's street there were people everywhere: little kids rushing in front of her on tricycles, teenage boys glaring at the short mannish stranger on their turf, young girls giggling to see her diddy-bop by in her d.a., her comb sticking out of a back pocket. Grandmas on narrow porches and mothers pulling shopping carts or pushing baby carriages glared at her suspiciously. She began to feel even shorter than she was and hurried to find Jessie's street address.

She ran up the steps and leaned heavily against the doorbell. Somewhere way above her a voice yelled down, "It's open, Frenchy, come on up!"

She bolted in the door and stood in the darkness of the hallway to compose herself and catch her breath. How did these two stand it here? Jessie looked as much like a dyke as she did.

"Hey, Frenchy, come on in! Help yourself to a paintbrush!" Jessie said at the doorway to her third floor apartment. "How do you like it, huh? Ain't it a palace?" Jessie grinned, paint all over her chinos and sweatshirt, her squarish face red from exertion under very short, home-cut hair. "Mary, c'mere, Frenchy's here!"

Mary came out of the kitchen, wiping her hands on a ruffled apron, and kissed Frenchy on the lips. She was wide-hipped and full-breasted, with dark, warm eyes. Her hair was permed in a short, neat style. "I'm so glad you came! I'm baking a cake for after lunch. Did it take long to get here?"

"Pretty long," Frenchy answered, disoriented by seeing her bar friends in their home. "Looks nice," she approved with a cool steady gaze around the living room. The aqua couch and matching armchair were neatly covered with a fitted plastic see-through protector. There was a white coffee table with curlique legs to match the legs of the chair and couch. Above the couch hung a gold-framed mirror. Two lamps with thick swirling bases on either side of the couch looked like modern art, and another lamp was suspended from the ceiling over the chair on a gold chain. The white floor-to-ceiling drapes over the window had not yet been opened. A cabinet, also standing on curliqued legs and adorned with scrollwork, was filled with tiny dishes and dolls and souvenirs. Frenchy walked to it on aqua and gold shag wall-to-wall carpet. "You really done this place up nice," she said.

Mary lifted her chin proudly and darted to Frenchy. "These are all our treasures," Mary explained, going on to tell the history of each item.

"Great folks, Mary's family," Jessie said. "Make me feel like family, too. Wish I could take Mary home to my folks, but they just wouldn't understand. Hey — how'd you get a Saturday off?"

"I've been up at the A&P so long, I work two on, two off now."

"Let me show you around," Jessie said. "Then you can help me paint."

Mary put her hands on her hips. "You can show her around some more, but our very first guest outside the family is *not* going to paint."

Frenchy was relieved; she didn't want to mess up her clothes with paint. She sat on the edge of the couch; its plastic folded, with a crumpling sound, beneath her.

In very little time, Mary brought a plate of steaming soup to the table and began to dish it out.

"Hey," Frenchy said in surprise, looking at Jessie, "since when do you wear glasses?"

Jessie blushed. "A couple of years. I always wear them at home, never downtown."

Mary sighed. "We're getting old, Frenchy. Jessie's twenty-nine and I'm not telling how old I am," she finished coyly.

"Come on," Frenchy teased, "Jessie couldn't have married an older woman . . ."

Mary scolded Frenchy, cutting her off. "You need some fattening up. You ought to settle down with a nice girl who'll take care of you." She got up, then called from the kitchen, "Whatever happened to you and Edie?"

Frenchy toyed with a fork. "You guys even got nice silverware."

Mary arrived with a steaming tuna casserole. "Nothing fancy, just a little lunch to keep us going till dinner."

Frenchy said, "Jess could put away three or four hot-dogs at Nedicks in one sitting. With the works. And coffee and pie for dessert." She laughed. "Those were the good old days, right, Jess?"

Jessie looked covertly toward Mary who was dishing out plentiful helpings of casserole. "Sure were," Jessie replied. "Not that I'd trade them for the good new days."

"What about Edie, Frenchy?" Mary asked again.

Frenchy was having trouble eating a second course. "She's okay. Haven't seen her for a few months. She don't come downtown now she's got this new girlfriend."

Mary looked shocked, disapproving, and sympathetic in quick succession.

"I don't care," Frenchy said. "We were through long before that. I mean, I liked Edie a lot. She was maybe my favorite girl. But she was looking for somebody I wasn't like, you know what I mean? Besides, she needed a smart girl. Not like me."

"You're plenty smart, Frenchy. All she had on you was an education and you could get one of those if you wanted to."

Mary was silent for a moment. "She wasn't our kind, is all. Here, finish this and I'll bring the cake," she said, splitting the rest of the casserole between the two butches.

"I can't Mary. Honest I can't," Frenchy groaned. She was still trying to decide if she should defend Edie to Mary. "How do you like being married, Jess?" she asked instead, pulling out a box of Marlboros and lighting one.

"It's great, Frenchy. She does all the cooking and cleaning, won't let me do a thing except painting and fixing stuff. Sometimes I feel bad, but in her family, that's how you're a good wife."

"They really don't care you're a girl?"

"No," Jessie said, pushing back from the table and unbuttoning the top of her chinos. "I mean, I guess they'd rather she had kids, but they're happy she's married to someone who loves her and who she loves. She said it was hard at first when she came out, with her mother telling her how she'd burn in hell. She met this girl at the factory back then. One date and she knew she was queer. She never did like men to touch her and this girl showed her why. One night her mother caught them making out in the hallway. They had a big scene. Her father wasn't home. They made a deal to keep it from him. But over the years I guess Mama couldn't keep the secret and brought the old man around. Now he talks to me about cars. Wants me to learn to play *bocce* with the boys. Wants me to help him put in his garden this year so's I'll know how. They figure to leave their house to Mary since she can't earn good money like the boys."

Mary bustled in, bearing the cake. "Now that Jess told my come out story, let's hear yours, Frenchy."

She was blushing. "You don't want to hear that."

"Yes I do. So does Jess, don't you?" She hugged her. "We were saying just the other night how we don't know yours."

Frenchy shrugged and crossed her legs under herself, secretly pleased by their interest. She lit a cigarette.

"I used to tell girls who asked me that I never came out — I was born gay." Frenchy wriggled a little on her chair, nervously looking to see how Jessie and Mary were reacting to her words. "Whatever, I was fourteen the first time I knew for sure. Me and Terry, a friend of mine, used to hang out together. Go to the candy store for egg creams, up to the RKO for Debbie Reynolds musicals. Our favorite thing was to dress up like guys and ride the subways."

"You? In your neighborhood?"

"We were like spies in a foreign country until we got out of our own neighborhood. Sometimes we'd go downtown to the wrestling matches at Madison Square Garden. There were always weird people there. They never noticed us. Sometimes we walked Broadway, pretending we wanted prostitutes."

Jessie and Mary laughed. "Ever get picked up?" asked Jessie.

"You kidding? We just had a great time being whoever we wanted, going wherever we wanted. Then we discovered Greenwich Village. The girls down there all looked like us!

"We'd heard of queers and we'd heard there were a lot of them in the Village, but neither of us ever thought of them being girl queers. Just fairies. We went running back to the Bronx so fast . . ."

Frenchy put out her cigarette and stretched her legs as far as they'd go. "After a while we started hanging out in Washington Square instead of Madison Square. And at Pam Pams."

"Good old Pam Pam's. Our favorite hangout," Jessie said. "I think it's a Dunkin Donuts now."

Mary asked, "How did you get boys' clothes?"

"My mother always dressed me in my brother's hand-me-downs. Terry ripped hers off." Frenchy shook her head, smiling. "I'd go over to her house to change. Then there was this basement passageway through a couple of buildings. We'd slip down an alleyway and into the subway."

"How old were you?" Mary asked.

"We met in sixth grade. I remember Terry best in gym class, when they'd give us dance lessons. How those droopy felt skirts we wore would cling together, all full of electricity.

It made me scared the other kids could tell how I was feeling about her, all that electricity between us."

"So what happened?" Jess interjected. "When did you finally do it?"

"Jess!"

"Aw, Mary, we're all girls."

Frenchy had a soft smile on her usually cautious face. "Even seeing all those gay girls downtown didn't tip us off to ourselves. When we finally figured out what was going on, what kind of scene we'd gotten into down there, we didn't call each other up for about two weeks. Then we did, and I went over there to change. Terry'd ripped off some new clothes and looked more like the gay girls downtown than ever. She was sitting on her bed watching my every move. We didn't say a word. When I'm mostly dressed, she pulls a tie out of her pocket and comes toward me. 'I bought this for you,' she says.

"Terry never gave me nothing before. It was embarrassing. 'Bought it?' I asked her, because she never paid for anything. She put it around my neck and started straightening my collar, her fingers touching my neck. I remember feeling all my little neck hairs stand on end, she was so close."

Jessie and Mary were holding hands, staring at Frenchy who was lost in her story. Frenchy took a deep breath.

"She kissed me. We fell on her bed and never got off it until we heard her mother come home late in the afternoon."

"And Frenchy the lover came out."

"Come on, Jess," Frenchy said, still self-conscious. She changed the subject. "What're the candles for?"

"For you! Didn't Jessie tell you? We missed your birthday so we thought we could celebrate today."

Frenchy was even more self-conscious. "You didn't have to do nothing."

"I knew she wouldn't come if I told her, Mary," Jessie declared.

"I hope you're not upset, Frenchy."

Mary lit the candles. She and Jessie sang "Happy Birthday," mortifying Frenchy even further. "Come on, make a wish and blow out the candles!" Mary insisted.

"I can't think of nothing to wish for." But when it came to blowing out the candles, she wanted to do that right. It was a matter of pride to quench all twenty-seven candles in one breath. Mary and Jessie cheered when she did it.

For a long time they ate cake and drank coffee around the table. Mary got up to do the dishes and Jessie offered to go for a walk in the park with Frenchy.

"No, thanks," Frenchy said, thinking about the gauntlet they'd have to run through the crowded neighborhood.

"Let's wait for Mary then and we'll all walk together. We'll take you to the busstop afterwards."

Maybe it would be better with Mary along. "Okay," she said, thinking how the stares and taunts never used to get to her like this. "I guess everybody's getting old," she said aloud.

"But you know," Jessie said, lighting a cigarette, "it's not as bad as I thought it would be. Sure, I wish I knew Mary when we were kids, but I don't know as I could have appreciated her then. I always wanted to go with a girl forever, but I didn't know how. It took Mary to teach me."

"What do you mean?"

"I can't really say. She just knows how to do it. I can even help in the kitchen, as much as she'll let me, without feeling dumb." She lowered her voice. "Even in the bedroom she knows how to make me stick around."

Frenchy winked at her friend.

"Not like you think," Jessie whispered. "I never thought

I'd want to go with a girl who liked to do it to me, but she makes even that okay. And I can't have her unless I let her, she says."

"You mean you're not butch no more?"

Jessie sat up tall. "Of course I'm butch," she said firmly. "You can see that. And I'm butch in bed too. But I'm more than that now."

Frenchy shook her head, feeling abandoned. "I went to a new bar once up on Sixteenth Street. I swear they didn't know what butch was."

"Yeah? I don't go for that. I still want to be man of the house. But it sure is different being married than being a wanderer. Remember our old theme song? *The Wanderer?* That Dion sang?"

"Yeah. You sure have changed, Jess."

"I sure feel good, Frenchy," she said as Mary came out of the kitchen. Jessie pulled Mary onto her lap and hugged her.

Frenchy left them making out while she went to use their bathroom. She wondered if it was easier to walk through a neighborhood when you were married and lived there, so they all knew about you and were used to you. Especially when your family lived there. Maybe you'd get some respect if they knew you were okay and didn't bother nobody.

She sang *The Wanderer* as she combed her hair, looking into the mirror of her friends' home. Twenty-seven years old or not, the old songs still fit her life best.

* * * * *

The long trek to Queens and back wore Frenchy out. She didn't feel like going downtown this Saturday night. Besides, the past year or so the old crowd had thinned out considerably; only this one or that one showed up. With all these young kids moving in Frenchy had begun to feel like one of those leathery older dykes who sat at the bar all night getting soused and watching the young femmes, hoping one would be looking for an old lady to take care of her. And if she found one, a month or so later the old lady would be back, hoping again, and still drinking.

She went to bed early and got up Sunday before her mother. She dressed in her blue jeans and left a note that she was visiting friends again. With the styles changing now she found she could dress almost the way she wanted to as long as she was going out and her mother didn't look at her too long.

Once she hit the street all she had to do was snap on her ID bracelet, buy a box of Marlboros, and when she was on the subway and out of her neighborhood, slick back her hair.

It was a beautiful warm day, the skies over New York cloudless, like an Easter Sunday when she was a kid, an exciting day when everybody would get dressed up. After church her mother would allow her to stay outside and play like on a Saturday. Today she had that same feeling; she could do with her Sunday anything she wanted. Since she had missed her usual Saturday night walk down 6th Avenue from 14th Street into the Village, the walk that helped her get into being Frenchy, she decided to go for a walk today. When she got to Columbus Circle she went over to 5th and headed downtown.

This early, she had the City to herself. She almost skipped at times from happiness at loving her city and being free to walk the streets. The long grey ribbon of 5th Avenue seemed to shine under the sun. The buildings along it, all tall, all dressed up with their decorative fronts and elegant ground-floor shops, were full of a magic different from what she found in the buildings in the Village. This was a straight magic which had to do with commerce, money, a world not hers. And the people who walked beside these buildings were dressed in a Sunday finery bought from those shops, earned in those buildings. Even the traffic lights, clicking green and red, seemed polished as if New York's most famous parade route were daily on inspection.

St. Patrick's Cathedral loomed before her, all spires and stained glass. Throngs of well-dressed people strolled sedately down its steps, down, down to where she walked. They seemed to disapprove of her in glances that refused to rest on her. She didn't care. They probably wished they too could put on their boots and go walking, carefree, around the City. She looked at the younger women with their parents or new husbands and thought, what a waste that they're with men. One in particular caught her eye and she walked partway down Fifth Avenue pretending to have her on her arm.

By the time she got to the House of Detention she was starved for breakfast and she wandered the unfamiliar day-time streets looking for a restaurant. People were beginning to emerge from brownstones for their papers, to walk their dogs. She ducked into a narrow place and ordered break-fast at the counter, reading a *Daily News* she'd bought next door. Mary was probably bringing Jessie her paper and breakfast in bed right then, but she didn't envy Jessie and Mary their cozy home. She, Frenchy, had her freedom, and she relished it. She put a toothpick in her mouth as she left the restaurant.

In and out of the narrow, sometimes cobbled, back streets of the Village she walked. The sun had grown hot and she welcomed the cool shadows cast by rows of brown-stones and the newer, fancy high rises. Here and there a shop opened to sell flowers, or hippie-type clothing or odd pottery she saw nowhere but the Village. A couple of times she swung by one of the bars, hoping the seedy-looking places would be open so she could stop in for a drink, maybe see one of her pals. Here and there she recognized someone from the bar and said hello if she knew her well enough. She followed one couple who came out of a rowhouse arm in arm. They picked up a paper, stopped at a bakery and sauntered back home, raising their faces now and then to the glow of the sun. One leathery old dyke walked her equally leathery old dog, looking carefree and contented as Frenchy felt. It was funny to see these women outside the bar, mingling on the streets with faggots and artist-types. Maybe they were cashiers too. Or worked in rubber factories. Had mothers and felt, as Frenchy did, that the world was changing too fast for them.

She ended up in Washington Square Park where she finished reading the *News* on a bench; then she simply sat in the sun wondering if she should go home. Several groups of folksingers had formed around the fountain, under the arch. Their competing voices and guitars, the constantly changing audiences, gave the park a busy aspect that absorbed her attention. Few gays were about, but straight tourists crowded around watching the singers and strollers. A co-ed game of volleyball had started, net and all, on the other side of the fountain. She would have liked to join but saw no gay players.

It was fun just to watch people enter the park. From 5th Avenue and slightly east came the well-to-do residents of the Village, walking fancy dogs. From the east and part of the south students spilled out of New York University dormitories in their mixed garb: sandals and button-down shirts, long-term visitors who tried to fit in. From the south the hippies left their coffee houses to be outdoors, some having spent whatever part of the night they could get away with sleeping on park benches. In the western corner old men and N.Y.U. students played chess and checkers on concrete table-boards while gays from the west side and tourists from the buses paused to watch. Though

Frenchy watched everyone with suspicion, especially the hippies and artists, she reveled in all the differences around her. She was just another type in Greenwich Village, a place where people went who couldn't fit in elsewhere.

A woman in a long colorful skirt and a shawl stepped out of the crowd around the fountain and walked toward her. As she got closer, she looked familiar. She was smiling. "I thought it was you," she said as she swirled to a stop and sat beside Frenchy. "Do you remember me?"

Frenchy couldn't imagine where she would have met someone whose earrings hung to her shoulders, who hung out at the fountain. Then she remembered. "Provincetown."

"I even remember your name. Frenchy, right?" She went on, "I always wondered if I'd see you down here. You said you went to the bars a lot."

"But I almost never come down here during the day."

"Remember Jenny? The redhead from Ohio?"

"Yes, a real nice person."

"We still write. Every year I say I'll go visit her, but between one thing and another... You know how it is."

Pam was charming — just like the sophisticated ladies you saw in the movies, Frenchy thought, making you want to smile and talk. Still, she hoped none of the kids would see her talking to a hippie. "So how've you been?"

"Groovy," Pam said and Frenchy winced at the word. Maybe Pam was too weird for her. She wondered what she would be like in bed and thought she saw the same question in Pam's eyes.

"You going with anybody?"

Pam laughed warmly. "I don't. Go with anybody that is. I'm a free agent, don't want to get tied down."

"Me too," said Frenchy, sitting up in excitement at finding a kindred soul. "But I been finding out how there's not many of us left. All my friends are getting married or not going to the bars. They just aren't any fun anymore."

"What a drag. I know what you mean, though. They want to stay home and watch TV!"

"And listen to drippy singers like Anne Murray and Lana Cantrell. There's not even any good songs left."

"You're into the wrong scene, then. I hear a lot of good music. Some really exciting jazz right here in the Village."

"I'm not a jazz fan. Sounds like a lot of mistakes they string together."

Pam smiled. "You're a breath of fresh air," she said, touching Frenchy's hand. That's when Frenchy realized Pam had been touching her all along as she talked. She was that kind of person. "Listen, I want to go for a bike ride so bad. I've been trying to hustle up someone to go with me. Want to come?"

"I got no bike."

"No problem. The guy next door lets me borrow his all the time. Come on, Frenchy, we'll bike up to Central Park. It'll be fun."

She hadn't been on a bike since she was a kid. She was a little scared of looking foolish, but she couldn't admit that to Pam. "I don't know —"

"Never mind you don't know. I want to spend the day with you. Come on. Let's get the bikes!"

Soon Frenchy was inside a tiny apartment that was an incredible mess — unlike anything she'd ever seen. Pam's colorful clothes were everywhere, thrown on everything. The walls were covered with paintings and with long-feathered hats hanging from hooks. There were no curtains on the windows. The bathroom had been painted black, and when Frenchy went to use it, Pam stuck her head in — shocking Frenchy who was on the toilet — to tell her there was a candle behind her if she needed a light. As Pam arranged to borrow the bike next door, Frenchy looked over the one-room apartment more carefully. There

was no TV or radio that she could see. Only a refrigerator
the size of a carton, a bed unfolded from the wall and laden
with junk; a large collection of tiny pipes and cigarette
papers; and, over the two-person kitchen table heaped with
dirty dishes, a wall of drawings of naked women making
love. She could hear Pam talking next door, but she didn't
approach the drawings; she squinted, trying to see them.

Pam yelled for her. She wheeled Pam's bike, smaller
than the neighbor's, to the top of the stairs. Pam was already halfway down the first flight with the neighbor's
bike. "Just pull the door shut, it'll lock by itself," she
called up.

The bike against her, Frenchy was balanced precariously
between the door, which she was trying to close, and the
stairs. When she finally worked her way to the top of the
stairs she couldn't imagine how she would carry the big
bike down all three flights, but she took a deep breath and
started. Halfway down, though her shaking arms told her
to stop, she told herself to continue. Pam didn't seem to
notice the sweatstains under the arms of her black sweatshirt or the redness of her face.

Now she had to ride the damn bike. She followed Pam,
who was walking hers, over to an uptown street. Pam swung,
skirt and all, over the bar of the men's bike. Frenchy, re-
duced to riding a girl's bike, gingerly mounted it and after
wobbling a bit, took off up the Avenue after Pam. Tense
and worried about potholes, passing traffic and parked cars
and pedestrians, her eyes fastened on Pam's back, she followed her every move. By 50th Street she felt like an old
pro and looked forward to riding the paths of Central Park.
She caught up with Pam at the entrance to the park, her
legs tired, but her head filled with the same exhilaration
she'd felt that morning walking down 5th Avenue. She
couldn't believe she was riding a bike in New York City

with a wild-living artist who wore big earrings and lit a candle in her bathroom.

"We'd better skip the Zoo," Pam said. "Too crowded for bikes. Where do you want to go?"

Frenchy was too embarrassed to admit she hadn't been to Central Park since she was a kid. "Any place is fine with me."

"God, I'm thirsty. Got any money on you? Let's get a couple of sodas."

Frenchy bounded off her bike to play the familiar role of buying a girl a drink.

They pushed off, Frenchy with a cigarette hanging out of her mouth and feeling more sure of herself, Pam talking to her as they rode side by side through the gentle air. Frenchy was hardly aware of the pedestrians they passed and was beginning to fall a little in love. At the lake she bought ice creams and they lay under a tree, surrounded by soft greens, the noise of the city muffled beyond the trees.

"Isn't this a gas?" Pam asked.

Frenchy was getting used to her hip talk. "That looks like fun too," she said, pointing her wooden spoon toward the rowboats on the lake.

"Want to go rowing?"

"No, no," Frenchy said, feeling old and worn by all the unaccustomed exercise.

"Next week, then. Okay? You free next Saturday? Pick me up at my pad. Early. Like eleven."

She remembered that hippies slept late and prowled around coffee houses at night. She asked, "Do you work?"

"I collect."

"You mean unemployment?"

"Is there anything else I can collect?" Pam laughed. "If there is, please tell me! I'll go apply!"

"I don't know. I've always worked," Frenchy replied a little boastfully.

"I work when I have to — at whatever I can get, to tell you the truth. Last year I had this job machine embroidering workshirts. A friend of mine decided to start his own business. I can get a job with him whenever I want because I'm good, but when my funds run out I'll try to get something in graphic art. I wish I could sell some of my work."

Frenchy asked, picking up both of their dixie cups and tossing them into a nearby trash bin, "Do you draw or paint or what?"

"Or what, is right." Pam laughed. She was sprawled on the grass, her skirt tucked under her legs, her head resting on an elbow. "I love drawing most. But there's less of a market for drawing, especially my drawings, than for anything else. I've done portraits which I'm pretty good at and watercolor landscapes. What do you do?"

"I work at the A&P in my neighborhood."

"That's all?"

"What else could I do?"

"Oh, write poetry or sing or knit, for chrissakes."

"No. I'm just a cashier. I'll be there ten years this year."

"In the same job?"

Frenchy nodded proudly, drawing deeply **on** her cigarette.

"You like it?"

"It's okay. I don't mind it. They keep **trying to** make me head cashier, but I'm not interested."

"Amazing," Pam said, shaking her head. "You're just a good little all-American dyke, aren't you?"

"What do you mean?"

"You work, pay your taxes, and screw around with girls on the weekend." She reached over and ruffled Frenchy's hair.

Frenchy didn't know how to take this. She combed her hair back in place. "What's wrong with that?"

"Nothing's wrong with it. It must be a good way to live. Do you live with a girl?" Pam half-crawled toward Frenchy and lay her head in her lap.

"No, with my mother." It still embarrassed Frenchy to admit this; she feared girls would think her a sissy. "She doesn't have much herself. Just my Dad's pension. So it makes it easier for both of us."

Pam looked up at Frenchy, then took the cigarette from her lips and dragged on it till it burnt down to the filter. She threw it toward the lake. "Can you row?"

"Me? Sure," Frenchy said, looking skeptically toward the boats.

" 'Cause I'm no good at that at all. Every time I try I get tangled up in other boats and somebody has to come out and untangle me." She laughed.

Frenchy looked down at this woman in her lap. She seemed to have nothing to hide — no hesitations. She trusted Frenchy as if they were best friends. The woman closed her eyes and nestled into Frenchy's lap.

"What a fine warm day," Pam murmured. "Want to fall in love?"

Frenchy laughed. "Okay," she said. "Why not?"

"Come live with me, Frenchy. What's your real name anyway?"

"Genvieve Tonneau." She'd been so confused by Pam's invitation that she let her real name slip. Never, never, did she tell a girl her name except once and when they broke up the girl had told everybody. She'd spent years living it down.

"What a beautiful name."

"Yeah, it really fits, don't it? Most of my friends can't even pronounce it."

"May I call you Genvieve? You know you have a beautiful face. Really a fine bone structure."

The woman was crazy. She made everything topsy-turvy. You didn't tell a butch she was beautiful. You tried to get the butch to say that to you. But she couldn't say that to Pam, who had heavy, thick features, thick eyebrows which almost met in the middle of her face, a long hooked nose and tangled hair. This was not a beautiful woman by her standards. Yet, she thought, there *is* something about her. Pam looked fierce and strong, like she was nobody's fool. "No, you can't call me Genvieve. I hate it and please don't tell anybody else my name."

Pam looked at her again, then sat up suddenly. "You are adorable. You really are. I could just hug you to death." She hugged Frenchy and rocked her back and forth in her arms. "You're *so* little and *so* cute and *so* tough. I don't know where I found you, but I'm not putting you back till I've had my fill of you, Genvieve Tonneau."

"Stop, hey, no!" Laughing, Frenchy protested, "We shouldn't be touching like this in the park."

"Why not?"

"We could get arrested!"

"Don't be so square. Nobody's going to arrest two women for hugging. Now if you reached up under my skirt, which is what I'd like you to do, *then* they'd have a case."

Frenchy stared at Pam. "That's what you'd like me to do?"

"Sure. Isn't that what you'd like to do?"

Holy shit, thought Frenchy. This woman was scaring her. She'd never known anyone so forward.

"Well," insisted Pam with a mocking smile, "isn't it?"

"I haven't even kissed you yet."

I should have known, Frenchy groaned inwardly. Pam had reached up from where she lay again on Frenchy's lap and pulled her mouth down to her own. She was kissing

Frenchy with her lips and tongue and teeth. Frenchy felt like a leaf caught in a storm. Nobody'd tried to kiss her since Mercedes. Giving in to this consuming passionate wet insistent kiss — in public yet — was beyond her.

Pam pulled away to breathe. "There. Now we've kissed."

As she wiped her mouth, Frenchy felt stirred by this woman who felt larger than life. This was a real woman.

"I don't play games, Frenchy Tonneau. I find you very attractive and I want to make love with you."

Frenchy tried to breathe normally, but her heart was fluttering. "Pam," she said thickly, turned on in spite of herself. "What the hell," she said, and leaned to kiss Pam again, to kiss her with her own controlled passion, hoping she would like it. But where would she find control? She reminded herself that Pam was just another girl. She'd been with plenty of different kinds of girls. She could handle Pam.

Frenchy lifted her lips to Pam's, then kissed her gently, brushing left to right, and finally stopping.

Pam opened her eyes. "You're good, beautiful, aren't you?"

Frenchy leaned back and lit a cigarette for Pam. They lay side by side, sharing the cigarette, not talking for a while. "Can you come home with me tonight?" Pam asked.

"No. I have to start back pretty soon. My mother's expecting me for dinner and I have to go to work in the morning."

"Yeah, I think it'll be a late night when we get together."

Strange chills went through Frenchy as Pam said this in her throaty voice. Her words sounded like deep, dark sexual promises of things Frenchy had never known. With effort she took her eyes from Pam's to look at her body, to measure the woman.

"You sure you can't come tonight?" Pam asked as Frenchy looked at her. She moved off her back and leaned toward Frenchy, her hips and breasts moving provocatively.

"Yeah," Frenchy said, her voice as throaty as Pam's. "Next week, after we go rowing."

* * * * *

Frenchy chuckled to herself as she ran up the subway steps at 14th Street. How her body had ached all week from last Sunday's exercise! How she had ached inside for the promise of a night with Pam. Hard as she tried to imagine it, she got no further than seeing them making out behind a tree in some remote place in Central Park. She checked out the Automat across the street as she passed, planning to take Pam there for dinner. She didn't know any other restaurants except holes in the wall, and hippie or not, this girl had class. Compared to Edie, she was cosmopolitan. Like Mary said, all Edie had on the rest of the kids downtown was her education. Inside she was plain old Edie.

Pam now, she knew a thing or two. She knew the world and how to get along. She had guts, living without a steady job, having her own place, knowing her way around the whole city — not just a few bars at night. Pam would be an education for her, and when she graduated she'd be a smoother, more sophisticated butch, able to take smoother, more sophisticated girls around the big city, taking cabs and eating at Tad's Steak City or some place as fancy. Maybe then she ought to go see Mercedes, show her the town. Maybe then Mercedes wouldn't hate her any more.

She left 14th Street more north than she usually did. It was fancier-looking up here. There were fewer shops and those she saw were expensive places she wouldn't dare enter. She wondered how Pam could afford to live in the West Village until she got to Morton Street where tenements stood side by side with brownstones. Still, the street had a kind of class to it with its arched doorways and barred windows filled with flowing ferns. Here she was in Greenwich Village, going out with a girl who lived on Morton Street. That made her feel a little better, lightened her heart heavy with thoughts of Mercedes. She didn't need Mercedes. Pam was an artist, a hippie, not some dyke as dull and lacking in prospects as herself.

Frenchy stamped out her cigarette. Her freshly laundered and ironed black sweatshirt was spotless, the collar of her white button-down underneath filled with starch from the Chinese laundry, her blue jeans sharply creased and her boots polished like she was going to Radio City Music Hall instead of rowing. She'd even polished her red pinky ring and it caught the sun, sparkled. She patted a Marlboro out of its box and slowed to saunter casually up Pam's street in case she was watching.

She buzzed the apartment, leaning against the wall to wait for the answering buzz that would allow her upstairs, wondering if Pam had tidied her place because she was coming. After a couple of minutes she realized this was taking too long and buzzed again. Then she checked the apartment number and gave a long buzz. Maybe she was sleeping. Could the buzzer be broken? But wouldn't Pam have told her, left her a note? Should she yell up to her window? But which was her window?

She buzzed once more, viciously. Then she stomped out of the vestibule and started back the way she came.

"Frenchy!" She had heard a window open; she looked up and saw Pam.

"Is it eleven so soon?" Pam's hair hung over the sill and she clutched some garment over her shoulders. "Come back, I'll buzz you up."

Frenchy hesitated, still mad. But she'd look stupider going away mad than going up. And Pam didn't know how she'd panicked. She went in and climbed the stairs.

The door was open and she slipped inside. If anything, the mess was greater. She shook her head affectionately.

"I'm in the shower," Pam called. "Make some coffee, would you? For Dorene too!"

"Dorene?" Frenchy glanced around the apartment.

"Hi!" A sleepy light brown face smiled at her from the bed.

Frenchy jumped half out of her boots.

"My, you *are* short."

All Frenchy could do was stare.

"I'm Dorene." A hand reached out from under the covers. Silently, Frenchy went over to shake it.

"Do you know where the coffee is?" Frenchy asked, unable to think of another thing to say.

"Cabinet over the sink." The woman pointed, sitting up, the covers falling, revealing her naked body. Frenchy quickly averted her eyes and pulled a chair to the sink to get the coffee down. "No, wait," Dorene said, when Frenchy had climbed up and was peering into the cabinet, "I think she left it on the table last night. Yeah, there it is."

Frenchy climbed down, feeling very undignified.

"Don't make any for me, though," Dorene said. "I got to be going. I'm due at work at twelve. Besides," she added with a smile in her voice, "I know this is your day with Pammy. I didn't mean to be here so late. We just didn't get to sleep till all hours."

Dorene quickly dressed and walked into the bathroom with Pam. Over the sound of the flushing toilet Frenchy heard her ask to use Pam's toothbrush.

Dorene said when she returned, "Pam'll be right out. Unless you want to go in. She likes these long, long showers."

In the face of all this intimacy, feeling like a customer at the A&P waiting for the customer ahead of her to leave,

Frenchy tried to act perfectly natural. "Does she just use this pot to boil water in?"

"Yeah, but you got to wait till the shower stops because the kitchen sink shuts the water off in there. You can fill the pan in there."

"I'll wait," Frenchy said quickly. Dorene was smiling. Frenchy realized she'd seen Dorene around the bars. Just now and then, though, and always in the kind of clothes she wore now — jeans and a leotard top, with a couple of shirts or silky jerseys over them and a lot of scarves and jewelry. She had wondered what her scene was.

"You an artist too?"

"I try. Indeed I do try, little one. I sculpt. I have to run now. Nice meeting you. See you around?"

"Sure," Frenchy said, holding the pot in one hand and the coffee in the other. "I guess so."

"Hello darling."

Pam had come up to Frenchy and hugged her quickly from behind. Frenchy turned around and sighed in relief. Thank goodness Pam was wearing a robe.

"I'll be dressed in a jiff, then swallow my coffee in one gulp and we're off." Pam looked out the window. "What a groovy day for a boatride in Central Park. You're impossibly romantic."

"I am?" Frenchy asked, looking for a spoon.

"Here, just pour a little in," Pam said, taking the coffee and the cup. "I suppose you're too butch to be any good in the kitchen."

"My mother does all the cooking."

"Can you tell when water's boiled?"

"Do you like it to have the little bubbles on top or the big ones?"

"Impossible," Pam muttered, throwing off her robe and pulling clothes out of various piles as if she knew what was where. Frenchy looked away again and carefully watched the water for signs of boiling. Pam said, "I think we ought to take the bus up to the park. I haven't got a lock for my bike."

"Okay," Frenchy agreed, beginning to see bubbles.

"Full of life this morning, aren't you?" Pam asked as she returned. "That's done enough." She took the pot off the stove.

Frenchy turned the burner off. She had decided not to let on that she was upset over finding her in bed with Dorene. After all, it was Pam's life — hadn't she said she was a free agent? Just because they had a date today and were going to sleep together tonight didn't mean she owed her life to Frenchy.

"I'm okay," she answered, smiling over at Pam who was drinking her coffee standing, one leg lifted and propped against the other.

"You've got the prettiest smile."

Frenchy scowled.

"And the nastiest scowl. Do you have change for the bus or should I hunt through my stuff?"

"No, I can pay for you, no problem." Frenchy rattled the change she had been careful to put in her pocket.

"Always prepared?"

"I try."

"How'd you like Dorene? She's my oldest friend in the City. We go dancing together about once a month. She's a fantastic dancer and she says I'm the only white woman she can stand to dance with. I take that as a big compliment."

Frenchy wondered if she was a fantastic lover too.

"And she's a fantastic lover too."

She felt challenged, and hoped Pam still wanted her to stay over. "Do you still want to go out today?" she asked.

"Of course! I'm up now. Otherwise I might have just pulled you into bed with Dorene and me." Pam turned to put shoes on. By the time she turned back Frenchy had swallowed her shock.

On the bus and on the street Pam acted as if they'd been lovers for years. Her kind of lover. She kissed and hugged Frenchy interminably, mussed her hair and teased her. By the time they were at the park Frenchy felt like both an adored child and a woman involved in a passionate affair. She paid for the boat rental and helped Pam in. The attendant pushed them off. The oars had been placed in the oarlocks and she dipped them and pulled. The boat moved a little, then a little more, then she hit the boat next to them. "Sorry," she called.

"Want me to navigate?" asked Pam.

Frenchy remembered how she had said she snarled traffic. "I'm okay. I just haven't done this in awhile." More like never, she reminded herself, wondering how to steer. But she'd watched the people on the water the week before and knew it had to do with just using one oar. Soon she had them in the middle of the lake, well away from the worst traffic, and she felt she could pull in the oars and light a cigarette.

"I forgot mine," Pam told her.

Frenchy loosened a cigarette and offered it to her, then flipped open her Zippo. She watched Pam's face as she leaned into the light. Their eyes met and Frenchy didn't look away as she lit her own cigarette.

"You weren't jealous of Dorene, were you?"

"Naw," Frenchy said, inhaling and looking at the tops of the buildings that surrounded the park. They looked so far away. She could hear birds singing. It was so peaceful. "Why would you think that?"

"You were so quiet before."

"I guess she might of took me by surprise a little." She rowed them back toward the little island they'd drifted away from. "I mean, usually in my crowd when you pick up a girl, she's not in bed with another girl."

"As long as you weren't jealous," Pam said almost teasingly.

Frenchy wouldn't look at her. "Didn't bother me."

"You're not a bad liar, Genvieve."

"Hey, I told you not to call me that."

"Which, liar? Or Genvieve?"

"Maybe we better go in," Frenchy said shortly, tossing her cigarette into the lake and picking up the oars.

"Oh, I'm sorry, Frenchy," Pam said, quickly shifting to sit next to Frenchy, almost capsizing them. "I didn't know you'd get so mad."

Pam looked altogether different, scared now. Frenchy knew she'd made her point, but kept her silence.

"Listen, if I ever say it again you can take me home, but let's not spoil today. I've been looking forward to it all week. Okay? Here," she said, "let me help row. Your arms must be tired."

Frenchy looked at Pam with a disinterested steadiness, then shrugged and took up her oar. They rowed in a lop-sided fashion until Frenchy told Pam to go back carefully to the other seat. Pam obeyed. That's better, thought Frenchy.

"Are you mad?" asked Pam.

Frenchy shook her head.

"I really am sorry."

Quiet, Frenchy kept rowing, very smoothly now, admiring the way her sturdy arms looked against their rolled-up sleeves, the red ring twinkling in the sun, her I.D. bracelet flashing. Pam took a small sketch pad out of her large bag and began to draw. Frenchy realized she'd never known an artist before.

After several minutes Pam tore off the page and handed it to Frenchy. "For you."

It was a drawing of Frenchy rowing, cigarette hanging

out of her mouth, her face stern. "That's good!"

"Thank you. It's a present."

"I can keep it?" She thought of showing it to her mother, but how could she explain who Pam was? Why she was smoking cigarettes? Maybe she'd show Marian at work. "Thanks," she said, melting a bit. "Would you hold it? I don't want it to get wet."

"If you'll smile now, I'll do a nicer one."

Frenchy felt a smile force its way to her lips. "I guess I'm too touchy about that."

"Your name?"

"Yeah."

"Hey, I think it's great you chose your own name. I should have respected it more. It's like learning to recognize an artist by the name she puts on her work. I learned my lesson." Pam sketched quick lines. "You really have a fine face."

"Thanks."

"Are you all French?"

"Every inch."

"You could be Italian. Or Spanish. What part of France are your people from?"

"Marseilles."

Pam looked up, surprised. "Really?"

"Yeah, why?"

"My cousin's family was hidden by a family in Marseilles before they came to America during the war. Was yours a fishing family?"

"Yeah, but they came here before the war."

"Why did they come?"

"I don't know. I never asked. Where's your family from?"

"Warsaw. In Poland. They're Jews."

"Oh." Frenchy understood now why the cousins had to hide. Why, she wondered, did she keep falling for Jewish girls? In all the years at the bar, no one in her crowd had been Jewish. Or Puerto Rican. Yet on her own, away from the bar, that's who she was drawn to. Was she looking for someone, something different? In a way she wished Pam were Mercedes, yet another way she was glad she still had time to be ready for Mercedes.

"There, isn't that better?" The sketch was of a smiling, carefree Frenchy.

"Pretty good," Frenchy said, much complimented.

"Not mad anymore?"

"I guess not."

They'd been drifting for a while. "I'm sure we've been out here over an hour. Maybe we'd better go in before it gets too expensive."

"Sure," Frenchy said agreeably.

It was a quieter, less demonstrative Pam who rode back downtown. Frenchy worried that she'd overdone her anger. She tentatively reached to hold Pam's hand.

"Gee," Pam said, "it's been a long time since anyone's held my hand."

"Do you mind?" Frenchy asked, wondering what had got into her to ask a girl's permission to hold her hand.

"Of course not. It feels good. Kind of trusting. Like I can lean on you."

"Want to go to dinner with me later?"

"Oh," Pam said, sitting up, "but you don't know what I had in mind for *you*." Pam's voice lowered to husky sexiness. "A spaghetti dinner by candlelight. At my place," Pam finished, whispering.

Frenchy thought of Mary cooking for Jessie.

"What do you think? We'll buy the groceries now, a couple of bottles of wine, I'll cook up a storm for you. Restaurants aren't really my scene." Frenchy was smiling, and pleased. "Don't tell me no girl's ever cooked you a dinner before."

"Not really. My ex, Edie, she'd feed me when I went out there, but it was always just because it was time for lunch or something."

"This will be a celebration. A happening!" When they got downtown Pam pulled Frenchy from store to store with her, buying the best kind of spaghetti here, the crispest Italian bread there, the freshest vegetables and hamburger in another place. Frenchy staggered under an enormous bag of groceries while Pam struggled with wine bottles and the door to her apartment. Frenchy lit the candle in the bathroom and shut the door. When she emerged, Pam had cleared the counter, the kitchen table and the couch. The bed was still empty of all but rumpled sheets from Dorene's visit.

"Where'd you put it all?" asked Frenchy.

"Away, away, away," sang Pam. "I'll deal with my closet tomorrow." She laughed, and sat Frenchy down on the couch. "Ah, my French lesbian, it's a pleasure to have you here," she said, putting her arms around Frenchy and leaning to kiss her. She ran her arms up and down Frenchy's back and chest, lingering at her breasts. Frenchy felt totally overwhelmed again. She wouldn't have dreamed of touching Pam's breasts so soon. She pulled back. "No, no," Pam said, biting Frenchy's lip gently. "Let me, let me, I want you." Frenchy flushed with excitement at Pam's words, that someone wanted her like this, that someone was making her feel like girls must have felt when she touched them. So what if Pam was acting butch? She wore skirts, didn't she? She was going to cook dinner, wasn't she? She was built like a femme, wasn't she? And she acted like a femme, except for this delicious arousing and touching.

"What about dinner?" Frenchy managed to ask into Pam's lips.

Pam pulled back. "You're right," she said, pushing her hair off her face. "We must eat, fortify ourselves for later."

She was laughing as she stood above Frenchy, large and bold and strong in a womanly way. Frenchy looked up at her as she would at a huge wave about to fall on her and sweep her away. Excitement was all mixed with fear in the pit of her stomach. As Pam walked back toward the kitchenette Frenchy pulled the seam of her jeans away from herself to dry.

Pam was no more organized in cooking than her housekeeping. Frenchy, used to her small, quick mother's movements in the kitchen, was mesmerized by the havoc of the larger woman's methods. As Frenchy sipped wine on the couch, Pam stripped, then lost, garlic cloves one after the other, sent onions rolling into her sink where she left them, selecting only those she needed, and made twice as much ground beef as she could fit in her small frying pan, leaving one batch to congeal on a plate amid a litter of pots, pans, bowls, boards and plates. Now and then she would fly to the couch to hug and excite Frenchy who was docile as a hypnotist's subject. Pam drank great quantities of red wine from a gallon jug on the floor, filling her jelly glass each time she stumbled over the bottle.

But when she changed from her sweaty clothes and returned in a long Oriental silk robe, the apartment was filled with delicious smells and the kitchen table was transformed. "Antiques," she explained as she set out delicate flowered plates, colored wine glasses, embroidered napkins and heavy, shining silverware. "I only bought two place settings of this silver — that was all the shop had — but they're keeping their eyes open for more for me. Isn't it elegant?"

"You sure got style, Pam."

"Oh, Frenchy, do you think so?" She sighed and sat on the couch next to Frenchy, a few dried flowers in her hand, looking like a picture, thought Frenchy, of a lovely woman.

"Sure I do, Pam. You look great, the table looks great, dinner smells wonderful."

Pam lay her head on the back of the couch, suddenly still and relaxed. She smiled gently toward Frenchy. "Sometimes all I want to do is settle down with some appreciative woman like you and take care of her. Play house in a big airy space where every moment is planned and predictable. From nine to noon I'd draw, then clean house and prepare dinner in a leisurely way the rest of the day. She'd come home from work at five. At night we'd read by the fire, then walk hand-in-hand up the carpeted stairs and make love for hours, every night, till we were ready for sleep. Oh, Frenchy." She sighed again as Frenchy leaned to kiss her gently, admiringly, lingeringly, her small hands gentle on Pam's neck and shoulders. "You do have a way about you, don't you," Pam said. "You make me feel respected, delicate, instead of the big schlep I am." Frenchy held Pam, simply held her, until the sauce began to burn and they both leapt for it.

Laughing, Pam said, "Typical, I can't even be quiet without screwing up."

"Listen, let me help," pleaded Frenchy. "I got to be good for something."

"Oh, I think I've figured out exactly what you're good for," Pam assured her, that salacious glint in her eye again. "But here." She handed Frenchy the bread. "Cut it in half, butter it thickly, put some of this garlic on it."

"Okay," Frenchy said, cutting the bread in half with great care and concentration, thinking of Jessie helping in the kitchen. "Of course I'm butch," Jessie had said, "but I'm more than that now."

Finally, Pam lit the candles and they sat down to eat. With Pam's glowing eyes across the candles, the meal was the best Frenchy had ever tasted. Their sexual excitement, their restrained desires, enhanced the common food. Garlic became an aphrodisiac, red sauce a sensuous texture. Half-way through the second bottle of wine, Frenchy vowed to step outside herself for the night.

She started by calling her mother. She was playing cards with the girls from work, she said, and would stay the night in Staten Island. Then she made up a telephone number and suggested that the phones on Staten Island didn't work right because it was an island. She did not normally tell such outright lies, but she wanted tonight to be special, totally removed from her mother. Pam meanwhile had put a bossa nova record on the stereo, and though it was not her kind of music, Frenchy danced back to the table to it.

"Can you bossa nova?"

"Never heard of the guy."

"Silly. Here, put your feet like this —"

Suddenly, she didn't want to pretend anymore. Didn't want to be civilized about seducing this woman. And she *was* a woman, not a girl. She fastened her eyes on Pam's lips as Pam was watching their feet. In one motion, Frenchy turned to Pam and caught her face in her hands, pulling it to her so she could kiss her with the same kind of passionate abandon, almost desperation as Pam's kiss the week before.

The remains of dinner got cold, the wine sat uncorked and undrunk, while the two lovers turned and twisted their wet mouths against each other, and panted, and struggled to the bed. Pam's robe fell off her shoulders, leaving her large, smooth shoulders open to Frenchy's hurried kisses, then fell further so that her heavy breasts lay revealed to Frenchy's open mouth and ceaseless tongue. Pam undid the robe's tie, but Frenchy slid it apart. Now it was Pam who was overwhelmed by the inspired woman who was no longer careful or hesitant, but everywhere on her, hungrily sensuous and everywhere. Pam caught Frenchy's sweat-shirt and began to pull it over her head.

Frenchy stopped, dead still, looked at Pam with shocked, glazed eyes, then tore the shirt over her head and calmly, quickly, went to turn off the light. With only candlelight in the room, the tiny woman quickly removed the rest of her clothes.

Pam groaned as their naked bodies touched. Frenchy groaned as well. With her hands, her mouth, her tongue, with her words, Frenchy brought Pam to climax, and then lay back. Pam, as if sensing that this was not usual for Frenchy, crooned and comforted as she stroked her, slowed when Frenchy tensed, stopped and just held her, then went after her passion and wouldn't let it go until Frenchy, too, had come, long and exquisitely.

Exhausted, they looked at one another in the candle-light. Pam finally laughed softly. "I knew you'd be good, but I never thought you'd be so passionate."

"You make me feel funny."

Pam laughed again, taking Frenchy's small body in her arms and rocking her, squeezing her tightly to herself until their breathing quickened. The bossa nova kept playing.

Seeing, hearing, feeling each other's desire, soon they were moving together again, a little slower, tireder, quieter. This time, Frenchy couldn't finish, but when Pam promised in her breathy whisper, "Later, then," Frenchy did, sud-denly, with a surprised groan coming from her lips, her eyes half-open, able to see the pleasure this gave Pam. She felt insatiable, as if she'd never feel the end of this need for Pam's touch, for Pam's incredibly soft, enveloping, exciting body.

On and on it went, Frenchy's night of fire, the only light the wavering sun of candlelight and then that too sputtered out. They fell asleep.

* * * * *

Sunday was a dark day. Frenchy showered at Pam's apartment, but had to leave because Pam was visiting her own mother on Long Island. Her body, under the steaming water, seemed new. Every thought of what had passed between herself and Pam the night before sent waves of excitement through her. More than once Frenchy groaned almost audibly as she remembered certain of their touches. Where was Frenchy the butch now, she asked her body as she soaped it. She would never be the same, never be able to look at a woman in the same cool, appraising way. Somehow she was one of them now, not something other than what they were; no longer could she hold herself apart from their common experience.

Dried and dressed, she sat with Pam at the table, the remains of dinner still piled in the sink. "I'd be glad to clean up while you go off to the Island," she offered.

"I'll do it tonight. Or tomorrow. I've got nothing to do then." Pam was dressed more neatly than usual.

They looked at each other with the memory of desire staining their eyes, its taste on their tongues, its power in the slight trembling of their hands when they touched.

"You take care, Frenchy," Pam said at the door, hugging her protectively.

"You too, Pam," Frenchy said, meaning it, wanting to say more, but not knowing what. She felt as if she would never see Pam again, as if their night had been a gift that couldn't be repeated. "Can I call you?"

"You'd better."

But Frenchy feared she might not, once the full impact of what had happened last night hit her. Even if she wanted to . . .

They ran down the stairs and walked as far as 6th Avenue together. Pam hailed a cab and Frenchy watched her ride off. Feeling as if something had been torn from her, she began to walk. At Sheridan Square she saw a subway sign

that said South Ferry and remembered that she had resolved, when she was at Provincetown, to visit the docks,
to ride the ferry. She went down the stairs and caught a
train.

She found her way to the ferry slip as if in a fog. The
terminal was huge and almost deserted, the boat larger
than she'd imagined and carrying few passengers. Another
kind of excitement, much different from last night, filled
her as she heard the blasts of the ferry's horn. She looked
down into the water and, as she had in Provincetown, felt
something stir very deep inside. Deeper than where Pam
had touched her last night. The loading platform clanged
closed and the boat moved out from the slip. The terminal
slid backwards in Frenchy's vision. The white water foamed
up powerfully under the boat, and again Frenchy felt that
sense of loss. The wind blew through her hair. She took
her comb from her pocket, but stood, comb in her hand,
transfixed by the receding city.

It was a foggy afternoon. Few pleasure boats were out.
She'd given the last of her cigarettes to Pam and decided
not to buy more, even when she discovered a snack bar
within the cavernous, echoing boat. A few people slept
on the benches on the bottom level where the water rolled
by outside the windows. Iron stairways clanged under her
feet. Eventually she found her way to the front of the ferry
where huge ropes lay coiled, and chains hung across the
bow. Wind pushed at her. She held onto a railing and swallowed mouthfuls of the wind, grinning at the salty spray
that began to coat her face.

Here, she could think of Pam. She licked salt from
her lips and remembered how they made love. How *she*
had been made love to. How, holding Pam, she'd felt as
this ship must on the undulating surface of the sea, hardly
able to enter the water at all, large as it was. Yet the sea
surrounded it, buoyed it up. And the pleasure of it, the

crazy, all-consuming pleasure of it! She stared at the Bay, lulled by its motion.

Land was approaching. She felt she could ride back and forth on the ferry all day. Strange that she was ending up where she told her mother she was going: Staten Island. And really, compared to last night, she hadn't done much more than play cards with most of her girls over the years, as she'd told her mother she had. She'd played hearts. And always won. Never got involved. Dropped each girl before she got too close. Then Mercedes had slipped into the deck.

As she paid her fare again and crossed to the returning ferry, the boat whistle sounded. It tore through Frenchy's heart like the memory of Mercedes. She'd wrecked things all right. Driven Mercedes from her with her game of hearts. The game she'd always played to please her mother.

And what if she stopped playing? A wave from a passing boat threw spray into Frenchy's face. Chilly and wet, she moved again to the front of the boat. As the boat neared it, the City grew bigger and bigger.

She stood at the bow, looking at the City with determination, her legs wide apart, her hands in fists at her sides. She felt as if she were going home, only not home to the Bronx. Home to a world of her own. Pam lived there: Pam and the Frenchy she was uncovering. Jessie and Mary lived there too. And Mercedes lived there. All of them, thought Frenchy, were doing okay out there on their own. When the ferry bumped the padded dock, Frenchy swayed, but didn't lose her balance. Humming a bossa nova, she went into the City again.

Chapter 5

Baklava
December, 1966

Frenchy's Saturday nights had changed. No longer did she willingly work until the last minute of a Saturday afternoon or even into the evening. She used her seniority to grab the choicest Saturday hours. She also used her good record and the high opinion of her boss to dare to wear pants — jeans — to work. She carried a big gym bag and changed into her boots, blue shirt and jean jacket after work right at the store, leaving through the big back storage room where no one else saw her. The bag she stashed in the tiny employees' lounge where she could change back to her work shoes and smock on Monday morning.

Almost ready for the gay scene downtown, Frenchy hurried along the A&P alleyway away from her mother's apartment, and walked several blocks out of her way to a subway stop in another neighborhood. She grabbed her pack of cigarettes at a newsstand outside the subway (her mother still had never seen her smoke) and dashed up the steps to the platform where she usually had time only to slick back her hair into its d.a. and pompadour before the train arrived. She checked out the car to make sure it hadn't picked up a neighbor from its previous stop, but nobody went into the City late Saturday afternoon except her. As usual she'd told her mother she'd be playing cards with the girls from work that night, and would be spending the night at one of their houses. She suspected this story might be wearing thin, but her mother was getting older and older, and beginning to fail, and she didn't seem to notice.

Pam, of course, was the reason for this change in routine. Frenchy was head over heels, not in love, but in *desire*, with her artist. They still had found almost nothing in common but their gayness, and Pam sometimes frightened Frenchy with her impulsive and irresponsible lifestyle. Yet they now had a bond deeper than any Frenchy had ever before shared with a woman. Frenchy, with Pam, had been able to throw off years of denial of her own womanhood, her sexuality. Every weekend she allowed herself to spend the night with Pam, to undress, to be made love to. Most exciting to her was that she did not feel threatened by the role she allowed Pam to take in their lovemaking.

She was still obviously as butch as she needed to be. If only all this had not happened too late. If only she could have changed sooner. . . . With Mercedes, it would not have been a matter of desire, but of love.

Tonight Frenchy was taking Pam to the bar. *If* Pam was in the mood. Pam never made promises to her any more, because Frenchy got too upset when she broke them. It was only because of the sexual spell Frenchy seemed to have woven around Pam that she managed to remember when Frenchy was coming and be home for her. In the weeks since the start of their affair, they had done little besides meet at Pam's tiny, cluttered Village apartment and make love. Frenchy had made it plain that she was getting itchy for the bar and Pam clearly wanted to accommodate her if only to guarantee that Frenchy would spend the night.

Frenchy often wondered what drew Pam to a short, uncultured bulldyke from the Bronx. Pam was so sophisticated, artistic, educated. Nor did it seem to bother Pam to want nothing but sex from another woman, as if preferring that her relationships not integrate too many aspects of her life. If she met the woman with whom she could share sex, art, intellect, food, lifestyle, ambitions — then, said Pam, she would have met her future and would have to settle down. But Pam wasn't ready to settle down yet.

So once more Frenchy skipped out of the Bronx the first chance she could get, and made a dash for Pam's place, even sacrificing her ritual walk into the Village. Somehow, these days, she didn't miss her first glimpse of the Women's House of Detention at all. Full of anticipation, she rang Pam's bell, knowing the pleasure they would give one another, excited to know she'd be in Pam's arms in a matter of minutes, and relieved that she'd found a place where she was more of herself than she'd ever dreamed possible.

There was no answer.

Frenchy remembered that first time she had gone to pick up Pam. Surely Dorene wasn't there today — it was 5:00 on a Saturday afternoon! And if she was — what would Frenchy do then? Pam wasn't the kind to say she'd go with Frenchy, not officially. They hadn't exchanged rings.

She didn't belong to Frenchy.

She rang again, angrily. How could she live like that, without knowing who would be in her bed that night? Frenchy felt a sudden pull at her heart: was Saturday night enough for her; did she see other women during the week, when Frenchy was working uptown? Sure she might, Frenchy slowly acknowledged, knowing Pam's voracious sexual appetite. Even as much as they made love Saturday nights, Pam probably didn't wait until the next week for more.

Discouraged, Frenchy leaned against the wall of the little vestibule, ringing one last fruitless time. The woman had made a fool of her. Stepping out behind her back while Frenchy let her do those things she did in bed. She felt used, violated. No wonder Pam didn't respect her — she was a femme for her.

Someone was struggling with the outside door behind Frenchy's back. Wearily, she turned to open the door, but then a smile transformed her face and she grabbed the door and yanked it open, Pam almost falling in on top of her, Frenchy catching the packages Pam dropped. She put her small arms right around Pam, packages and all.

"Frenchy, am I glad you're here. I wouldn't have made it another step. Look what I got!" she said, stepping back from Frenchy. "Dinner! Ever had artichokes?" Frenchy made a face through her smile. "And noodles. I'm going to make this great noodle dish: kugel. And in here, look!" She began to dig in a series of smaller bags.

Pam's round gold bracelets clinked on each other as she raised her purchases in triumph. "For tonight!" She held a pair of loose, black, oriental-looking trousers against her denim skirt, and a white low-necked top embroidered with multi-colored stitching. "For going to the bar tonight.

I have the perfect jacket upstairs. You'll never know I don't go there every week!"

Frenchy looked skeptical as she led Pam upstairs, but was glad Pam hadn't done anything really crazy, like buying butch clothes, because she would have refused to go.

"I'm really psyched up for tonight, Frenchy." Pam unlocked her door. "Whoops, better not put these on the bed, we might need it." She smiled over at Frenchy who had collapsed on the couch. Pam put the grocery bags on the kitchen table and sat next to Frenchy who had pulled off her boots. "Feet hurt? Cashiering is so hard on your feet." She began to massage Frenchy's feet through her socks, her back to Frenchy, who felt a stirring between her legs as she remembered Pam's broad fleshy naked back.

"How've you been?" Frenchy asked.

"Frustrated," Pam teased, looking back at her.

"How has your week gone?" Frenchy was thinking about the dozens of lovers Pam might have seen in the past week.

"Lonely," Pam answered, pulling Frenchy's socks off slowly, and kissing the bare, tiny feet.

"Do anything exciting?" Frenchy asked, beginning to realize that this crazy woman was making love to her feet and she, Frenchy, was getting turned on.

"Not till right now," Pam murmured, pausing to turn Frenchy's feet so that she could reach her soles.

"Oh," Frenchy gasped, as Pam's tongue ran, dry, over her soles, one after the other. Frenchy leaned to pull Pam to her, but couldn't reach her. "Pam," she said, "Pam."

Pam was nibbling at her ankle and sliding one hand up under her pants along her calf. Just when Frenchy was about to embarrass herself and say please, Pam turned with a small smile toward her, and began to unbutton her pants. Then she moved up and slipped one arm around Frenchy's shoulders, her hand inside Frenchy's pants, where she found, and increased, the butch's wetness. Frenchy came, quickly and without inhibitions, as amazed at herself as she'd been the first time. She laughed as she scrambled up to reverse their positions.

"What's so funny?" breathed Pam.

"We haven't been in the house for five minutes."

"It's been a long week. And I've wanted you every minute of it."

Reassured that there was no one else, she doubted that Pam's near-celibacy would last. Eagerly she watched Pam remove her clothes. They stayed on the couch until hunger for food overtook them. As Pam made dinner, Frenchy poured wine and set the table. Over and over she felt desire for Pam well up in her, fighting with her need to visit the bar, to see the kids, to be her other self. She'd been, after all, Frenchy the bar butch a lot longer than she'd been Pam's lover.

They finished supper and even did the dishes — a week's worth — which Pam allowed Frenchy to wash while she showered and dressed in her new "bar clothes." Frenchy had been careful to take her good shirt off when they made love and still wore an old shirt of Pam's which hung to mid-thigh.

"Voila!" said Pam.

Frenchy was amused to see how Pam's bar clothes had been transformed into an outfit that was Pam's alone, and she felt the desire triggered again by this gypsy-vision. Pam had wrapped a scarf around her hair like a long headband and her long dark hair ran richly down her back under it. She had put on a beaded shimmering belt, her gaudiest dangling earrings and several rings. She'd painted her nails. The white blouse had puffy sleeves and tight cuffs, colored embroidery clashing — almost — with the colors of the band, the belt and the earrings. "Well, what do you think?"

"You look groovy!" Frenchy laughed, purposely using Pam's word.

"Do you really think so? Will I fit in at the bar?"

"Baby," Frenchy said, shaking her head in wonder, "You'll always stand out no matter where you go. You have a way of doing that."

Frenchy stood, legs apart, hands on hips, cigarette hanging from her lips, shirt open over her pants.

"Don't move," said Pam, quickly sifting through a mess to find her sketch pad. "I have to draw you. I just melt to see you like that." As she drew she talked. "When you tell me how good I look, and I look at you saying it, I can't tell you what a thrill it gives me."

Frenchy shifted, half-embarrassed, half-pleased.

"Don't move! I want you just like you were." Pam's face was flushed, but her look was intent as she drew. "Sometimes I wish I looked like you myself. I'd like to make women feel the way you make me feel when you stand like that, so butch, so I can just see your little butch breasts under your shirt." Relaxing a little, Pam's pen strokes became longer, firmer, more sure. She sighed. "But I just don't have the body for it. Or the discipline. How do you do it?" she asked admiringly. "How can you just stand there and look so damned attractive like it was the most natural thing in the world, like you don't even know you're doing it? Don't you know what a fine body you have, how good it looks, how good-looking your face is, especially all serious like that?"

Thinking an answer was required, Frenchy shrugged.

"Do keep still, just a few minutes more. I'll try to keep you amused." Pam was smiling again. "I wish you could feel my heart pounding, I wish I could show you how much I want you. But it's better to wait sometimes. We'll have our own private erotic scene going in front of everybody at the bar." She was nodding as she spoke and Frenchy wondered what she was cooking up for them now. She knew that look.

"I'm getting excited just thinking about you later, darling. How I'll look right through your clothes remembering a hundred other ways I've seen you walk and sit and lie. I'll think of you like that, nude, when you're only showing the world what you want it to see. Just a little longer now. Stay still. When you're paying for my drinks I'll imagine you last week, in the shower, coming as you leaned against me. When you're dancing with one of your old femmes I'll think of your legs open, waiting for my lips and my tongue. And if I think you're not paying enough attention to me I'll remind you by the way I touch you, and where, by the way I move against you when we dance. How delicious," Pam said as she put down the pad and pencil.

It was hard even for Frenchy to go out into the Greenwich Village streets after that.

Full darkness had not yet descended. It was too early to go to the bar. She and Pam joined the people who seemed to drift aimlessly along the streets.

"Let's go over to the coffee house," Pam suggested.

"The coffee house?" Frenchy looked as if she had just tasted something bad.

"Not for long, Frenchy. Please," Pam said, with her most winning smile, the smile that had coaxed so much from Frenchy already.

Frenchy wasn't giving in. "Why?"

"For dessert!" Pam declared.

"I'm too full for dessert."

"Not for this, you aren't. Ever had baklava?"

"Sounds communist."

"You're so delightfully *square*. And you're chicken."

"I'm not scared. Just don't like all those bearded creeps."

"Come on, I know the waitress. She'll seat us in the back. Ah, Frenchy, my mouth is watering." Pam's eyes glittered.

Frenchy pursed her lips. "All right," she said. Pam grabbed her hand as if to take her there before she changed her mind.

"Too damn dark in here to see who's what anyway," Frenchy complained when they were seated by the steaming front window. Afraid one of her bar friends would see her, she turned her back to the street.

Pam laughed. "That's why they wear beards. So you can tell which are boys."

Reluctantly, Frenchy grinned at Pam. When the waitress came Pam ordered for both of them.

"Who wants expresso?" asked Frenchy.

"You'll love it. There's nothing better than expresso with baklava."

"That's what you say about everything."

"Only if I'm in the mood," Pam claimed.

A great whoosh came from the back of the room and Frenchy started. "They're blowing the place up," she said, only half-joking.

"Darling, this is not a communist plot to assassinate you. That's the expresso machine. This is a little Village restaurant that's been here forever and I hope will stay here forever, serving the kinds of things you can't get anywhere else. The owners are capitalists like the owners of the A&P. They just don't make as much money as the A&P. But they would if they could."

The waitress put the order on the table with their bill. "Thanks," Frenchy said. She looked to Frenchy like a thin duplicate of Pam. Maybe all these artist types were just like Pam. How could she like these drafty old places with nothing but wine and beer and strange food and no jukebox? What kept these people sitting around for hours? It just didn't seem American. Frenchy tasted the expresso. "Argh," she spat at its bitterness.

"Baklava first," Pam instructed, waving some on her

fork. "Then you can appreciate the expresso."

Frenchy tried it. The thing was so small and flaky it crumpled under her fork.

"Tiny bites, darling," Pam suggested.

She tried again, got a tiny piece on her fork and put it in her mouth. It was heavenly. She scowled at Pam, picking up the tiny expresso cup again. It did go well with the dessert.

"Well?" asked Pam.

"Well what?"

"Isn't it great?"

"I like it okay," Frenchy conceded.

"You're impossible!"

Frenchy shrugged and broke up a tiny bit more.

"If you don't want it, I'll finish it for you."

"That's okay," Frenchy assured her with a martyred air.

They ate in silence. Frenchy, while enjoying the food, glanced sharply around. Whatever they were, communists or hippies, they were certainly straight. A woman sat with a man at almost every table.

"At least do you like the music?" Pam asked. Classical tapes were playing.

"It makes me itchy."

Pam sat suddenly despondent over her uneaten baklava.

"How come you're just sitting there?" Frenchy asked.

"Because you won't even try."

"What do you mean, try? I'm eating, ain't I?"

"Yes, but Frenchy, I *like* this place. I'd like to come here again with you. And I like some of the people."

"They're all straight."

"Oh, no they're not. Is that what's wrong?"

Feeling remorseful, Frenchy admitted her real discomfort. "I don't belong here. They're all staring at me. They know I belong down the street in the Swing Lounge."

"You said you can't even see them. How can you tell they're staring at you?"

"Straights always do."

"These people are different, Frenchy. Look, see those two guys in beards over there with the woman? They're fags."

"What about her?"

"She's a fag hag."

"You mean a faggot moll?"

"She only likes fags."

"Right."

"And that man over there is a far-out sculptor. He's teaching Dorene. That's his wife. But they know Dorene and I are gay and they don't care. The same with that group who just left. They're going to another coffee house later. They asked me during the week to go. They're all straight."

"I don't trust them. Why'd they want you to go?"

"They like me."

"Even though you're gay?"

"Yes."

"I don't know."

"What's there to know?"

"I just don't like being around them. I can't explain it."

"You're prejudiced."

"I am not. I got black friends."

"Not against blacks. Against straights."

"Maybe I am. I don't see why I shouldn't be. They'd as soon lock me up as let me be on the street. You see how they look at us. The tourists from New Jersey over here to sightsee on Saturday nights. They stare at us like we're something the tour guides put here for them. They hate me. And they think you shouldn't be with me."

"These people aren't tourists."

"No, they're used to us. Once they were tourists, though, and I bet it took them a long time not to stare."

"They're my friends."

"You can have them." Frenchy knew immediately she'd gone too far. "I'm sorry. I never knew any straight people to like gays."

"You never had the guts to let any straight people *know* you're gay."

"Guts! You think I'm stupid? It's none of their damn business. They can come on as friendly as they want, and turn their backs on you anytime they want. The whole *world* is straight. *I'm* going to tell them I'm different? That's like, like, going to war without a gun!"

They glared at each other.

"Maybe —" Frenchy said after a while.

"Maybe —" said Pam at the same time.

They laughed. "Go ahead," said Frenchy, lighting a cigarette.

"No, you go," said Pam, taking it from her while Frenchy reached for another. "No, let's share this cigarette."

"I don't want to. You tongue them."

"I *what* them?"

"Tongue them, get them all wet. I like them dry."

"Crazy," said Pam, shaking her head. "We're so different. Go ahead, what were you going to say?"

"Maybe some of them are okay. You're right, I wouldn't know. But I still think I'm right to be scared of them. What did you want to say?"

"That you could be right. These people, especially the men, might turn against me if they had to. You know, if the Nazis came or something. But they'd get me for being a Jew anyway, so why should I hide being a lesbian? Maybe I'm just more used to feeling exposed than you because I'm a Jew. Maybe I live with their dislike and suspicion too easily."

"Like you said, we're so different," Frenchy said, almost touching Pam's hand.

"You can touch me in here, no one will say anything. I've touched other women right at this table."

"Did they look as queer as me?"

"Maybe not."

"I better not. Anyway, I like the expresso. And the — what is it?"

"Baklava."

"And I'd like to have it again sometime. I just wish there was a gay coffee house somewhere."

"Me too. But you can't have everything."

"It's late enough now. Want to go to the bar? The kids ought to be just about getting there."

"After dressing up, do you think I'd miss it?" Pam rose and swung her jacket over her shoulders.

The lovers joined the crowds on MacDougal Street. Jewelry stores seemed to battle with each other for space to sell native American, African, Mexican merchandise. The bars along the streets and up the alleyways were filling up and jukebox music stole out of them to draw the crowds in. Frenchy kept an eye on the Swing Lounge, one of the bars she frequented, but no one she knew went in.

Pam walked slowly, dawdling despite the chilly fall air, looking in shop windows, reaching to touch Frenchy and whispering to her. Frenchy slowed her normally brisk, aggressive and confident walk to match Pam's, aware of the stares they attracted, while Pam seemed oblivious. As Pam pointed to bracelets she would like to wear, Frenchy stared down a man who, seeing her, grabbed the hand of his date.

The crowds and stores thinned as they neared Washington Square. It was darker. Frenchy could hear dry leaves blowing across the pavement. She took Pam's hand as they passed through the park.

The closer they got to the bar, the more eager Frenchy became to be with her own. There, in that smoky dark place owned by racketeers, fueled by poor liquor, so crowded she sometimes could not sit and had to wait in long lines to use the toilets, where she danced on a packed floor to music most often sung by straights, she felt at home, accepted. She paid the bouncer at the door for this acceptance and entered with Pam.

They stood, just inside, Pam blinking to adjust her eyes, Frenchy breathing in relief to be there. She hadn't ever been away from the bars this long. "Frenchy!" she heard someone call in welcome, and her homecoming was complete.

She looked at Pam, inspecting her for acceptability — and found her all wrong. Yet surely all her friends would recognize how she and Pam felt about each other. Like they felt about their girls. That's what made them all belong. Pam looked overwhelmed by the bar.

"It's okay, Pam," Frenchy said. "These are our people."

It was Pam's turn to look skeptical. They went to join Jessie, Mary, some others at their table. "Where you been?" Jessie asked, thumping Frenchy on the shoulder. She was more dressed up than Frenchy was used to, with a turtleneck under a Madras shirt. Her hair was cut more stylishly too. "We ain't seen you since you come out to the house. Like my new duds? Mary's got great taste." She said all this while suspiciously eyeing Pam.

"I been busy," Frenchy said. "What're you drinking?" she asked the table. She ordered a round, including a glass of chablis for Pam. As she made introductions she could tell the others were torn between admiration for Pam and disapproval. This was their pal Frenchy's new girl, but boy had her tastes changed. The longer Jessie stared, the more disapproving Mary looked.

It was a ragtag group, a mix from years of hanging out at the bar. Hermine, a heavy bleached blonde, had been married to a man before her sister-in-law brought her to the bar. She was from Brooklyn, but had adopted the gay life so completely she'd moved into the City. Her dream was to own one of those tawdry jewelry shops that catered to Village tourists. Next to her was Beebo, an immigrant from Connecticut. As a teenager she'd been thrown out of her house because she was gay, and she had never recovered. She was tall, but stooped, as if cowering from anticipated blows. Because she was so tall her friends had nicknamed her after a character in one of the gay paperbacks they passed among themselves. She worked in the garment district, sewing.

Everyone was gossiping and laughing except Pam. "Want to dance?" Frenchy held out a hand to her. "What's the matter?" she asked when they had squeezed onto the floor.

Pam had to shout. "I'm not used to this. I don't fit in."

"Sure you do. Everybody's gay!"

Frenchy tried to calm some of Pam's fears. Pam wasn't, Frenchy assured her, so different from her friends at the table. "You just don't understand them," she said. "You'll see when we hang around with them for a while. They're all nice people. They'd do anything for you."

"But why do they dress like that?"

Frenchy looked over at them. Beebo, as usual, was in her ill-fitting jeans; a turquoise and black striped muscle shirt exposed her thin pale arms. Like Jessie, Mary was dressed up. Her frilly white blouse fit tightly across her breasts and rounded stomach, and she wore black knit pants and white cut-out heels. Hermine was all in black, with blue eyeshadow and pencilled brows.

"Like what?" asked Frenchy.

"Why does that one wear sunglasses in the bar?"

"Beebo's been around forever, baby. Sunglasses used to be cool. They're part of her now. Like you wearing all that Indian jewelry. They probably don't understand that."

"Don't you like it?" Pam asked.

"I like it a lot on you. Now, if Beebo wore it she'd look pretty silly, right?"

They slowed almost to a stop and swayed together, feeling the desire again. Frenchy touched Pam differently, more intimately.

"Frenchy," Pam said, "I'd like to, but I don't fit in. I don't know what to say to them."

"You don't have to say anything. Just be my girl."

It worked, somehow. Frenchy, reminded of Pam's desirability, acted possessive and proud. Pam seemed to become comfortable with her own quietness and felt free to touch Frenchy, to lean over and kiss her, take drags on her cigarettes, wetting their tips to remind Frenchy of their intimacy. Soon the others were asking how they met.

"I'd never been in the Ace of Spades before," Pam told them. She squeezed Frenchy's arm, while Frenchy tried to look nonchalant. "And this cute woman from New York, she stuck in my mind all these years. When I saw her a month ago I knew just who she was. And," she said, looking at Frenchy, "I knew I wanted her." Frenchy looked back at her with sexy eyes.

Beebo asked incredulously, "You were at the Cape, but you were never in the Ace? What do you do at the Cape?"

"Visit friends, go to art shows, the beach."

"You have friends up there?" asked Mary, looking impressed.

"Someone's always renting a place up there. And then the rest of us visit. I lived there one summer. The summer I came out, as a matter of fact," Pam explained.

"When was that?" Beebo asked innocently.

"Oh, years and years before I even met Frenchy."

"You've been out years and years?" Hermine looked surprised, as if the group had decided Pam was new to the gay scene.

"Yes," Pam said and from that moment the group opened more to her. Soon Pam began to tease Frenchy, apparently more comfortable.

"Cut it out," said Frenchy the next time they danced.

"Why? I thought you liked it, lover."

"Not in front of the kids," Frenchy ordered.

Pam was hurt. "Why?"

"Because I said so," Frenchy said, the self she always was at the bars, forgetting Pam didn't know this side of her.

"I don't have to take this from you," Pam said. "I'm not your wife, you know."

"Oh, shit. If only we had more than Saturday night," Frenchy groaned.

"What do you mean? What difference does that make?"

"We have to get everything in on one night. I want to come here, you want to go to your places. We both want to make love all night. I wish I lived down here."

"It would help, wouldn't it," Pam said. Frenchy for the first time felt it might be possible. Dancing slowly, they looked at one another for a long time. Could they make it work? Would it help to live together? Frenchy felt a surge of courage. She could work it out at home, she knew she could.

"Frenchy, why don't you move in with me? Just to try it. Maybe you can get a job down here. I'd really dig living with you."

The music stopped. "Let me think about it, Pam," Frenchy said, wondering where this courage was coming from. She felt as she had on the prow of the ferry — master of her fate, riding into the city full steam, ready for anything. Suddenly, she didn't want to go back to their table. She wanted to go home with Pam and stay there. Make love endlessly. Go out on Saturday morning and buy the *News*.

Come back to Pam and make love, be fed, and stay, stay, stay with her girl.

Frenchy said, "Let's go home."

* * * * *

Later that week, Frenchy decided she could no longer put off the idea of moving out on her own. She had to tell her mother now, while her need fed her courage.

She stood outside the kitchen door. Her stomach felt like a meat grinder, churning and churning. She nearly lost her courage, but then she tightened her lips, fisted her hands, stepped into the kitchen.

Maman was in pincurls. Her grim little face surveyed Frenchy as if conducting an inspection. She pointed with her chin to Frenchy's place at the table, then set a plate of pancakes next to juice and syrup.

Frenchy wavered, almost sitting, then decided to stand as straight as she could. "Maman," she began, her voice barely audible. "Maman," she said louder, "I decided."

The face didn't change, but Maman's eyes rose to meet her own, as if daring her to say these words.

"I'm moving downtown. I want to try it out." Now she would sit, hide behind her meal. She chewed automatically, longer than usual, as if trying to swallow sawdust.

Maman had turned her back, her little shoulders bowing under this mountain of suffering. "*Je ne sais quoi,*" she sighed as she scraped the griddle clean.

Frenchy knew she should answer something, anything, but she just stuffed more pancake into her mouth.

"*Sacre Dieu,*" said Maman. Was she about to cry, leaning over the sink? No, she straightened her back, not unlike Frenchy had a few moments before, and with a slight gesture of one hand disapproved, accepted, declined further talk on this subject.

Was this it, then, wondered Frenchy? No scene, no tears, no anger? Was this all she'd feared for so many years? Her mother must have been waiting for this news for as long as Frenchy had been avoiding it. Perhaps she'd suspected it was time. Perhaps she had plans of her own. Frenchy's brother would be visiting that evening. Maybe she would learn her mother's true reaction then.

She rose. "I'm late, Maman," she lied, bending to have her cheek kissed. It would be better to leave now, in case her mother was only in shock and the worst was yet to come.

"What?" asked Maman, as if she'd been far away.

Frenchy accepted the kiss and left, guilt as heavy in her as the pancakes.

* * * * *

Frenchy's arms once had become tired ringing the register. Now she didn't even know she was doing it unless someone watched her every move, trying to catch her making a mistake. But she didn't make mistakes.

"I think you overcharged me," said grumpy Mr. Regan from her building.

He always thought she overcharged him. "Look," said Frenchy, "I don't have time for this today."

"What?" asked Mr. Regan, who was hard of hearing.

Frenchy considered all the rude things she could say without him ever knowing and chuckled despite her annoyance. She'd been remembering the scene with her mother and brother the night before.

"On the tuna fish!" Mr. Regan shouted. "It's on sale. You charged me full price."

"Must have been another item the same price," she shouted back.

"No, no," he yelled, almost gleefully pushing the tape at her.

"All right, all right, skinflint," Frenchy muttered, examining it. She couldn't believe what she saw. She took every item out of the man's bag and checked it against the tape. The line at her register lengthened. The old pig was right. "Sorry," she muttered ungraciously, rebagging the items and calling the head cashier for a void slip.

"Whatsa matter, Genvieve?" called Marion from the next register after Mr. Regan had shuffled away, counting the fourteen cents Frenchy had refunded. "You losing it or what?"

"I must be sick," Frenchy joked. But she was worried. She *didn't* make mistakes. Was it because she was upset over moving out of her mother's house?

"Want to eat together?" called Marion.

"Sure." She could use somebody to talk to.

They met in the smoky, dirty lounge and grabbed two milk crates to sit on out in the alleyway beside the store. Unwrapping their sandwiches, they smiled at each other, glad to be off their feet and not having to say it after working together so long.

Frenchy remembered how attractive she'd found Marion when she'd first come to Frenchy's store. Seven years later she enjoyed the warm comraderie she shared with Marion, since then a mother of two.

"Hey," Marion said, "are you going to tell me what's the matter or make me ask?"

"I told my mother I'm moving out. Then last night she tells me *she's* moving out."

"This is great news!" Marion said, neatly folding her lunch bag for re-use.

"Yeah, but it's taking some getting used to. My brother

Serge has to move to Florida for his company. I didn't know she wanted to go with him. And she thought she had to stay up here to take care of me."

"So with you moving out she's free to go."

"Here I thought she'd be moping around the house... Still, it's kind of a shock knowing she won't be around at all." She lit a cigarette. "What I want to do, see..." She drew nervously on the cigarette, "is move in with this friend of mine downtown even before Maman goes to Florida, just to try it out. Then I can decide to live downtown or not. If not, I could take my mother's apartment. It's rent controlled. Until she moves, I could eat supper with her, make sure she's okay."

"Sounds like you planned it perfect."

"I'll tell you, Mar, I'm scared about it. I don't know how it'll work out with this particular friend of mine." Frenchy blushed. "I'd be paying half the rent downtown and my mother will just have to cough up her share out of the cash she's been salting away for Serge and me when she dies."

"I admire your guts, Frenchy, I really do. If I'd had what it takes five years ago I'd never have married that guy. But at least I got the kids out of that deal."

They stared at the ground, Frenchy marvelling at how everything was suddenly working out for her. "Guts," she laughed. "It took me so many years to do this."

"What's making you do it now?"

"I don't know, Mar, to tell you the truth. Maybe just because I'm getting old. Maybe so I won't miss any chances when they come along. Maybe because my friends are all settling down. This girl I might move in with, she's been on her own for years and years. She never thought to do it any other way. Now *that's* what I call guts."

"Where's she live?"

"Downtown."

"You already said that. Where?"

"Morton Street."

"That around Wall Street?"

"No," Frenchy hedged further. Everybody knew the Village was full of queers. "Near Fourteenth."

"Oh, the Village," Marion said. Frenchy blanched. "Boy would I ever like to live in the Village. I love it down there."

"You do?"

"Yeah," she said, looking at her watch. "Hey, the half hour's almost up and I got to go to the little girl's room. Coming?"

Frenchy shook her head. She was always too embarrassed to share a bathroom with a straight girl.

"See you inside, you lucky stiff. Ah, to be single and on your own in the Village. What I wouldn't give..."

What had Marion meant? Could she be queer? Or want to be? But she had two kids. She'd heard of lesbians who married and had kids. She'd have to keep her eye on Marion.

But meanwhile, she felt a little more sure of herself. Her plan seemed reasonable and she'd get along just fine on her own. Even if she wanted to, she couldn't back out now. Serge had told her mother Florida was more like Marseilles and the old woman was anxious to move there now. She and her mother both would get by — she hoped.

At least it was Saturday again. In less than four hours she would be with Pam, telling her what she'd decided, free of her mother's air of martyrdom and being told by Pam that it would work out, that they would have a wonderful life together in Greenwich Village — Frenchy hoped.

The next four hours went fast, without mistakes now that her mind was clear. With her heart beating to a bossa nova beat, she went downtown. Pam was home, waiting. She had even cleaned up the apartment. Frenchy didn't know where to look first, at the impressively neat room, the shining kitchen, the drawings neatly matted and hung on the walls, or at Pam, who lay completely naked on the bed, fanning herself with a long green feather. On the stereo, Bob Dylan sang *Lay Lady Lay*.

"Close the door, lover. I may not be modest, but I don't want to be arrested either."

"Hello." Frenchy couldn't think of anything else to say.

"I thought since you couldn't wait for me to get my clothes off last week, I'd save you the trouble."

"Thank you," said Frenchy, still standing in the doorway even after she'd closed the door, feeling vaguely repulsed at the sight of the naked woman on the bed. Not that she didn't like naked women — but there was something wrong with this. It didn't do anything for her. She preferred Pam in her sexy clothes, at least to start with. She walked over to the bed and sat uncomfortably next to Pam, looking down at her, knowing she should touch her.

"I can see you're not in the mood," said Pam, suddenly sweeping herself off the bed.

Frenchy had just noticed a row of drawings of herself Pam had hung on the wall. Smiling, she turned to see Pam put on an alluring robe. Then she was up off the bed and holding Pam. "You took me by surprise," she explained. "I never walked in on a naked lady before."

"I wasn't naked, I was nude. And you didn't walk in on me, I was expecting you."

"Okay, I'm sorry. Want to try it again?" Frenchy asked, hoping Pam wouldn't want to.

"No, the mood is gone."

Pam was sulky. Frenchy was afraid they would have another fight. "I just wasn't thinking about you that way when I came in," she said. "I was excited to be telling you what's happened this week." She poured out the story of her mother's move.

"So what are you saying?" Pam asked.

"That I can, I might. If you still want me to, that I think I could," she stuttered.

"You want to live with me?"

"Yeah," answered Frenchy, blushing.

"Far fucking out!" cried Pam, whirling, her robe swirling around her.

Frenchy grinned timidly, still unbalanced by her entrance, but feeling more like herself. "You're glad?"

"Glad! Oh, Frenchy, darling, what do you think all this work has been for? Look at this place! Didn't you even notice it? And me arranging a big seduction scene so you'd be glad to come home to me every day?" She paused, looking breathlessly at Frenchy. "I'm so happy!"

"But why?" Frenchy asked, genuinely puzzled, though pleased, that Pam wanted her there. Pam just wasn't the type to settle down.

"Why? Because I want your body." Pam hugged her ferociously. "And I like your company. And for however long we last I know we're going to be white hot. And because I care about you," she said, suddenly soft. "I want to make life a little kinder to you." Quickly she raised her voice again. "Whatever my evil motive, this calls for a celebration. I got my unemployment check yesterday. Want to go out to dinner?" She laughed affectionately. "Some place other than the Automat?"

"Sure," Frenchy said, uncertain whether she was being teased. She stood taller. "But I want to take *you* out."

"But darling, it would genuinely give me pleasure to buy you a fancy dinner."

"No."

Pam looked hurt.

Frenchy was surprised. "You really want to that bad?"

Pam nodded. "Not if it would hurt your pride too much, though."

Frenchy thought about her pride. No girl had ever wanted to take her out to dinner before. She was supposed to pay for the girl, but she was also supposed to give the girl what she wanted. What a dilemma. Was Pam really going to be hurt? "Listen," she suggested, "what if we pool our money because that unemployment is all you got to live on, and take *ourselves* out to dinner?"

"You mean *share* the price of dinner? That's okay with me. Are you sure it's okay with you?"

"I'll try it. Besides, I got to watch my expenses now."

"Maybe we shouldn't go where I had in mind, then," Pam said, looking mysterious.

Frenchy was intrigued. "Where?"

"My Aunt's Place. It's a faggot restaurant a few blocks downtown. The food is very fine and the service makes you feel like you're at the Ritz. Also, you might be more comfortable there without straight people hassling you."

"Sounds worth it to me. One last splurge before I have to pay two rents."

"Two rents? You mean you're still going to pay for your mother?"

Pam sounded angry. Frenchy realized that she was right to be mad, that she shouldn't have to support her mother. But she just couldn't cut herself off from her like that. "Just half. I'll explain over dinner. Okay?"

"All right. I'll see if we can get... No, you'd better call, Frenchy. See if you can get us reservations. It's in the book."

Frenchy grinned. She'd never made reservations anywhere before. This would be the start of her new life on her own in the Village. She looked for the pile of clutter where the phone book usually was. "How am I supposed to find anything in this house now it's neat?" she called to Pam who was already rummaging through drawers for clothes.

Pam laughed. "Make a mess, lover, then you can find it."

* * * * *

A month after she moved in with Pam, Frenchy noticed when she woke up on a Sunday morning how last night's tobacco smoke still hung in the air. The steamy heat held odors in the apartment. Almost as strong as the smoke smell was the garlic Pam had fried for dinner. It had smelled good at the time. Frenchy moved very slightly to get more comfortable, not ready for Pam to waken yet. The covers shifted and she smelled their bodies and their bodies' smells on the sheets which had not been changed for three weeks. She was not used to doing these things for herself; Pam didn't seem to see a need. She wasn't dirty — nor was Frenchy scrupulously clean; but she could smell that it was pleasanter to change the sheets more often.

It was late Sunday morning, perhaps 10:30. Bright daylight filtered in through the break between drapes. Frenchy looked at the sleeping woman beside her, a mound of pale flesh with disheveled hair and a puffy face and breath that reeked of cigarettes, wine, garlic and unbrushed teeth.

She felt bad not liking to wake up next to Pam, especially as Pam was ready to make love most mornings, even the mornings Frenchy had to catch the train for her long ride to work. Pam's heavy nakedness and sometimes unwashed body bothered her first thing in the morning; she felt her attraction much more at night. During the day, over breakfast, or sitting around the apartment, she also felt Pam out of sync with her life.

Would she feel this way about any girl she lived with? Edie? No, she would be nice to wake up next to, and real nice to spend the day with. But she wouldn't be anywhere nearly exciting as Pam at night. After Pam, she realized, Edie was boring. Who else? Mary? She didn't find her attractive any more, though she saw why Jessie did. Mercedes? Well, she was a different story. She could live, breathe, and die next to Mercedes without ever being bored or disgusted or irritated. Life could never be anything but exciting with her. But — there was no Mercedes in her life. And there *was* Pam. She slipped out of bed to take a shower.

She mused as she took a shower. If she was lucky, Pam wouldn't wake up while she left to buy the *News* and pick up breakfast. This was still her favorite part of living in the Village — walking the streets on a Sunday morning, free and easy, seeing kids from the bar who lived around the neighborhood. She was even beginning to know the shopkeepers. She no longer wanted to stay late at the bars, but rather get home, make love and wake up early so she could hit the streets and belong to a real daytime world. Be Frenchy Tonneau right out here in broad daylight, have a key to an apartment where she belonged.

If she could only get Mercedes out of her mind. Wouldn't it be great if it were Mercedes, not Pam, who lived in this apartment. Mercedes whom she made love to. Mercedes whom she came home to at night. Mercedes with whom she walked the Sunday streets.

As if fleeing her thoughts, she ran down the steps and into the street. When she got home maybe Pam would be awake and cooking pancakes. Two things she couldn't regret about Pam were sex and food. She wondered if Mercedes could cook, and banished her from her mind again. Instead of getting more involved with Pam as she had expected, she had become more obsessed with Mercedes, as if she were growing away from Pam. What would she do then? She couldn't face going back to the Bronx. Her mother would be gone in a month and she had to give the landlord a decision. Maybe they could sublet. But what if the relationship with Pam ended? What would she do then? She couldn't go on living with her. Now that she and Pam had moved to a larger apartment downstairs, she couldn't afford the apartment by herself.

The Sunday morning walk chilled her. She headed home. At least in Pam's arms she could forget her worries.

An upbeat Bob Dylan song was blasting on the stereo. Pam was in the shower singing along at the top of her lungs. For all Pam's faults, she certainly knew how to enjoy life, and it was good to get home to her. Maybe everything would work out. Maybe she should take that promotion the A&P had offered when she requested a transfer. They needed a head cashier in the Village store. She wasn't sure she wanted to be a head cashier, but the money was better. Of course she could handle the job, she told herself. The boss had wanted to promote her for years. But she hadn't wanted to rock the boat. What if they found out she was a dyke? They might keep her on if she was just a cashier, but in a more important position, they might get rid of her.

She wasn't going to worry anymore, she reminded herself, and poured orange juice, bright and frothy, in glasses for herself and Pam. She knocked at the bathroom door.

"Come on in!"

Pam's smiling head came out from behind the shower curtains. "Great! Just what I needed. I have a hangover from mixing wine with Scotch." She poured juice into her mouth, trickles of it escaping down her chin. "Good," she breathed, and handed the glass back to Frenchy. "What are you going to do today?"

"I don't know. How about you?"

"I forgot to tell you. Dorene called yesterday. She wants to show me some exhibit of African art up in Harlem. Want to come?"

She was stunned. Pam was going to spend time with her

old lover? And she wanted her to come too? And Harlem?
She thought for a moment. Maybe she'd see Mercedes up
there...

"What do you think?"

"How come you're seeing Dorene?"

Pam turned the shower off and emerged wrapped in
towels. She believed she didn't have to do laundry as often
if she used a lot of towels at once. "Why not? We've been
friends for years. No matter who else we're lovers with."

"You're still lovers now?"

Pam frowned at Frenchy's consternation. "I don't mean
actively, but you never know what's going to happen. I
mean between you and me. Me and her. Her and somebody
else."

"She going with somebody?"

"Some Spanish chick."

Frenchy's heart stopped. It couldn't be Mercedes. It
couldn't. "You know her name?"

"The Spanish chick? Yeah, let me think." She brushed
her teeth. Frenchy had to wait till she was finished. "Something unusual. Long. Nereida, that's it, Nereida. Why?"

"Thought it might be someone from the bar."

"Come on. Help me get dressed."

Frenchy trailed after her, confused. Were Pam and
Dorene still lovers? Might Dorene know Mercedes? Was
there a chance she'd see Mercedes if she went along today?
She knew she wouldn't be comfortable with Dorene.
Especially with Dorene *and* Pam. They were both artsy and
high class, she wouldn't fit in. Maybe Nereida would know
Mercedes. Would it be worth the discomfort? Ah, she was
being stupid, these women wouldn't know Mercedes. She
was a street dyke like Frenchy.

"I think I'll stay down here. Maybe clean house a little."

"Sure, okay," Pam said, distracted. "I don't know what
time I'll be back, so go ahead and eat if I'm not here." She

was halfway to the door, slipping into her sandals. "Sure you don't want to come?"

"Yes," Frenchy said, returning Pam's kiss.

"*Ciao*, lover. Don't go running after any little chicks you see, Mama'll be home soon's she can be."

The door closed behind her.

* * * * *

She tried to be cool walking to her apartment, but how do you walk butch with a shopping bag hanging off your arm and groceries towering over your head? At least, she thought, the place would be clean when she got home. Jessie and Mary were coming over, and Pam had promised to clean all day. After seeing Jessie and Mary's house, Frenchy knew hers had to be spotless.

She struggled up the stairs to the apartment, wishing Pam would meet her on the stairs and help her — but maybe she was putting the finishing touches on the apartment.

The door was ajar; she pushed it open and stared between the two grocery bags. The house was a worse wreck than when she'd left that morning. Pam sat at her easel, back to Frenchy, painting. Frenchy counted to ten.

"Hi, lover," called Pam. "Come see what I've painted for you. It's my first erotic water color!" Two women on the canvas were making love.

"It's very nice," said Frenchy, putting the bags on the table.

"You don't like it," complained Pam.

In a low voice, Frenchy asked, "Did you forget Jessie and Mary are coming tonight?"

"Oh, I did!" she cried and became a whirlwind.

Within half an hour the house was relatively neat. In another hour it was relatively clean. Pam began to prepare dinner. Frenchy was exhausted. Instead of resting before the guests arrived, she had worked harder and faster than she had all day. She was still wearing the same bedraggled clothes. Pam had done wonders, and Frenchy wasn't angry any more. She'd swallowed the anger when she learned how overcome Pam had been with the need to do her painting, so overcome she'd forgotten everything else. But she felt their relationship was now hopeless. She sat and stared at the painting, impressed with its bold lines, unembarrassed to see the acts Pam portrayed. Pam had asked her to pose sometime. It might be exciting, but damn it, she'd rather have a woman who cleaned once in a while instead of painting dirty pictures. She made herself a stiff drink and went to shower.

The shower helped. So did clean clothes. She put on Pam's favorite record, *Nashville Skyline*. She never playeа her oldies, as Pam called them, because Pam didn't like them. But they both liked some of Pam's music. Pam didn't play jazz, so Frenchy didn't play the Shirelles. It was fair, but she missed her music. She went up behind Pam in the kitchen and kissed the back of her neck. "The place looks great, lady."

Pam turned. "I'm really sorry." Her hands were covered with flour; she didn't touch Frenchy. She looked truly contrite.

"I know you are. I'm sorry I got so mad before. I just think if we could maybe keep the place up all the time, then we wouldn't have to go through this." Frenchy was toying with Pam's breasts.

Pam groaned quietly. "Keep that up and this quiche won't get cooked."

"What's a quiche?"

"It's like a meat pie, only with egg. We're having crabmeat and peppers in it since that's what we had in the house. It'll work out, darling, honestly. There's a groovy dessert in the oven already. If you just set the table, I can go change as soon as I finish the crust."

"Okay," Frenchy said, eyeing the sinkful of dishes. Maybe she'd get those out of the way before Jessie and Mary arrived. She was going to make this evening work. She mixed herself another drink and brought one to Pam.

When the buzzer sounded at 8:30 on the dot, they were ready and had even been sitting down for a few minutes to relax. Pam looked great, Frenchy thought, in her red and yellow kimono over the wide black pants and a black leotard top. She couldn't resist touching Pam's breasts once more before going to the door. Pam pulled her back and grabbed her at the crotch.

"I want you thinking about me tonight. All night," she said.

Frenchy nodded, trying to act butch with a hand between her legs. She had regained her composure when she let Jessie and Mary in.

She knew immediately that they were not impressed. The music was wrong, the apartment was far from perfect, Pam was dressed too weird and she'd left the easel facing the door so that it was the first thing to strike anyone walking in. She could see Jessie and Mary try to avoid looking at it. She accepted a bottle of wine and took their coats.

"Nice pad," said Jessie, obviously trying to impress Pam with the slang.

"I love your drapes," said Mary, going to them and stepping back as she discovered they were bedspreads.

Frenchy said, "Someday we're going to get real ones. If we ever have any money!"

They all laughed in commiseration.

"Here, have some cheese and crackers," said Frenchy. "What are you drinking?"

Two drinks later, the quiche was on the table. Frenchy was tipsy, Pam red-faced and sweating from cooking. The apartment was stifling. No one had relaxed. Pam put some classical music on the stereo and Jessie and Mary looked at each other. But the quiche was a novelty and delicious, and soon Pam and Mary were exchanging recipes while Jessie and Frenchy talked about the old gang.

"Remember Donna? And her cousin Marie from the Island?" asked Jessie.

"Sure do," said Frenchy, wondering if she would have been happier if she'd settled down with Donna back then. "The night you went with the cousin I broke up with Donna and brought out Edie."

"Did you? That night? You Frenchman, you," Jessie teased admiringly, a little high on the dinner wine. "What'd you do? Go to her place?"

"No, we made it on a bench somewhere. A subway stop I think." Frenchy laughed.

"You know, Edie's got that other chick, Mercedes, living with her."

Frenchy laid her fork down. She stared at Jessie. Mercedes — at Edie's? This was the last way she ever thought she'd connect with Mercedes again. "No," she managed to say, unable to hide her shock.

"Not like *that*, man. She just lives there. Edie's still going with that black girl."

Still shaken by the news of Mercedes, she asked Jessie several more questions about her, trying to be cool by asking about Edie at the same time. But Jessie didn't know much more.

"Man," sighed Jessie, "those were the good old days. Life wasn't complicated at all. Seems like there weren't no bills to pay. No complications with girls except never enough of them. You just went out and had a good time. If you had the money you spent it. If you didn't you made your cover drink last."

"Now you don't even get a drink for the cover!" Frenchy said, with effort pushing Mercedes to the back of her mind.

"Yeah, but you can have all the toilet paper you want!"

Frenchy was laughing too. "Remember? They used to hand it out, one piece at a time?"

"I used to hold it in so's I wouldn't have to wait in line."

"Back then we *could* hold it!"

"Say, remember Kitty?" Jessie asked, serious. The other women were talking about embroidery now. "That real tall femme? Used to go with Beebo? Killed herself. She came in with this guy one night, all over him. Couple of weeks later, I heard she was dead."

"Wow."

"But there's good news too. Remember Paulette? In the wheelchair? The bouncer used to carry her down the stairs."

"Sure do. She was a sweetheart. I never knew how to act around her. I was always afraid I'd hurt her or something."

"Well, somebody figured it out. Her and old Shirley Faye got married. Ceremony and all, in a church."

"Shirley Faye? The softball player? She got herself a good butch then."

"And Shirley Faye got herself a good woman."

"What are you boys carrying on about over there?" asked Mary.

"Just the old days, the kids we know. What's happening to them. Frenchy isn't around as much anymore and she misses all the dirt."

"It's funny," Mary said, "Jessie and me get to the bars just about every week and we live way out in College Point. You two are right here in the Village and hardly ever go."

Frenchy was putting on a Judy Collins record. "Somehow, living down here, you see enough queers that you don't need to go to the bar so much. You know?"

"I think so," Jessie answered. "We miss a week of not seeing no gay people and I feel like I need a fix."

Mary agreed. "Family and the people at work are nice, but it's just not the same as your own."

"I never used to feel that way," said Pam, pouring more wine for everyone. "But since Frenchy moved in, I do more. I don't care as much about seeing the old group I went to coffee houses with. They're mostly guys and they don't understand my work."

Jessie and Mary looked embarrassed. "What kind of work do you do?" stammered Jessie.

"That kind of thing," Pam said, pointing at the painting on the easel. "Though I've never done figures in water color before."

Jessie blushed, looking at it, and Mary wouldn't look at all.

"I didn't understand what Pam was trying to do at first," said Frenchy, trying to help her friends' embarrassment. "And I'm not sure I do now. But as Pam says, the straights have their great artists always doing pictures of lovers, why shouldn't we? I got to agree with that even though sometimes I still have trouble looking at them."

Jessie was peering nearsightedly at the painting. She looked at Mary. "I guess it's kind of nice," she said.

"You couldn't put it on your wall, though, could you?" asked Mary.

"What if I gave it to you," Pam said. "Where would you put it?"

"A real painting? By a lesbian?"

"By me. Artist and lesbian." Pam reached for Frenchy's hand over the table.

"I'd put it right over the couch," said Jessie staunchly.

"You wouldn't!" Mary objected.

"Yes I would. Who comes to our house who doesn't

know we're lovers? Look, we go to your sister's house and there's that little statue of the two naked people kissing. And the dirty cartoons your other sister has in her bathroom downstairs. I don't even like looking at them. Why not put something of our own up?"

"Because it's, you know, what we *do*."

"You think they don't know what we do? Talk about it? Let's show them. Let them get more used to the idea. Let it be in the open more. Then it won't look like we're ashamed or got something to hide. Besides, I would like to have a picture of two women doing it to look at. Makes me feel sexy."

Pam laughed. "Right on! I think that's great. Those are some of the things I want to do with my work!"

"Maybe you have something there," admitted Mary. "Do you have any more?"

"Let's go in the living room and I'll show you."

"I'll clear the table," Frenchy offered.

"You will?" asked Jessie, astonished.

Frenchy hitched up her pants and began stacking dishes. "Sure," she said, "why let a lady do all the dirty work?"

Jessie looked like she was thinking about that one as the three went to huddle over a stack of Pam's drawings. Within a few minutes Frenchy could hear little murmurs of enthusiasm from the group. "Oh, I like that!" Mary exclaimed more than once. "Hey, we never tried that!" Jessie guffawed at one point. Frenchy was so proud of Pam she started right in doing the dishes, sleeves rolled up to show the little muscles of her upper arm. It had been a good idea to ask friends over. Maybe it would work out with Pam after all.

Chapter 6

Lavender Skies
Spring, 1967

Listen, I don't kid myself anymore. I have it good now: a career, a home where I can be myself, a kid who makes my life better. But I'm still me. And it can all disappear, just like that. One little thing and Humpty Dumpty falls off her wall. I'm being careful with myself. I've got too much to lose.

Still, I'm proud of what I've done. See how much better I write now? I have some education.

With Esther and Edie's help I sat down and looked at the catalogues. I liked science in high school and I knew I wanted to help people, and I wanted to make decent money in a job that would be around for a while. And I like nuclear medicine, I really do. Going into the hospital every day, wearing a white coat. I especially like giving therapy. People who are as miserable in their bodies as I once was in my mind — I can help them feel better, some of them. Others — it can be so sad.

They didn't think I could take it, you know. After my first year of school, this counselor called me in. They'd been checking out my records. You have to be stable for this job, they said. I told them I was stable, now, more stable than somebody who never went through what I did. It took awhile, but seeing this counselor a couple of times a week was good for both of us. She was convinced, finally, and I learned even more about how to stay well. Now the patients and staff all think I'm good, respect me. My father would be proud. I think I made the right choice.

The course was offered by a community college, didn't cost much, even with getting my G.E.D. at the same time only took about two years. Because I've always read so much, Esther said.

Lydia. The poor kid didn't understand why she couldn't live with me after I stopped being so "sick" and being put away all the time. Why couldn't I live with Grandma and her and my two sisters and their kids? Or why couldn't she stay here? She loved Edie and Esther. Esther and Lydia were close right away because they're both so dark. Lydia is darker than me, darker than anyone in my family, so it was always she and Esther against me and Edie.

I'm listening to old records as I write this. It helps keep the gay fever down. Keeps me away from the bars. I'm afraid of what would happen to my life if I went back to the bars. I sit here for hours listening and dreaming of women and yet stay in one piece because I'm not drinking or getting hurt in a love affair. When I get to the point where I want to ask Edie and Esther to strap me down because the fever's on me so bad, I come in here late at night with a glass of seltzer and a pack of cigarettes and I sit and listen, dancing, loving women in my head until I'm exhausted.

But back to Lydia . . . It hurts to write this.

Our neighborhood made up my mind for me. Some kids told her I was queer. How they knew it or why they said it I don't know.

But they told her I'm queer and they told her what a queer is. The kid wasn't even upset. She just wanted to know was it true.

I just stared at her.

"Hey, Ma," she said. She'd just turned ten. "They said it like it was a dirty word. But I don't think so."

I knew I couldn't freak out on her. For maybe the first time I wouldn't allow myself the luxury of carrying on when I was upset. "Just because your mother is, doesn't mean you have to be, little one."

"What if I wanted to be?"

"Sure then. Whatever's right for you." And I wasn't thinking; this was instinct. Instead of warning her what a hard life she'd have, I'd let *her* decide.

How did I deserve this special child? Was it her intelligence that made her see things more clearly than others? Or did I pass along something of myself?

"And Aunt Edie and Esther are too, aren't they? I can see they love each other a lot," she rushed on. "Are they ashamed?"

I was laughing through my tears and trying not to hug her to death. "No, they're not ashamed. But all those hateful people, they make you ashamed of yourself and your own. Because of them we have to hide who we are. We have to be careful especially about Edie and Esther. They're teachers and could lose their jobs if people knew."

"Why?"

How do you explain something like that to a kid?

"Straight people are afraid gay teachers will teach their students to be gay."

"But the straight teachers teach us to be straight."

"For some reason, I don't know why, they're afraid. So they want to convince kids that being straight is right."

"Weird," said Lydia, moving away and picking up the teddy bear she's had since she was a baby; he probably gave her more security than I did.

"Can I go tell Edie and Esther I know they're queer?"

I laughed again. "Some people don't like being called queer."

"You mean gay?"

I explained the history of the word lesbian. "This woman Sappho lived on an island and taught school. All the girls in that part of the world would go to her school. They all loved her and learned to love each other. It was okay, see, to be like me back then. The island was called Lesbos. Like we're from Puerto Rico and we're proud to be called Puerto Ricans."

It seemed to make sense to her. "Then can I tell them I know they're lesbians?" I grabbed one last hug from her and we went off to find Edie and Esther.

I can't say I hadn't felt proud to be gay before that. Sometimes, all dressed up to go out, I'd strut around. Or dancing with a pretty girl who was making eyes at me . . . But that was only sometimes. Not enough. And not as I had felt that moment, knowing my daughter knew I was gay and thought it was okay.

So I was thinking about Lydia and feeling pretty good, when Esther came down here a little while ago, all sleepy-eyed.

"Did I wake you with the records?" I asked.

"No, no. I was lying there and lying there and couldn't sleep," she said, sitting heavily on a chair near me.

I got up and put on a new stack of records.

"When I hear you playing these records I know you have to be wanting," she said, leaning back and laughing a little.

"Yeah," I admitted because I can't resist Esther's warmth, "I'm wanting. But I can handle it."

"You're wanting," she said again through a yawn.

Something about the way she was talking made me suspect it wasn't me, but herself, she was talking about, that it was Esther who was a little bored with her life, who was wanting. The thought terrified me. What if something was wrong between her and Edie? I needed to know.

"You sure you're just worried about me, girl?" I asked.

She didn't look at me, but I could feel her closing up. "If you don't want to talk about it," she said, rising, "I'd better get some sleep."

I watched her go back upstairs. I'd never seen her in this mood. It scared me. Esther and Edie had become a fixture for me, the one thing in the world besides Lydia I could depend on.

It occurred to me, as it sometimes did late at night, that all I had to do was put some shoes on and go downtown for that part of my life to start all over. Going in to work every day, since I got out of school, was not a habit I couldn't break. I was tired, really tired, of being sober and sane and regular. I liked parts of being crazy. I was still part crazy, but had to hold it in. And I was tired of no sex and of being a mother. I felt like I was tied down to this damn house, to Edie taking care of me like a goody-goody white girl, to Esther psychoanalyzing me, to Lydia hanging onto me.

What it feels like here sometimes is dull desert. All white, bleached out, bland. Nothing to excite me, upset me. Deserts are supposed to be beautiful once you get to know them. But this white, middle-class neighborhood is still an unfamiliar desert for me. I miss my neighborhood,

where every night in the summer some wino walks down
the street singing drunkenly in Spanish. Where there's always
a siren going by. My heart gets so heavy, it's too much to
carry — this keeping myself from any life real to me so I
can keep life.

If only I were strong enough not to go crazy. Or still
crazy enough not to have to be strong.

I'd set the record changer wrong, *Downtown* was playing over and over. Why shouldn't I get out? What *if* it set
me off? What *if* I kissed a girl and lost my head and disappeared for a week? I had enough money. If Edie and
Esther didn't like it I'd get my own place. Downtown. Go
out every night if I wanted to. I could work second shift.
Why not?

Because it would drive me crazy, that's why, I answered
myself. What would I do on my own, without anyone to
help me, to hold myself together? Then I did cry. Because
I did need holding together. I wasn't anything but a near-
empty bag of tricks.

I crossed the room and shut off the stereo. I'd never
go downtown again, much less live there. I didn't have what
it took. I was a messed-up PR dyke hiding in a white girl's
house. And I had the fever. Gay fever. I wanted a girl so
bad . . . I had to stop wanting. Had to shut it out. If only
Frenchy were different, if only I could have felt safe with
her, if she could have understood. Because it's Frenchy I
see in my mind when I feel the fever.

I climbed the stairs to bed slowly, shaking.

* * * * *

That was one of my bad nights. I was lucky the stack
of records didn't wind down to Timi Yuro's *Make the World
Go Away*. That would have finished me for good.

The whole next day I was distracted and worried about

Esther and Edie. I hurried home after work.

"Edie!" I said, not expecting to see her there in the kitchen getting supper ready as always.

"What's wrong?" she asked, startled.

"I don't know. Something is. You tell me." Lots of times we've had a wordless communication; she wasn't surprised that I was tuned in to her distress.

"Rosetta is what's wrong."

"Another girl? For Esther? You want me to beat this Rosetta's head in?"

"Oh, Mercedes, I wish it were that simple," Edie said, collapsing in to a chair.

"Does she want to leave you?" Edie shook her head. "She wants to have an affair and *still* go with you?"

"Yes," Edie said with such misery in her voice I could hardly stand it.

"Maybe I should go beat on Esther."

"I can't believe it. In the beginning she wanted me so badly, she said she'd never want anyone *but* me. Maybe if we'd had an understanding that we might want to see other women . . ." Her voice broke. ". . . Then I could understand it, try to go along with it. But this just came out of the blue."

"Is she black?"

"Yes. She sings with Esther."

"I can see the attraction." Edie looked up at me, surprised. "Edie, you know what a problem it's been for her to live two separate lives. Half with you, half with her own people. I'm surprised she wasn't tempted long ago to try an easier way."

"But it isn't any easier. She knows that. The problems are just different." Edie sounded as if she were pleading with me.

"Yeah, but when you're working on one set, sometimes the other set looks easier to handle. I should know."

"The grass is always greener," she said bitterly.

"You said she doesn't want to leave you."

"How long can that last with this cutie in the wings?"

It was time for me to get a hold on things. I couldn't afford, for Edie's sake, to think of the consequences her breaking up with Esther might have for me. I had to get Edie in the mood to fight. "You *want* to lose her?"

"No," Edie flashed back, angry.

"Then why give up like this? She'll never come home to a woman who acts like a loser. Not when the cutie is all smiles and sunshine."

"Let her have the smiles and sunshine then. If she wants to give up all *we* have together, then let her."

"You just said you didn't want to let her go."

"Mercedes, stop it. I don't want to, but what can I do?"

"Hey lady," I said, walking over to her and taking her hands. "You've had other problems in your life. You didn't just sit back and let them happen, did you? Then why this?"

"Maybe I don't know how to fight this. I can't turn black."

"You won't have to. If you were black, Esther probably wouldn't have been interested in you in the first place."

"You think so?"

I smiled at her. "You *weren't* black, were you? Sometimes it's these obvious things that are hardest to keep sight of."

"How do you know all this?"

"*Somebody's* got to think this out. Maybe I've already thought it out about myself." I had Edie interested, I had to keep her like that. "So let's start there. Esther wouldn't have loved you in the first place if there wasn't *something* good about you, right?"

"I guess so."

"We have to figure out what it is and make sure we remind her of that. The cutie may offer her other things, but she can't give her the same things you do. You know?" My brain was working so hard I felt like I was back in school.

"She's new," Edie said, beginning to cry again.

"That's where we can start. Newness might not be a bigger attraction than what Esther already knows."

"Still," Edie said, taking a deep breath and getting control of herself, "we just don't know. It's all up to Esther. If she doesn't forget the value of the things I can give her, then I have a chance. But if she decides she doesn't want those things anymore . . ."

I sat next to her and put my head on her shoulder. "You're giving up again, Edie. Sure, the final decision is hers, but you get to influence that final decision. Is she coming over tonight?"

"She's singing. With *her.*"

"They can't do much when they're singing."

Edie was able to laugh.

"Don't assume she'll be with Rosetta if she doesn't come here, Edie. This is pretty heavy for Esther, too. She might just go to her sister's house, where she can be alone to think."

Edie looked up. "That gives me an idea. She could have a space of her own here."

"Good thinking. A place she's used to, but where she'd be more alone than with her cousins crawling over her."

"After dinner I'll clear out the sewing room. If I make it comfortable . . . But you know, somehow this isn't kosher. I'm using the house to lure her back to me. Rosetta is probably poor and can't fight on the same terms."

"But that's one of Rosetta's attractions. She's more the poor side of Esther. Rosetta'll fight with her own weapons. You have to use what you got."

"That makes sense," Edie said slowly, blowing her nose and wiping her eyes.

"Besides, you share your house enough, there's no reason

to feel guilty about owning it. Where would I be without your house?"

I could see I'd convinced her. She was beginning to believe she didn't have to stand there and watch Esther go. "How about that dinner you're talking about? I'll go up and get started cleaning things up in Esther's room."

"Okay. And I'll be thinking too, about my winning points." She smiled sadly.

I went upstairs and got to work.

* * * * *

The tension in the house was awful. Afraid for both of them, I was a mess. Edie was trying to show Esther what she offered her and yet leave her enough space to think in. Lydia, on the weekends, tiptoed around the house, as if afraid to upset the delicate balance of anyone's feelings. And Esther, Esther the joker, the one who was always there to help you through a rough spot, walked around moody and obviously torn apart by her feelings.

Lydia was staying with her grandmother during the week. She had ties in the old neighborhood she needed to keep and was more comfortable in a school with her own. Soon after she left that Sunday evening Esther came home from church. Early. Edie and I looked at each other. Esther went into her room and stayed there. Edie fooled around the house for a while then went to bed. I had just settled into *Make the World Go Away* when there was a padding on the stairs and I felt Esther come into the room. I was smoking and drinking seltzer, doodling pictures' of girls faces on the margins of a magazine.

I'd never seen Esther so gloomy. She'd obviously been crying and her hands moved nervously on each other: wringing, scratching, cracking her knuckles.

"How are you doing?" she asked.

"Doing okay."

"It don't sound it from the song." Just then Timi was at her most desperate. I moved over and put my arm across Esther's shoulders in a friendly way. I hoped she didn't mind. Esther hung her head. I guessed I better take my arm away, but I stayed next to her.

"I'm all tore up about this, Mer," she managed to say. I really hoped she wouldn't cry in front of me. I mean, I loved Esther, but I never felt that close to her to want to see a butch — which is how I thought about her — cry in front of me. The old ways are strong.

"When I get near Rosetta," she blurted, "my mind just swims away. There ain't nothing but this big puddle of my body melting toward her so I just know it's going to wash over her some day when I'm not even noticing what I'm doing. I can't keep away from her, Mer, you hear what I'm saying?"

"I sure do."

"I wouldn't have chosen this to happen, no way, but it is and all's I can see to do is let it happen till it's all over."

I didn't say anything, but I got to wondering why Esther hadn't let it happen so far if she wanted it so much.

"She's in my mind so strong, there's no room for Edie, but I know I didn't just stop *loving* Edie. That's not possible is it?"

"You would have known it was coming, I think."

"You're probably right. She works where you do," she added.

"What's her last name?"

"Young."

"Technician?"

"Nurse's aide," Esther said as if confessing it. "She's only twenty-two. Saving money to go to college."

"Sounds nice," I said without really meaning it. Esther picked up on my empty words.

"I know it's plain ridiculous to say I can't help myself, but that's how I feel."

We were quiet for a while. I let Timi sing once more. She was really wailing, sounding like a gospel singer. I got up and shut off the record. Time for me to say something. I didn't want to sound preachy. "When I used to go drinking," I said. Esther looked up. "I knew where it would lead, to the looney bin or some other kind of trouble. I'd say to myself, I don't want to go through this. And my self would say, but you *got* to, you feeling bad, girl. You feeling so damn bad, what else can you do?"

Esther was looking at me like she wanted me to go on, but that was all I was going to say. All I had to say. I sure didn't have any advice, not with the mess my life had always been.

A long time later she asked, "You ever feel like this, Mer?"

"I used **to.** I was just thinking about it. This little femme named Nancy. Me and Frenchy were hanging out downtown, you know?" This was going to hurt — but I thought maybe it would help. "We'd both sit there and talk about the chicks and she'd tell me who she was hung up on and I'd point out some cute ones. After a while I felt like I ought to be having some feelings too so I picked one out and got this crush on her. After a while I was feeling about her almost like you are about Rosetta. And I could've had her, I know that. But, you know, I sat in that damn chair next to Frenchy night after night and never did a thing but stare at Nancy. All week I'd dream about her at home. I couldn't wait to get down to the bar and see her. But I never even asked her to dance."

"Why?"

"It was Frenchy I was in love with. You couldn't have torn me from beside her."

"I don't understand."

"Me neither. I didn't know it was Frenchy I wanted. For a lot of reasons. We were both butch for starters, which meant I couldn't love her like a femme. You know what I'm saying? I had to let those feelings out, but there was something stopping them from going where they ought to be going."

"But you never let yourself feel for Frenchy."

"Oh yes I did. One night. But it didn't work out. It takes two to work something out. She wasn't ready. I wasn't either, but I was readier than her."

"Why don't you see if she's readier to work it out now?"

" 'Cause I can't teach it to her if she doesn't know. And she'll come to me when she knows. I hope."

And I hoped Esther knew I was talking about her, too.

She was quiet. She finally asked me, "What were the other reasons you couldn't feel like that about Frenchy?"

I'd thought so much about all this I could tell her. "I wanted more from Frenchy than I'd ever wanted from any girl. I wanted her for life and that meant learning new rules, meant we both had to settle down, stop running around. She wasn't bigoted, but she did have some stupid stubborn ideas about racial stuff I knew would get in our way. She lived with her mother and I didn't want any girl who was going to run home to Mama every night after making love with me. There may be more. You get the picture? It was a very scary thing."

"So you just aimed your feelings elsewhere."

"And fooled myself with them for a long time." I was getting sleepy and wanted to lay my head on Esther's shoulder. I sat next to her again, but that was as far as I could go. Always this barrier between us.

"But you don't know Rosetta," she said.

I didn't answer.

"But then, I guess I don't either." She shook her head like she was clearing cobwebs out of her brain. "I don't know," she sighed, rising. "I just don't know. I have to get some sleep. Got to go to work tomorrow."

"Me too." I turned off the lamp and took my cigarettes and glass. She stood in the doorway while I rinsed out the glass.

"Thanks for talking to me." She shuffled back up the stairs.

I felt so useless. What could I do? I'd said all I could.

Suddenly, the tension left my body and I slumped against the sink. "Ohh," I groaned. I'd come on so sure and strong, and I couldn't even have the girl I wanted. Was love ever easy? I'd thought once you got past the beginning you could settle down and be happy — like Edie and Esther.

* * * * *

The next morning at work I searched for a nurse's aide named Rosetta Young. If she sang with Esther she probably worked the day shift. I just wanted to check her out and size up the opposition. I asked around on break and at lunch. I'd gotten to know a lot of people and especially everybody gay, but it was harder to find gay girls than fags. The few lesbians I knew about were so obvious most of us tried to stay away from them at work, afraid people would catch on by association. So I figured my best chance was with the gay boys. Finally, about halfway through my fifth cup of coffee (I'd had one with every group I questioned to make my search look casual) I found a fag who knew a fag who roomed with a dyke named Rosetta.

"She's cute," he said. "Works on the fifth floor. How'd you meet her?"

"I haven't — yet. Friend of mine's interested. But," I whispered, "my friend wants to get to know her in her own way. I just want to get a look at her. So don't say anything, okay?"

"Sure, doll," he said and I changed the subject.

There were only fifteen minutes left of lunch. I got away and rushed to the elevator, already filling up with workers getting back to their floors. I checked my watch, still trying to look casual. I thanked my lucky stars for nametags.

Two aides were at the nurses' station, probably ready to take off for late lunch. Having picked a name from the floor chart, I told the ward clerk I wanted to check on a patient I knew. The aides eyed me and I tried to read their tags. The ward clerk told me that that patient had just checked out. I snapped my fingers, pretending disappointment. I hadn't figured how to get out of that one, and at this point I was going to be late getting back to work. The name tags were still too far away. I chatted with the clerk until both aides headed for the elevator.

Rosetta was the tiny, delicate-looking girl. She talked real soft to her friend, but glanced shyly toward me a couple of times. She was truly beautiful. More competition than Edie could handle in that category. Real petite, with dark, dark skin and lively, laughing, yet shy eyes. Her hair was long and tied back in a severe way that made her eyes all the bigger. I wondered how anyone that size could lift heavy patients. I wondered, also, if Esther's attraction was mostly physical.

I was back at work by ten past. Now that I knew who she was and where she worked, I wanted to fix things, make everyone feel better, relax myself. How?

I couldn't decide what the hell to do about talking to Rosetta or not, so I lived through the week in a frustrated sweat. Before things had become so rocky between Edie and Esther, Jessie and Mary had asked us all over to their house for the coming weekend. Something, I hoped, would be resolved by then.

Esther didn't show Friday night. Usually she went to

her sister's to get her things and joined us by dinner. Edie waited to start dinner, face drawn. By that time Lydia had arrived. She took one look at us and knew something was wrong. The minute she could get me alone she asked what was happening.

"Esther hasn't come home yet is all. We don't know any more than you do, kid." I was so worried I hadn't even properly greeted her.

She gave me a hug and kissed my cheek. "You sound like Frenchy now."

I froze. Edie had wanted to see Frenchy again and asked her out to the house. I made myself scarce, went up to Harlem to see the old gang. But Lydia was there, eager to meet Frenchy who must have become by then, a mythical figure to her. When Frenchy's name was mentioned around the house it was carefully, in hushed tones, as if dropping it would set off tremors in the earth. And after she'd met her, Lydia was still awed by Frenchy — in love, I suppose, just like her mother. She'd told me Frenchy had played with her, like a kid. I'd like to have seen that.

"She calls me 'kid' too. Hey, Ma," she said, "why don't you come with me and Frenchy next time?"

"Next time?"

Lydia looked embarrassed. "If there is a next time."

"Did she say there would be?"

"Yeah."

"Then there will. Frenchy's like that." Lydia hugged me again and stayed close to me. "Come on, I don't want to leave Edie alone that long."

That night was when I started to learn how to cook. Edie just couldn't. I knew if she was going to eat, I'd have to concoct something that would appeal to her. I made a mess, but she ate. The appreciation in her eyes made me want to cook again. After dinner Lydia normally practiced her drums, but that night silence was the only sound in the house. It was spring outside, though, and we managed to get Edie out on the porch.

"There's nothing like spring in New York City," I said once we were settled. "Shoves up through the old concrete like it's too strong for even eight million city people to ignore."

Edie sniffled. She hadn't cried yet that night, but I was expecting it. If only she'd talk. The crazy Queens houses seemed full of gloom next to the blossoming lilacs. Across from us were a few semi-attached houses, a four-story building that must have been built around 1920, a few aging houses like Edie's. The vacant lot at the end of the street was going crazy with wildflowers. Just the scents of spring, mingled with the gritty smells of sidewalks and subway trains, made me half crazy. To hold a hand, to kiss a girl, to dance all night long . . .

The darker it got, the brighter the old lavender lilac bush outside glowed and the deeper was Edie's silence. Around us life went on: the almost-summer noises of kids playing kickball in the street, babies crying as they were bedded down, the muffled rumble of the subway. Edie's eyes kept glancing up the street toward the subway. Her hands lay motionless and white-knuckled in her lap.

Lydia was running out of stories to tell us about school. "Ma," she said, startling me, "when we go to Fire Island do you think Frenchy will be there?"

"How should I know?" I hate it when I'm short with Lydia like that, but why was she bugging me with Frenchy tonight of all nights?

Edie stirred. Maybe it was seeing my pain. Maybe she thought something was going on in Lydia's head — like she wanted to push me into a marriage in case Edie's failed.

"Why don't you ask her if she'd like to go to Fire Island with us for the picnic?" Edie suggested to Lydia.

It was my turn to sit rigid, staring ahead. I could see how that lilac bush might become monstrous, glowing more and more, menacing me with reminders of spring urges.

"Could I, Ma?"

My nerves were brittle thin ice I could feel everywhere in my body. My mind felt as if it would crack open and everything inside spill out. If Frenchy was seeing Lydia, then maybe she was trying to say she wanted to see me. If I said yes, would that make Esther appear on the street? If Esther came home would that guarantee things would work out with Frenchy? I fingered the little herb bag around my neck, as if it were full of hopes, not weeds.

"Ma?"

"If you want to, Lydia." I wasn't going to influence this thing one way or the other. Then I smiled at myself. Here I'd told Edie she should fight, take an active part in winning back Esther, and I was refusing to take a step to help Frenchy.

She conferred with Edie over dates and times and where exactly we'd all be on Fire Island. Soon afterward I heard her in the basement playing her drums along with some of my Supremes records. Like mother, like daughter, I thought. She studies my records for their beat, I study them for love, for the beat that runs through my life.

Edie and I sat there in the glowing dark, listening to my child beat drums like some crazy tribal witch. I reached over to take Edie's hand. It was ice cold. "We both got our troubles, don't we?" I asked.

She looked at me mournfully. The sky behind her head was lavender. I felt so much love for this woman — I'd never realized it before. She'd done so much for me and we'd shared our lives for over two years.

"Why couldn't it be you and me in love?" I asked regretfully. "We both want the same things."

"Life isn't like that." Edie sighed. "For some reason we have to earn with blood everything we have."

"I don't like to see you suffer."

"And here I've only been suffering two weeks. Look at you."

"I'm not suffering, just waiting," I said.

"Think she'll come to you?"

"I think between you and Lydia she won't have any choice."

Edie laughed. It was good to hear. "We aren't conspiring you know."

"Maybe not on purpose, but you got something going."

"Yes, we both love you and want to see you happy."

I squeezed her hand, tears coming to my eyes. "Want to go in yet?"

"I keep hoping she'll walk right up that street there, getting bigger and bigger till she fills up my life again." Our awareness of Esther had made her so real I half-expected her to be just out of eye range. Mothers began to call their children in for the night. Crickets chirped in the grass. Even after two years this sure was a new New York to me.

"Edie, I think she's somewhere thinking."

"How long will it take her?"

"How long will you give her?"

"A while. I've been doing as you said and showing her, even telling her what she'd be missing if she left me."

"She can't have both of you? Not that I think she should," I hastily added.

"I don't know." In the deepening darkness I could hardly see her face. "I worry about that a lot. I couldn't live with the pain of knowing she was with another woman — a woman who might take her from me for good. Or change her in ways that would change our relationship. And I would change too — from the pain and resentment. It might well kill my love for her. I'm risking all of her to refuse to give away part of her. But am I forcing her to refuse a part of herself she needs to express? So many, many questions."

"And I don't have answers. Except you shouldn't forget that whatever her decision is, it'll be hers. You haven't made it for her. And you have a right to decide how you want to live — and love — too."

"Still, it's as if I'm attaching conditions to myself."

Like the conditions I'd given Frenchy. I wouldn't put a clamp on a whole part of me to fit her and the way she thought she had to live. I was forcing her to change if she wanted me. Maybe I didn't have the right either — but did she have the right to demand me with the clamp on? "We all do," I said. "Attach conditions. I don't think we'd be human if we didn't. The conditions we have to have to survive, the ones we take on out of fear."

"Why do you think Esther wants this woman?"

I took her hand again. "I have an idea. I think she's all plugged up inside. I think, much as she loves you, she hasn't let herself love you all she can yet. Maybe because you're white. Maybe because she's scared of committing herself. Who knows?"

Edie was staring at me. "I've always felt that too," she said.

"So this unused love, or energy, whatever it is, has to go somewhere. I think it spilled out on some handy woman."

"But what is she afraid of now?"

"Let's hope that's what she's trying to figure out."

"I still want to know how you know all this."

I laughed bitterly. "When you've been to as many shrinks as I have — shrinks to make you straight, shrinks to make you stop drinking, shrinks to teach you how not to act like you're Puerto Rican, shrinks to teach you how to be a woman — you learn the things between the lines."

"They really tried to do all those things to you?"

"Oh, yeah. They're the only ones who can be right, you know. First I thought it was only white American men shrinks who stuff that crap down your throat. But I saw Indians, Orientals, blacks, once in a while a woman. I think they can't get to be doctors unless they're totally normal according to the white American men at the top. Psychology — the religion of normalcy." I laughed. "How's that for a dumb P.R.?"

"Pretty good, Mercedes." Edie was laughing with me. "Pretty good." She looked around one more time. "I'm getting chilly. I can't keep us out here all night. Either she'll come or she won't."

"Wherever she is," I said with sureness, "she's thinking about you."

"And you. And Lydia. Thank you for being family. That's one of the plusses I have over the other woman."

"Still can't say her name?"

Edie put her hand against her heart. "It hurts." She paused. "I do think our lesbian family is important to Esther, you know."

We walked inside. "But don't forget," I teased, "with you pushing Frenchy at me so hard, I may run off into the sunset anytime."

"We've talked about what would happen if you found someone," she countered. "Not necessarily Frenchy Tonneau."

The name jolted me like an earthquake. "And what did you decide?"

"Oh, we came up with all kinds of solutions to losing you." She smiled. "Lydia would go to Queens College eventually and live here during the week and with you and your lover on weekends."

"That kid is a born commuter."

We were hugging when Lydia came in.

"Consoling each other?" she asked innocently.

"Lydia!" I scolded through my laughter.

"That's all we need," Edie said, "is for Esther to walk in now and catch the two of *us* together."

"Edie," I said, "she won't be home tonight. She needs this time. Don't expect her."

Edie nodded. "Will she be back tomorrow night? What will I tell Jessie and Mary?"

"The truth. And we'll cancel. It would be too painful to go there without her. We'll wait till we're all together."

"Optimist."

"Right. Shall we all go to bed?" I asked, stretching my hand out for Lydia.

"Sure." Lydia smiled at us, obviously reassured by our talk and laughter that somehow everything would be all right. How I longed to spare her all the suffering that would go into making things work in her own life.

* * * * *

The weekend's agonized waiting couldn't have been worse if we'd all been locked in the House of D waiting for bail money. We didn't go to College Point. By Saturday night there was no convincing Edie of Esther's fidelity. She believed that the little worm, as she now called Rosetta, had gotten at her own bad apple. Which meant, of course, that Edie no longer had a lover since she wouldn't share her.

"Well, maybe," she said at one point, "if Esther finds out the worm's not very pleasant in bed, she'll come home with her tail between her legs."

Lydia giggled at the idea of Esther with a tail until Edie started to cry.

"Can't we go find her, Ma?" Lydia pleaded.

"You can't stop somebody from doing what they think they have to," I said, wishing my own mother had told me that at the age of twelve.

Sunday, knowing the worst was over, Edie felt better. We did what marketing we could at the few shops that were open, including the produce market off Roosevelt Avenue. Lydia earned some pocket money on occasion working for Henny, a tall older woman Esther and I suspected of being gay. She saw Edie was down and shooed us out of the shop, telling us we should go somewhere nice and relax. Reluctantly, Edie let me lead her to a bus and we smelled the flowers over at the Queens Botanical Gardens for a couple of hours. It got us through the day more pleasantly than I would have thought possible and the next thing I knew it was Monday morning. I wondered if Esther would show up for work. I left early to find out if Rosetta had.

I had never told Edie about tracing Rosetta because I didn't want to mention her physical beauty. But if she was at work, I decided to call Edie and ask if Esther was at school. We could conjecture from there.

Rosetta was with a patient. After the tension of the weekend I needed to do something positive. So I waited. When she came out, I approached her. I tried not to look angry.

"Excuse me, but do you sing with a woman named Esther?"

Her eyes lit up. I wondered how much power I myself would have had against such beauty as hers. I said, "I'm a friend of hers and was expecting to see her. She wasn't around all weekend. Was she at church yesterday?"

"No." Her voice was very quiet, almost timid for a woman so attractive. "No. And was the director upset. Esther never misses. She didn't even call. I thought maybe there were *family* problems?"

I knew what she was trying to ask. But I wouldn't give the worm the satisfaction of showing I understood, no matter how much I liked looking at her. "Wish I knew. Thanks," I said, tearing my eyes away. Mmm-mhm, I thought, butching it up as I walked down the hall. Esther has *some* good taste in women. I wondered how soon I could handle a relationship, Frenchy or not. Things were beginning to really get to me. Beginning! Hell, they'd got to me long ago.

But I still had time to call Edie. After a long time, she came on the phone, breathless. "I'm sorry," I said quickly. "You probably thought I was Esther."

"No. Actually I was afraid it was bad news, like she'd been in an accident."

"I have news slightly better than that." I explained how the worm worked in the hospital with me and hadn't seen Esther either.

Edie was naturally suspicious of my source. "She's not lying?"

"She seems pretty innocent. And Esther wouldn't pick a liar."

Edie laughed. "Obviously she's not here either. Hang on, let me ask if she's called in."

I held on, visions of Rosetta's eyes in front of me.

"Mer, she asked for some time off to go South, someone in the family was sick. Think she could have gone there?"

"Sure, but if she did, it's herself that's sick. Look Edie, she doesn't call you; she doesn't call church; she doesn't call the worm. That's just not like her. I bet she ran home to Mama."

"Where life was simpler. She said that the other night."

"Then that's where she is."

"But putting us through a weekend like this?"

"She couldn't make all those phone calls." The damn operator wanted another nickel. I fed her. "When she can talk again, that's when she'll show her face. I know that feeling well. Things get too much for you. You run away through liquor or the crazies or going home to Mama and you got to build up strength till you can take real life again."

It sounded all too appealing to me. In hiding, like Esther, I could screw up all I wanted, even love a woman for a few days, then come back again and live day by day.

"Why didn't she know I'd help her?"

"You *have* to be alone," I said, too harshly.

Edie was quiet. Probably wondering what I was mad at. All of a sudden I had to get off the phone. "I got to get to work. Talk to you later."

"Are you all right?"

"Yeah. Just late." I hung up on her. If only I could get away too, I thought, feeling panicked. Just get away from all these problems. This day-in day-out everything's-the-same. I was fed up. I felt crazy.

Chapter 7

How To Make Something into Something Else
Spring, 1967

Frenchy and Pam were putting a jigsaw puzzle together on the kitchen table. While both were increasingly restless spending so much time at home in bed or eating together, Frenchy was at a loss to recognize the exact source of her discontent, much less propose an antidote. It was Pam who had stopped at Brentano's and bought a huge and expensive puzzle with one of her last unemployment checks, despite owing Frenchy a considerable amount of money. Frenchy's mother had left for Florida, but Frenchy still paid her share of the apartment in the Bronx in case she should need it. That, and Pam, were keeping her nearly insolvent.

Outside, the Sunday afternoon streets were empty. Sunlight was fading, taking with it all the splashes of color that made the disorganization in their small apartment almost attractive in the daytime. At night, Frenchy thought, sighing as she stretched and looked around, it was just a mess. "What do you say we clean up tonight," she suggested lazily.

"Ah! That's where it goes!" said Pam with satisfaction.

"This could take all night," Frenchy warned.

"All night? These puzzles take weeks!"

"Weeks? Where are we going to eat with this on the table?" Frenchy got up and paced, bored.

"Oh, we'll find some place," said Pam, absorbed in the puzzle again.

She looked over Pam's shoulder, then looked down at her own feet and wiggled her toes. Living with Pam, she had learned the joys of bare feet. However, in an uncleaned apartment, she had also learned the hazards and wore bandaids on both feet. "How about it?" she asked.

Pam leaned back against her. "Now?" she asked, tilting her head back and rubbing it against the workshirt covering Frenchy's breasts.

"Not that. Cleaning." She didn't feel like making love. She was upset by the state of the apartment, the way her life felt.

"But we're doing this, Frenchy."

"Like you said, it could take weeks. Aren't we going to clean for weeks?"

"Sounds okay to me," said Pam, moodily turning back to her puzzle.

"Doesn't to me," Frenchy muttered. She was thinking of her trip to Edie's and how nice the house had looked, big as it was and with four people living in it.

When Edie had called to invite her, she'd hesitated, afraid Mercedes would be there. But Edie had tactfully reassured her and she'd gone. It had been disconcerting, seeing Mercedes' eyes in Lydia's face. But she liked the kid.

She'd been determined not to mention Mercedes, but Edie did it for her when Frenchy asked questions about how the housekeeping tasks were shared, looking for a model for her own. They all shared the jobs, Edie had said, except for Mercedes who couldn't, or wouldn't cook. It wasn't her kind of thing. So Mercedes, it was clear to Frenchy, was still butch.

Mercedes had gone back to school and now worked in a hospital, operating the machines that could diagnose illness, other machines to help with the cure. The more Frenchy thought about Mercedes studying such hard stuff, then working in a hospital, wearing a white coat, talking to doctors, the farther away she seemed to get. Her heart had begun to ache that evening in a new way as she talked to Mercedes' child and was warmed by what had become her family circle. Just when she felt ready to love somebody deeper and differently than she ever had before, and live more like Jessie, or Edie, she'd found Pam — and couldn't make it work with her.

Later, at Frenchy's shy urging, Esther had talked about the difficulties in her relationship with Edie. Mostly, she'd advised, "You have to talk about it. Talk till you're blue in the face." Esther had stopped herself there, looking puzzled in a silly way. "At least, till *Edie's* blue in the face." They'd all laughed. Then, more seriously, she'd continued. "Especially about that, about being black and being white." Frenchy had felt there was a special message in that for her — not about her and Pam, but her and Mercedes.

Before Frenchy left, Lydia had asked, "Are you coming to Fire Island this year?"

Even now her heart beat faster as she tried to answer that question. All the old crowd would be at the annual Fourth of July picnic on Fire Island. And all of Edie's new family. Should Frenchy go? Mercedes would be there. Would she want to see Frenchy? There was time to decide yet. And Lydia, meanwhile, had gotten Frenchy to promise her a day in the City together. What would Lydia think of this home, this mess, the feeling in the apartment she shared with Pam — not of family, but of camping out?

"Then go ahead and clean it, lover. I don't feel like it."

Frenchy sighed again and bit her lip. She looked around. Everything seemed to be Pam's. Almost timidly she said, "I don't know where your things go."

She felt like crying. Since that weekend in Provincetown when just about everything made her cry, she'd gotten in the habit of letting herself cry more and more. She seemed to do it often. But if she cried now, Pam would press her to her breasts and she would feel comforted into thinking everything was all right. "Pam," she started to say, but couldn't think of what to say next.

Pam had apparently heard the frustration in her voice and turned around. "Hey, I'm sorry. If you want to clean, we'll clean, Frenchy lover. Let's do it. It'll be fun."

Overjoyed, Frenchy watched Pam begin to sort things while she searched out the broom and dust pan. They didn't have a carpet sweeper or vacuum so Frenchy hoped Pam would help her shake out the big rug.

"Look at all this dirty underwear!" Pam marvelled. "It's a good thing my family gives me underwear for my birthdays or I'd never have enough." She made a pile for laundry, pulled out some clean clothes, began to stuff them in the closet. Frenchy was happily sweeping the kitchen and cleaning the countertops. "Speaking of underwear," Pam said, "I have one of those pesty yeast infections."

Frenchy stopped. "What's that?" she asked, frightened.

"You never had one?" Pam asked, incredulous. Then she answered herself. "No, of course you wouldn't have." She looked up at Frenchy. "Don't worry, lover, it's nothing to get upset over. I mean, it's not VD or anything like that."

Frenchy began to polish again.

"But if I have it, you probably do too." Frenchy remembered the strange smell the month before, right after her period. She'd worried briefly that it might be the first sign of cancer, then forcefully put that out of her mind.

"Are you itchy down there?"

Frenchy shook her head, realizing that she might be, a little — she had an urge to scratch.

"Do you have a nasty discharge?"

"Cut it out, Pam."

"Well, Frenchy, it's important. Lovers usually pass it on to each other and believe me, you'll be miserable if you let it go."

"Let me worry about it then."

"We'll just be passing it back and forth," Pam said in a warning voice.

"I can handle it." Embarrassed, Frenchy swept viciously.

"What do you think, butches are immune?" Pam joked. "Maybe you used to be immune, but you aren't now!" Frenchy didn't respond and Pam grew quiet, folding and sorting again. "This is what I hate about cleaning up," she said. "It just makes more work. Now we have to go to the laundromat."

The buzzer sounded. "Saved by the bell!"

Annoyed, Frenchy venomously hoped it was just somebody trying to get in to rob an apartment. But there was a knock on their door.

"What a sight for sore eyes!" said Pam, throwing her arms around Dorene. "My girlfriend here was introducing me to slave labor."

"Don't you know this girl doesn't know *how* to clean?" Dorene teased Frenchy. "Before you moved in with her I never knew she even had rugs, they were always so covered with her junk."

Dorene and Pam laughed while Frenchy smiled without enthusiasm.

"What are you doing here anyway, Dor?" asked Pam.

"Missed you is all," Dorene said, kissing Pam lightly on the lips. She glanced over at Frenchy who had stiffened. "Hey, just kidding. I'm not pining after her or anything. But she is my best friend, you know."

Feeling she was being unreasonable, Frenchy made more of an effort to be friendly. Still, when she saw Pam wasn't paying any more attention to cleaning, but was explaining to Dorene her latest work, she knew the battle was lost for the day. She put away the broom and sat on the couch, leaving the friends alone. She picked up a magazine and leafed through it, then moved over to the puzzle and tried to fit in a few pieces. She thought of going out, but she was hungry. Pam was a great cook, but ate so irregularly that Frenchy often had to fend for herself. Maybe she'd make some eggs. But that's what they'd had for breakfast. She took spaghetti from the cupborad to mix with some of Pam's leftover sauce.

Pam and Dorene were walking toward her, moving in the close way of people familiar with one another's bodies. "I have two more unemployment checks coming," Pam was saying. "It's too soon to get a job."

"But you'd love this."

"Are you cooking, Frenchy? I'm hungry too. Why don't you make some of that for all of us?"

It was one thing to heat something for herself and Pam and maybe burn it, or not get it hot enough — but to cook for Pam *and* Dorene?

"Why don't you make some of those sausages you brought home yesterday?" Noticing the look on Frenchy's face, Pam moved to her. "Did you ever cook sausage?" she whispered. Frenchy shook her head. "Look, it's easy. Just put them in the pan and keep turning them until they're brown all over, then pop them in the sauce. *Voila!* Can you handle it?"

Frenchy knew she was being challenged and said, "Sure." It did sound easy. So while Pam and Dorene talked, she pulled out pots and pans and began to cook. It felt funny, cooking for them. She spattered hot fat on her shirt. "Shit," she blurted.

"What's wrong, Frenchy? You need help?" called Pam.

"Nope." Pam would suggest she put on an apron. Damned if she'd wear an apron on top of cooking for them, she felt enough like a girl. She took out a cigarette and lit it one-handed while she stirred the sauce. It wasn't easy, but she was doing it, and feeling pretty confident.

The spoon hit the bottom of the saucepan and she felt a lump. What was this? She put her cigarette down on the edge of the counter and peered into the pot, exploring the whole bottom with the spoon. It was covered with goo. She spooned some up, scraping the bottom of the pan. The sauce was sticking. Why in hell was it doing that? She took a drag from her cigarette. Maybe the flame was too high. She turned it down and looked at the sausages as she heard another spatter of fat. "Shit," she said again, but to herself this time. They were blackening on one side and not cooking at all on the other. She'd forgotten to turn them.

"Okay," she said to herself and returned to the sauce, noticing on the way that she'd burned the counter with her cigarette. She threw it in the sink and heard it sizzle to a soggy mess — the way she hated to see Pam's cigarettes. The stuff on the bottom of the pan was thicker and she thought she'd better try to scrape it off and mix it in with the rest so Pam wouldn't see it. She turned the heat down more, but little specks of black began to appear. What had she done now, she wondered, close to tears. She began picking out the little black specks, then ran to the sputtering sausages and gingerly turned them again as they spat at her. There were grease spots on her shirt and spatters of sauce where the bubbling stuff had exploded at her. She started, finally, to ask Pam's help, but Pam and Dorene were sharing a joint, giggling and cuddly with one another.

Disapprovingly, she turned away. She didn't like dope, it made people act strangely. How would she ever set the table with all this going on? She went back to work on the black stuff again, figured out that it was burnt sauce, said the hell with it and scraped out all the solid stuff, threw it in the garbage and added some water to replace it.

Pam stood behind her. "I'm here to help, lover. Want me to take over or to set the table? I sent Dorene down the block for some Italian bread and wine."

Frenchy sighed in relief. "I'll set the table. You might want to spice things up a bit.

"Hey, you did pretty good for the first time, hon," Pam praised.

For once Frenchy was glad Pam was too stoned to notice details. "Thanks," she said proudly, moving to Pam and kissing her neck. Pam was more than ready for her and fell on her, kissing her lips, her face, touching her breasts. A little too ready, thought Frenchy. Had Dorene gotten her in the mood? If Frenchy hadn't been there, would Dorene be getting this?

"Hey, hey, she'll be back any minute," Frenchy warned.

"I don't care. She'll wait at the door till we buzz. We have her dinner. Besides, she's broke, you have to give her money for the bread and wine."

Frenchy didn't want to make love like this, much less to a stoned woman. But Pam apparently couldn't keep her hands off her. So she became her old self, unfeeling inside, yet sensitive to Pam's needs as she reached under her robe and found Pam's warm, soaked vulva. It gave her a rush of feeling until the thought occurred that Pam had been like this when she sent Dorene out for bread.

"Frenchy, Frenchy," Pam groaned and Frenchy remembered to stroke her, to bring her to climax. She held her a few moments afterwards, her mind on the dinner, on Dorene, until the buzzer sounded. She disengaged herself, leaving Pam leaning against the refrigerator, her smile sultry and satisfied.

"Dinner's going to burn," Frenchy said.

"Mmm," said Pam, still not caring.

Frenchy let Dorene in and took the bags from her. Dorene took in Pam's state and winked at Frenchy. Frenchy wanted to belt her. Instead, she didn't ask how much everything had cost.

The sausages were in the sauce and Pam was putting water on for spaghetti. Suddenly Frenchy wasn't hungry anymore. How many times a week was she supposed to want spaghetti, she wondered, forgetting that she had decided to make it herself. She set the table.

Dorene was in the kitchen sampling the sauce. Dorene really was a lovely woman, Frenchy thought. Tall and slender, completely unlike herself and Pam. Graceful, with a handsome and strong face, its brown color almost as light as — Frenchy paused with a plate in midair to feel the weight of Mercedes' name on her tongue. How long had it been since she'd last seen her? Since she'd first met her? And still she could feel like this. She didn't understand why that attraction should be so much stronger and different from how she felt about Pam, why it seemed younger, cleaner, more promising somehow. Was it simply because she wasn't actually living with her? Would it all be just as hard? Or harder because Mercedes was Puerto Rican? But Edie and Esther were together. And surely their difference in background wasn't any greater than the difference between Pam and herself or Mercedes and herself.

Everyone sat down to eat, Pam and Dorene still stoned

and talking soft nonsense, Frenchy lost in her thoughts of Mercedes. She remembered sitting down to another table a few weeks ago, remembered spending time with Mercedes' own daughter.

Mercedes having a daughter. On the one hand she couldn't stand the thought that Mercedes had been raped, had been swollen and in pain with an unwanted child. On the other hand, look at Lydia. How could she do anything but like such a high-spirited kid? She remembered Lydia's pride in the trap drums she was learning to play. The child seemed separate from the mother, but somehow her existence enhanced the mother's.

They had finished eating, but Dorene and Pam lingered over their wine. Frenchy talked only a little with them, and they hardly seemed to notice her distance. The way they looked at each other, the way they knew how to move around each other in this house, the way they took care of each other, maybe Pam and Dorene were meant for each other — like Esther and Edie. Maybe she wasn't made like that, able to give so much to a girl. Edie had never asked for it, nor had Frenchy known she could ever have that kind of love with a girl. Besides, she and Edie weren't meant for each other in the same way. That was a special feeling, more like a steady warm spring rainfall than a summer downpour. More like riding on the Staten Island Ferry than a big ocean liner. More Frenchy's speed.

She caught the words "yeast infection," and tuned into Pam's conversation with Dorene again. Pam had better not embarrass her, not reveal that she'd given herself to Pam or to any other girl like that.

"So I'm celibate now," said Dorene.

"I suppose I ought to be," said Pam. "When did yours start?"

"About a month ago. I ignored it as long as I could, but I know I can't be celibate much longer. As a matter of fact, if I knew somebody who had it already who wanted to sleep with me, I'd probably do it tonight! Anyway, I gave in and went to old Dr. Gracey."

"That pig?"

"He's cheap and his cure works."

"Yes, but — yuk! The clinic gives you a tube of ointment and an inserter. You can do it all yourself."

"Yeah, seems like I have to do *everything* myself these days," Dorene laughed, winking at Pam.

"Hey, don't look at me," Pam said. "You probably gave it to me."

Frenchy rose to clear the table. "We'll do the dishes," Pam offered.

You damn well better, thought Frenchy. She was enraged. So Dorene had had her infection only a month. For Pam to get it, that meant they'd been together since Frenchy moved in. Come to think of it, Dorene practically lived there anyway — was always just leaving when Frenchy got home from work, stopping by even when Frenchy was there. Didn't she have a lover of her own? What happened to her Spanish chick? But then — Pam had been her lover before Frenchy came on the scene. Maybe she thought Frenchy was the intruder and Frenchy should leave. Maybe Dorene had realized that she really wanted Pam. That would explain the increase in her visits.

Strangely, she didn't feel jealous. Instead, it was becoming more and more clear that she was going to have to make some decisions, and soon.

She left Pam and Dorene in the kitchen throwing Ivory suds at each other and she went to the telephone. If Edie approved she'd take Lydia to the zoo or something. More likely something. That kid didn't seem the zoo type. Frenchy chuckled to herself as she dialed, wondering where fathers *did* take their kids.

* * * * *

Sunday mornings were still wonderful. When she went out to get the *News* and baked goods, she knew more and more people on the streets and in the shops and could nod hello, even talk awhile.

There seemed to be a whole society of dog walkers in the Village whose contacts cut across the gay and straight worlds. Poodle owners, for example, whether they were the most effeminate of gay men, or the most synthetic of painted women, were always talking in the street. And the often unattractive owners of the most unattractive dogs seemed to find one another attractive over their common leashes. Frenchy, she'd buy herself a Sheltie. Gentle as a collie, but smaller, easier for her to handle. But not yet. Not till she knew what she was going to do. Meanwhile, she walked the nearly empty Village streets on Sunday mornings as if she were in a small country town and knew every neighbor.

Mondays, though, were not so good. Now that she had her promotion and worked a few blocks from home, Mondays — like this one — were awful. Her new duties were harder and she hadn't learned them yet. She loathed supervising. The disciplining, the need to be everywhere at once, the demands and needs of the customers, the cashiers, the managers. But she would succeed. She would do it if it killed her. And once she did succeed, damned if she wouldn't ask for a demotion back to her old job. If only Pam had gotten a job she wouldn't need all this money. And it wasn't that much more, really, than she would get working some nights and weekends extra if she wanted to, as a cashier.

Thursday was her day off, and by Wednesday she would always have things more in hand. Not that she liked the job any better, but she felt more on top of it. She would slack off a little, let her mind wander. And how her mind wandered these days. To Pam, and the apartment, and where her life was going; to Lydia and Mercedes.

The Saturday before had brought the Pam problem to a head. Pam asked how she felt about Dorene staying a few nights as she was between apartments. Out of a growing indifference she agreed to let her stay. The first two nights Dorene had slept quietly on the couch, going off about her business all day, arriving home late at night. The third day she'd stayed home all day with Pam. The house was airless and more dishevelled than usual when Frenchy got home; Pam was still in her robe, Dorene in very short shorts and a T-shirt. Frenchy could tell she wore no underwear. The atmosphere was thick, moist-feeling.

That night Pam had wanted to make love. Because Dorene was in the next room and her light was still on, Frenchy refused. Pam said Dorene wouldn't mind. Frenchy said *she* would. All she wanted was to go to sleep. She'd had several crises at work that day and had to be in early to reprimand a cashier. She was very anxious and knew she needed to be fresh and clear in the morning.

Dorene came in and sat on the edge of the bed, softly whispering to Pam, while Frenchy tried to sleep. She showed her annoyance by tossing and turning, but finally drifted off. She came awake suddenly, into silence, but somehow felt Dorene's presence. Then she heard Pam's breathing, a soft rustling of hands moving under sheets. She sat up. Dorene had climbed under the covers. When they saw she was watching, Pam reached an arm toward Frenchy to draw her to them, touching her breasts. Frenchy bolted out of bed.

"I am *not*," she said firmly and too loudly, standing to her full height with her hands on her hips, "interested in your perverted sex." She stood there in her pajamas glaring at the two women.

"You're not interested in sex tonight, period," said Pam, not unkindly. "And I am. So's Dorene. I can't see anything wrong with making love with her. If you want to join us, do. You can watch if you want."

Having the presence of mind to take the clothes she'd need for morning, she went out to sleep on the couch Dorene had vacated. She was a little frightened. Girls had told her how much she'd hurt them — was it her turn now? If it was hurt she felt, it didn't go too deep. If you have enough lovers, she thought, maybe it can't.

Although she knew Pam and Dorene were making love in the next room, she slept dreamlessly. In the morning she went to work, meted out the required discipline, and survived the day. On her way home she stopped at the rental agent's office to ask about an apartment in Pam's building she knew was vacant. It was clear to her that she'd never go live up in the Bronx again. The Village, filled with people like her, had claimed her. The agent was glad to rent the tiny place.

Pam, mercifully, wasn't home. Frenchy extracted her belongings from the mess, and after a dozen trips up the stairs to her new apartment she was finished moving. She left her old key with a note to Pam: "You can give this to Dorene. I moved upstairs as I think it's better for both of us. I need to know what to do and I can't do that here." She hesitated, not knowing what parting words to use. Should she thank Pam? Invite her to visit? She wanted to say something final, something to set the tone of their new relationship, but she had no idea what it might be. She caught herself reaching between her legs to scratch and remembered the ugly words "yeast infection." She left the note on the kitchen table and, quickly, afraid Pam would return, searched for the phone book and found it under several old newspapers. There he was, Dr. Gracey. If he cured Dorene he must be used to this sort of thing. And Frenchy would rather make an appointment now, while she was alone, than from a pay phone somewhere. She dialed his number, noticing the abbreviation Ob-Gyn next to his name. A ladies' doctor. She had never been to a ladies' doctor before. A receptionist answered and gave Frenchy an appointment. When she had asked why Frenchy wanted to see the doctor Frenchy had mumbled something about itching and hung up.

Frenchy came quickly out of her reverie about breaking with Pam. One of her cashiers was calling for help with a return. For the next hour there was a steady flow of long lines, too few baggers, and enough voids to keep Frenchy from thinking again. Then it was lunchtime. Normally she'd amble around the Village streets, eating lunch in a fast food place, feeling a part of things, relishing her sense of belonging. Today, though, she had her appointment with the ladies' doctor.

All morning she hadn't allowed her anxiety about the visit to enter her mind. Now as she sat on the cold leather chair in the waiting room, fear consumed her. She was by turns cold with it and hot from the embarrassment of what was about to happen to her. The receptionist showed her to a room and left her with a flimsy paper gown. "You know how to use one of these, don't you?" the receptionist had asked crisply, and left before Frenchy could mutter an answer.

Should she leave the opening in the back or in the front? Should she get up on the examining table or sit in the chair? Would he use one of the needles in that big bin on her? Her feet were cold on the floor, and her bottom was cold on the vinyl chair. The paper gown seemed full of little holes designed to let the air in. She settled finally on the table, painfully aware of how the chill made her nipples stiff like when Pam touched them.

"And how are you doing, young lady?" Dr. Gracey said as he entered. He looked her up and down. "Hm," he commented as he read the scant information on her chart. He was a tall, heavy older man who wore a wedding ring. His white hair was slightly long, his moustache full and stained from tobacco. His hands were cold as he gave her a quick general exam. "And where did you pick this up?" he asked. Was he being sarcastic? He disappeared, returning all too soon with the crisp receptionist. She stood through the exam, arms folded, scowling, thinking who knew what.

"Feet in here," barked the doctor.

The metal stirrups were ice cold.

"Scoot down more and raise your knees. We only need half a table for you, little one," he laughed.

The stirrups, throught Frenchy, would make a good weapon. They looked ugly enough. How would the doctor like to be beaten to death by cold stirrups? But maybe that was why he kept a witness in there, to protect him from humiliated dykes. How had Dorene stood this?

"It's a yeast infection, all right," he told her. "I'll just paint you up and you'll be fine in a week or so. No sex till then."

Paint her up? A week or so? No sex?

But before she could think how to ask without sounding more foolish than she felt, he was between her legs again smearing her with something wet.

"All set, little one," he said finally. The receptionist whisked out the door. Dr. Gracey wrote something on her chart and told her he'd prescribed something for her. Then she was alone in her rumpled paper gown, staring at a hideous purple stain on it. On her legs. Down there. How was this going to cure anything? How could she go back to work like this? Would it come through her pants?

The receptionist slapped a small grey package on the counter inside the door. "For you," she said. Frenchy waddled over, clutching her gown closed behind her and breathed in relief to see it was a sanitary pad. She'd never been so glad to see one in her life.

She had to hurry the few blocks back to work. Why did she feel as if she'd been assaulted? As if the man had molested her? No man had touched her down there since the doctor she'd had as a kid. Did every woman feel dirty after such an exam? Or was it just because she was gay? She shuddered. Why did straight women let men touch them? How could they stand it? She'd never let it happen again, ever. There must be lady ladies' doctors.

It was with relief that she saw the long lines at the store, the harrassed face of her boss. She could push what had happened back where it belonged. No one would know she was painted purple down there, had rubbed the itchy parts raw before she'd made her appointment. No one would know the receptionist had aimed one last parting shot at her before she'd left: "Try wearing skirts once in a while," she'd suggested. As if skirts could cure anything. She'd swaggered out the office door in answer, combing her hair back. The next time she wanted some damn man to touch her, that's when she'd wear a skirt. They made her feel as naked and vulnerable as those paper gowns. It was one thing for a femme to wear them. Reaching up a thigh under a skirt, now that was sexy. But not her, not to stop some itching that should never have happened, damn Pam, not to cure anything in the world.

She found herself yelling at the stockboy. She'd have to calm down. She was short a bagger and one missing bagger could really throw you off. That doctor had made her blow her cool. She found herself begging the manager for a replacement bagger as the disgruntled customers glared at her. Finally, vengefully, she bagged herself, between voids and writing up the next week's schedule which had to be posted before she went home that day. And there were always more voids when the customers waited too long; they got ornery and watched the cashiers extra hard, then the cashiers got nervous. If only her friend Marian from the Bronx A&P were there, they would laugh and exchange exasperated looks. But a supervisor couldn't make friends with a cashier. That would show favoritism and upset everyone. The other department heads were all men and she wasn't interested, especially today, in being friends with any man. "Watch out for them," her mother had always told her, "they want only one thing."

Soon people would be getting out of work and the commuter rush would begin. Then she'd be even busier, but closer to going home. Her legs ached. She wished that Pam were still around to massage them. Pam had come to see her, of course, hadn't cried or carried on, but was sorry they couldn't work it out. A couple of times Frenchy suspected Pam was hinting that they could still sleep together, but Frenchy, by this time, was suffering so from her infection that she had no interest in sex. Especially if this was what it got her. Besides, she was repelled by the idea of sharing. Or threesomes. She shuddered as she erased an error on the schedule. She had enough trouble taking her clothes off for one girl. Pam had asked her for dinner a couple of times, but Frenchy hadn't accepted. Not that she held anything against Dorene either. She just didn't feel good being with both of them.

Her first act in her own place was to scrub it. That was easy because she lacked any furniture. Her first night she slept on blankets on the floor. The next day she had a hardware store cut her a piece of foam rubber the size of a double bed. Over the next couple of weeks she visited second-hand stores and bought herself pots and dishes, lamps, a couple of comfortable armchairs and a low table. A monk's cell, she thought when she'd finished. She returned to the thrift store to buy drapes and a spread. If she'd learned anything from Pam, it was how to make something into something else. An old bedspread became curtains, a frayed linen tablecloth her bedspread. When she realized the bedspread would have to be cut in half so she could open her curtains and let light in, she decided there was no reason curtains had to open from the middle and was proud of her ingenuity when she pushed her curtain aside in the mornings. She'd taken her old clock radio from Pam's apartment, and now all she needed was a TV. But it would be a while before she could afford one.

In the meantime, she had bought a half a dozen old lesbian paperbacks and a stack of comics at the thrift store and had settled down to a quiet bachelor life. She was footloose and fancy free now. She had a good job, some nice friends, a place of her own. Best of all, she lived in Greenwich Village. This was enough. This was the life . . .

Someone needed her on the floor again. She realized she'd been rubbing her crotch against a chair and stopped. This itching was unbearable. Why had she let the old man paint her private parts like some fancy tramp if it wasn't going to work? She made one last adjustment in the schedule, but held off posting it till she was ready to leave. Otherwise, the girls would ask for changes. For one last hour she went out to face the music. As cashier, she enjoyed the store more when it got busier, her automatic actions seeming to free her mind more for her own thoughts. Today she looked forward to the end of this hour when she could pick up a can of beans, some hotdogs, a six-pack, and go home to rest her tired feet and read. And scratch.

Frenchy walked home. She remembered the first time she'd gone to that building. How different her life would have been had Pam not looked out the window. She'd probably be living in Florida, wishing she'd had the guts to stay in New York by herself. She trudged up the stairs with her bundle, the *News* under an arm. Someday she was going to buy the *Times,* just to see what all the fuss was about. Someday, she thought, she was going to do a lot of things.

Her phone rang as she stepped inside her apartment. Lydia wanted to visit her that Sunday. Frenchy's heart warmed at the sound of Lydia's voice and she told her she was welcome.

* * * * *

It was Sunday morning again; Frenchy stretched for the sheer pleasure of it on her thin foam pad. The sheets were clean, her boys' cotton pajamas were freshly laundered, and it was gloriously early. Even the newsstand would not yet be open. She allowed herself the luxury of remaining in bed. Alone.

She was almost glad the yeast infection had kept her from picking a girl up and bringing her home for the night. Now she could savor her Sunday morning. But what, she wondered, would she do for a sex life? Maybe Wednesday nights would be good to spend with girls. Nobody was around Wednesday nights, though; maybe she could get her day off changed. At this moment she felt so free of any need for sex she decided not to worry about it. Besides, after her passion for Pam, she didn't want sex with just anyone. She didn't want to be faced with making love like she used to. She'd really have to trust someone before letting herself be touched again. So what was the sense? Living down here in the Village she could go to the bars anytime, have a few drinks, eye a few girls, and come home satisfied. Wasn't that what all the fuss was about? To be in your own world, to share being gay with somebody else, to touch, as deeply as you could, another lesbian?

She could see, now, how much she needed the gay world. How she had lived for her Saturdays all those years in the Bronx with her mother. How the rest of her time had been a poor shadow of life. How her relationships hadn't meant anything unless they were with someone gay. How anything she did meant nothing unless it was centered around being gay. How she as a person and her life had been meaningless unless she was being her real self.

Living with another lesbian had made everything mean more. Like food. With her mother food had been a matter of necessity, her meals borne like the time between Saturdays. With Pam — and now cooking for herself — food was different; she was feeding somebody important, a lesbian who had a place in the world. Cooking and eating with another gay girl was fun. Sometimes it was a game; sometimes it was sexy; sometimes they could talk. Always, it was good to spend time with another lesbian. She wanted to become good enough at cooking to ask girls, or her friends, over for dinner. And she no longer wanted to be dependent on someone else feeding her, as Mercedes still was on Edie, as Jessie was on Mary — these butchy women couldn't feed themselves. She, Frenchy, could earn her own money and she would cook the food she bought with it. And she liked feeding herself, liked nurturing this lesbian she was, this lesbian other gay girls liked, this lesbian who would someday be someone's special lover.

Suddenly she remembered: this was the day she would take Lydia to the ballgame. Hurriedly she checked the clock — they wouldn't meet for hours yet. Would Mercedes bring Lydia to her? Or was the kid old enough to travel the subways by herself? She indulged herself in a memory of Mercedes walking along the beach in Provincetown all those years ago. Mercedes was trusting her daughter to Frenchy. Would she ever again trust herself?

She got up out of bed, anxious. She hadn't seen Mercedes in so long... Maybe she wasn't beautiful anymore. Maybe she'd changed in other ways, lost that special quality

of hers that had drawn Frenchy to her. Maybe she wasn't
so tough anymore. But then, neither was she.

She brushed her teeth, examining her eyes in the mirror.
Could anyone tell that she wasn't the same? That she'd been
touched by a woman in a new way? Did she look reachable?
The night she'd touched Mercedes... Was it *this* weakness
she'd seen in Mercedes' eyes? If someone saw it in her own
she'd do as Mercedes had done — run. Unless — unless it was
someone she wanted to tell about having changed, about
wanting to be touched. Someone she trusted, who revealed
herself to her, too. Did Mercedes understand that Frenchy
hadn't been ready for her then? Didn't know or want to
know this side of herself? Didn't know she could even
learn, that it was possible?

Frenchy turned the shower on, stood with one arm
testing the spray, then stepped under the water and felt
its warm flow wash away a whole part of herself. You had
to give a girl more than sex, more than things like flowers
and drinks, more than compliments and courtesies. You
had to give her part of yourself.

She surrendered to enjoyment of the water, the smell
of the soap, the feeling of being clean. She thought about
singing in the shower and realized that for the first time
she wanted to. And could! There was no one to hear...

A sudden warm constriction inside her caused the
mood to vanish. She had forgotten — it was time for her
period again. She reached and her fingers brought up blood.
Then she realized she no longer itched. And neither did
she have cramps. As a matter of fact, instead of crampy,
she felt sexy. All warm and needing someone to touch her
there — hand or tongue. She squirmed under the water at
the thought and grinned. Me? she asked.

She'd long ago finished washing, but she stood there
enjoying the feelings, wishing she could stay till her period
was over. This was another way of being all right. Would

she always feel like this now — this good? Walking around the Village on Sunday morning wouldn't hurt, she decided. She turned off the shower.

Dressed in her Sunday blue jeans, white shirt and heavy sweater, she chose her jean jacket to wear out. Pam had decorated it for her and she still felt self-conscious in it. Across the back, red letters outlined in black spelled out her name. There were designs stitched around the button-holes and the collar: seagulls and waves, suns and moons. What would the kids at the bar think of it, she'd wondered, just as she sometimes worried they could tell she was no longer stone butch. But how many of *them* were now? Jessie had changed; Beebo didn't strike her as the type; others regularly switched depending on the girls they were seeing. It was her own opinion she feared most. No one would kick her out of a bar for liking sex. Maybe they would lose some respect for her, since she was always the one who was toughest — and proudest of her ways. If she lost a little face — wasn't it worth it?

She walked tall along Morton Street despite the lumpy sanitary napkin. Thumbs looped in her jeans, she sauntered to a newstand and bought the *News*. A dyke couple from the bar was there.

"Hi!" she said cheerfully.

They looked up at her, bleary-eyed. "Hi, Frenchy. You look pretty bright-eyed for this time of day."

"Just got out of bed," she explained proudly.

"We didn't get to bed yet," they chorused.

Frenchy pitied them. They probably hadn't even had a good time, sitting in some all-night place with a few friends saying the same things over and over, dancing by leaning against each other, and all this was supposed to be fun, exciting, the thing to do. Now they'd sleep all day, laze around their apartment in the evening, disoriented, and have to get up as usual Monday morning. These women lived in the Village, had each other. Why wasn't that enough? Did they still feel outside of things? Still feel the need to insulate themselves from the hurt of being gay in a straight world by spending so much time in bars? It was disheartening to think her own happiness would soon dissipate. There had to be a way to make the gay life less hard, some way to make the straight world hurt less.

But today the sun was shining, and Frenchy walked down Sixth Avenue to a French bakery she had discovered. The long line of customers there was part of the Sunday morning ritual. She studied the delicacies behind the counter. Maybe she should get a box of cookies or something for Lydia to bring Edie and Esther and her mother. Maybe they shouldn't go to the stadium at all, maybe they should do something downtown. Then Frenchy could show Lydia her place. She ordered her breakfast and a box of delicacies for Lydia.

Chapter Eight

Crazy Nights
Spring, 1967

Yeah, it was on me, suddenly, the craziness. I was almost relieved. Now I could choose to go with it — or ignore it, just walk into my assignment where I'd concentrate on work till it went away. I felt it pulling me back toward the door out of the hospital. I could go back home, get dressed and go downtown. I longed for the sight of midtown Manhattan in daylight. The fancy buildings, the crowds, the traffic. Soon the bars would open in the Village. Cool and dark and romantic. A girl would wander in. Look down the bar at me. I'd smile, pick her up, touch her. The thought sent shivers down my back.

Edie, I thought. I used the thought of her to pull myself back into the corridors of the hospital. The hospital. But all those years they kept putting me in hospitals . . .

I walked the corridors crazy to get out.

The corridors began to shrink. The voice paging people on the loudspeaker began to echo. My head felt like it would explode. What was wrong with me? It had been so long since I felt like this. I had a choice. I could stop it — could I stop it?

"Mercedes," a gay guy was saying. Was I in the bar already? "Are you all right? You look sick."

I turned to look at him and realized I worked with him. This wasn't a bar. "I look sick?" I repeated stupidly. "Yes," I said, "I'm feeling very sick." I had sick time coming. A few days at least. "Will you tell them? Tell them I'm sick. I got to go home."

"Sure, Mercedes. Can you get home okay?"

"I'll take a cab," I yelled back, already filled with exhilaration. I burst into the sunshine and whirled around, my white jacket billowing. I ran to the subway, ran and ran. At home I stripped off my clothes, lay naked on my bed, feeling as high as if I'd been drinking. I hugged myself. My head was in this strange cloud that seemed to insulate me from all my worries. I touched my body. It was still me, firm, solid. Smooth and good to touch. But I could wait. I would find a girl to touch me. Some cute little girl like Rosetta. But I didn't want Rosetta or anyone like anybody I knew. Yet if I saw Frenchy, I'd, I'd — throw myself at her. No, of course I wouldn't. I'd run like hell to another bar and pick up someone else so fast Frenchy's head would spin.

I held my herb bag, a little calmer. Still driven, but calmer. I had to do three things: dress, get the emergency money from my bottom drawer, and write Edie a note. Not that it was any of her business. But it was, I reminded

myself through this sudden hostility. My absence would
be really hard on her, with all her worry about Esther. I
didn't want to think about that. I'd tell her I needed some
time for myself, that I felt close to the edge. Could she
take care of herself? Maybe she would call Lydia to come
stay with her.

She could call Frenchy to come over, give her my bed.
I caressed it lightly, thinking of Frenchy in it.

I wrote my note and went downtown.

* * * * *

It was night. The craziness had worn off a little. All
afternoon I'd wandered the streets and the tunnels under
the buildings of Manhattan. What a wonderful warm spring
day. Each time I passed lilacs I got a little more drunk on
their smell. My body tingled with anticipation. This night
I would be with a woman.

By the time the sky was lavender again I was hungry.
Feeding on my own excitement, I hadn't remembered to
eat. I went down to Chinatown. Marie and I used to go down
there when we were together. For the price of subway fares
and a couple of dollars we could have a feast. They never
knew what to make of us — two little dykes talking Spanish
and eating Chinese.

This night I looked around and saw a little place that
looked friendly — a few tables and a family running around
waiting on people. As I sat down this little kid came up
to me with a cart. I took something off it and she marked
a pad of paper. Whatever it was, it was great. Someone else
came by with a big pot of tea. I'd never had such good tea
in my life, not even the *espiritista's*. There I was, still a
crazy little Spanish dyke smiling my head off and eating
everything they brought me. I walked out of there as high

as I'd been that morning, and I bought some gum to cover all the garlic I'd eaten.

I strolled into a bar chewing gum and feeling real at home. I ordered a Coke.

The place was nearly empty. It wasn't right in the Village, but below it, I knew I wouldn't see anyone I recognized there. The lanky blonde bartender was the type who minds her own business. Some women played pinball, others sat around in groups or couples, no singles that I could see, but it was early. I smiled into the mirror, reading the backward lettering on the window: GOGIE'S BAR. Below it I could see my collar was crooked. I went into the bathroom, combed my hair and washed up the best I could, fantasizing about where I would sleep that night.

A woman was sitting at the bar when I returned. I smiled at her, taking her by surprise as dykes don't smile much at strangers in New York City. And suddenly I knew what I'd do, because any girl I picked up would have to know our night together would end. I'd lie about who I was. I'd be on vacation. Visiting from some place out of town. Then I could leave whenever I needed to and nobody would question me. If the girl asked about my New York accent, I'd say I grew up there. This was perfect, I thought, and the girl alone at the bar was a sign it would work out. Let it, please, I prayed. I needed this so bad.

I looked closer at the chick, but decided to take my time. Maybe she was meeting someone. The jukebox began to play something light and new, just what I needed. I hoped this bar didn't *have* the oldies on the jukebox. More women came in. I was still nursing my Coke. I ordered another; it was better for me than liquor. I felt too good, I didn't have to fake a high with booze. Occasionally a woman asked the chick at the bar to dance — so, like me, she was looking for somebody. I worked on my story and realized how rational I sounded to myself. I wasn't drinking and I was thinking things out pretty clearly. The only bad thing was taking a vacation when Edie needed me. But at least I didn't add not leaving a note onto her troubles, as Esther had.

Maybe I wasn't crazy to do this. Maybe I wasn't crazy at all anymore. I startled myself thinking: maybe I never had been crazy. Or maybe I was just as crazy as I needed to be. Maybe someday I could tell when I needed to stop, to get away, and I could plan it. Maybe I was doing something absolutely normal. That thought took the fun out of things, and I laughed quietly to myself. In the mirror I saw the girl from the end of the bar as she moved next to me. I offered her a cigarette.

She asked, "Are you shy or not interested?"

She sure wasn't shy. I gave her a look in the mirror before I turned to light her cigarette, then looked up from the match into her eyes. She didn't look away. "Let's say I was enjoying the suspense," I told her, and she laughed, exhaling. This was the life.

"Do you hang around here all the time?" she asked.

"I haven't been around in a while."

"Going with somebody?" She had the low sexy voice I'd been dreaming of.

"No. You?"

She shook her head slowly, and we smiled. "You don't go out much?"

Suddenly I wanted to tell the truth. "I was sick for a long time. I've been recovering, straightening out my life. The bars aren't the place for that." So that we could hear over the jukebox, her face was excitingly close to mine.

"Now you're ready for the bars again?"

"I've been ready for a long time, baby," I said pointedly. Then I turned away from her. "But not the same way. They're not a way of life for me anymore. I'm here because

I need to be, but I can't say when I'll be back."

"I'm used to that," she said.

I couldn't tell if I'd heard sadness in her voice so I looked at her again. All I saw was that seductive glitter in her eyes. She was a pretty girl. White, with softly waving brown hair, those glowing brown eyes and a wide, sensitive-looking mouth. Maybe I *was* dreaming; she was too good to be true. I wasn't sure I even wanted to know who she was, but I figured I'd be safer knowing. "What's your name?"

"Candy."

"You come down here much?"

"Only when my husband's out of town."

That shut me up.

"He doesn't know I do this. It would hurt him too much."

"Does he go out of town often?" I saw her drink was empty and ordered her another whiskey sour.

She shook her head. "Once a year, to a convention. He's a dentist."

After all I'd been learning about myself and being gay, and finally accepting myself for the first time these past few years, I was saddened by this woman who couldn't live openly with herself. "Why did you marry a man?"

"I couldn't live this way, the gay life. I couldn't tell my friends, my family. I've gotten used to his income, to staying home and being cared for. He doesn't ask much of me. I told him before we married I didn't want kids, so I don't have to worry about that."

"But . . . living a lie like that?"

She lowered her head. "Sometimes it makes me sick. But most of the time I'm too comfortable to give it up."

"You only go with a girl once a year?"

The sexy smile replaced her troubled look. "Makes it even better," she half-whispered, leaning close to me. I inhaled her whiskey breath with the feeling someone had just dropped me off a cliff and I was free-floating in space. I knew I'd be taking all those sick days I'd been thinking about. Hey, I told myself, this is how she wants to live — you won't have any ties to her afterward.

"How long has it been for you?" she asked, reaching to gently stroke my shaking hand.

"Over two years."

"What happened? You flipped out?"

"It's that obvious?"

"To me. I've done it too. Before I knew I was gay. Then again when I found out I was. That's one reason I hold onto the marriage. Keeps me steady."

We looked into one another's eyes. "I understand," I said, understanding a little more about me too. My marriage was to Edie and Esther.

"There's something about your eyes," she said, "and the lines of your face. It's all there." She'd been touching my face.

I touched hers, too, seeing the beginnings of the lines she was talking about. Lines of feeling. "I don't regret them. Some of those times were the most intense of my life," I said.

"Yet you don't want to repeat them."

"You never know if you're going to come back."

"I call this time, when my husband goes away, my crazy time."

Our lips were almost touching, we were so close. "You want to go crazy with me, baby?" I asked.

She touched my lips with hers and I could feel how much she'd longed for this kiss. Even more, I could feel how much I wanted it. We just sat there, breathing on each other's lips, afraid to kiss harder for the control we'd lose, yet not wanting to separate.

"Let's dance."

She wasn't arguing. The bar had filled, but wasn't

packed — it was Monday night — but there were enough women to make it cozy and anonymous. We stepped together and the feel of her soft, needy body against mine was more delicious than all the Chinese food in the world. I wished I hadn't eaten. I felt coarse and heavy where I wanted to feel light and charming. I pressed her to me and she sighed, like she was exhaling just enough to make herself fit against me. She felt too good to me to move. And for all her aggressiveness, I knew I'd be butch. She was so womanly, all soft curves in her ladylike clothes. You could tell, too, she didn't belong in the bars. Maybe the cut of her clothes, the careful styling of her hair. I wouldn't fall in love with her for life, she wasn't my kind, but for a few days she was just what the doctor ordered.

We left at the first fast song and went to her hotel. A nice one, not too expensive, in the Village. She had taken a room already so there was no hassle.

"What do you tell your husband? Doesn't he call you?"

"I say I go to the sea. That I can't stand to be in the house without him."

"And he believes you?"

"Yes. He knows I love the sea, that I'd spend all my time there if I could. We usually rent a place on the Cape in the summer, but I tell him I go to Maine for these trips, where it's wilder."

Wilder. The way she said the word, scared me. But just for a minute. Then I knew she was telling me how I should love her. She turned to me. I grabbed her upper arms and pulled her to me, kissing her harder than the first time. Not hurting her, but harder. I kneaded her arms and she wrapped them around me tightly, clinging as if I were holding her up in a strong sea. She bit my lower lip and sent a hot sharp message into my body. This first one would be fast, I knew. Neither of us could wait and I took her clothes off, quickly, then my own. We looked at one another. She was beautiful —

full, pendulous breasts, a little belly just round enough —
all womanliness. What surprised me was her body hair.
There was so much of it, I hadn't expected it on her. From
between her breasts it traveled in a line to her navel where
it widened and grew very thickly down onto her legs.

"Do you mind?" she asked.

I thought: how she must suffer, waiting for rejection.
I wondered how much this had to do with her craziness,
with staying with a husband who at least knew her. I knelt
before her and began to kiss her through it, pulling tufts
of hair with my lips, blowing at it, until I reached between
her legs with my hand. Perhaps I did mind, a little, but
only because I wasn't used to it. My hand was so wet with
her it was all I could do to overcome my excitement enough
to ask, "What do *you* think?" before I tipped her onto
the bed.

She sat on its edge while I spread her legs and began to
touch her with my tongue. All that hair felt strange on my
cheeks, but she soon fell back, gasping, and all I knew then
was woman feel, woman sound, woman wet, woman smell.
I didn't tease her, I couldn't, I wanted her to be coming and
never stop this first, overwhelming time. It was powerful
for her. She was lovely during it, too, moving so slightly
and sensuously, crying so quietly to me, touching me so
gently on the head all the while. What a beauty. When I
joined her lying across the bed there were tears in her eyes
and behind them, stars, just like there were supposed to
be. It was very gratifying, knowing what pleasure I could
still give a woman. I wiped her moisture from my face on
her, laughing to myself about her natural towel, and I kissed
her lips. She pulled me down to her and I could tell by
her touch that it was me, now, she would give me what I'd
just given her. For a second I longed for Frenchy, then she
touched the sadness out of me. She was good. Not as much

because she was experienced as from a real desire to please me.

"What do you like?" she asked, and the question turned me on even more.

"Show me my choices," I whispered, teasing. Didn't she trust herself to be able to tell? But I wasn't getting away as easy as that. This wouldn't be the fast and easy release I'd given her. She touched me everywhere, gently, hard, with her hands, her fingers, her lips, her marvelous breasts. She wasn't choosing, she wanted me to tell her. I did and came the instant she touched me with her tongue, just lost, lost, lost in whirlpools of the feeling, one ring of sensation dying and another, just as strong, beginning. I don't know how long it took, but I was downright embarrassed when she stopped. I was still feeling it, though faintly, and too wiped out to pull her back to me. I held her lightly.

Later, we turned on a radio. We danced, naked, to a Spanish station.

She'd never been with a Spanish girl before and I think she liked the idea. It made me seem sexier to her. I had to teach her love words in Spanish and that excited her. She made me tell her what I was doing as I loved her, in Spanish. Then she made me ask for what I wanted in Spanish, and I had to wait till she figured out the translation. Yes, she was a tease, a little kinky. She liked to hear the words of love between women. She had some other tricks I won't go into, too, and after the second day I'd gotten pretty tired of it all, a little over-satisfied, if you know what I mean. I was glad I'd told her from the start I couldn't stay with her the whole week.

I called into work Tuesday from a phone booth. Said I was still sick, that I might be in Wednesday, but certainly Thursday. And I called Edie Tuesday night.

"I'm sorry," I said as soon as she said hello.

She was great. "Mercedes, I'm just glad to hear from you. Your note said it all. *I'm* the one who should be sorry. You didn't need all this strain. And you've been taking it all on yourself."

"Thanks for understanding. It took me a while to figure all that out."

"I was glad of the time. I needed to start thinking and stop relying on you to do it all for me. Are you really having a vacation?"

"I think I've had enough. There's something creepy about being cooped up in a hotel room with a stranger."

"Oh, *that* kind of vacation."

"I needed to, I couldn't stand it any more. But, listen, I'm not sure I'll be back tomorrow. I think I'll stay one more night with her. She *is* good, you know."

"No, I don't," Edie laughed wickedly.

"Then I'll spend the day alone tomorrow. I should be home at dinnertime tomorrow night. Okay? And I'll call if not. You'll be all right alone tonight?"

"Fine. I haven't finished what I'm working on. It's a love letter. It may be too late, but at least I can try to put it all down. And I'm readier for bad news too. I know I'll survive."

"Yeah, me too." I could tell she was grinning on the other side of the phone. Like me.

"So, go back to your creepy stranger and enjoy yourself."

"I'm going to insist we go out somewhere tonight or I'll be home sooner than I planned!"

"Then I'll see you whenever!"

It was hard hanging up. She was all the plain regular normal everyday things in my life. Why couldn't I fall for her? I almost dreaded going back to Candy and felt a chill down my back as I thought of her. That's just what she was like, too, like candy, kind of sickly sweet. But then, she was beautiful and sexy and could be fun. If I could get some clothes on her and get her out on the street, I'd feel more normal.

When I got upstairs I realized I'd exaggerated her bad points. She was all dressed and ready to usher me out the door to dinner, a great little Mexican restaurant she just knew I'd love. This Spanish stuff was really getting to me, but that's what I got for picking up a white dentist's wife. I could humor her for one more night.

It was cooler than the night before, as if we were going backwards into winter. I put my arm around her and she snuggled into it. We walked along like any two women out for a night on the town, except it was only Tuesday. The part of the Village where she took me was interesting, all little criss-crossed streets, like the area Lydia had described where Frenchy lived. I wanted to run into every building and check names on mailboxes.

"How far *is* this place?" I asked, shivering.

"Around the corner. You're not used to fresh air," she said, leaning to kiss me.

She might be sickly sweet, but that didn't mean I didn't enjoy the sweetness. I felt very sophisticated, walking with a beautiful woman in the night under a lavender sky turning to violet. We found the restaurant and I ate sparingly, not particularly liking all that hot food. Then we went on to the bar where we'd first met. It seemed smaller, smokier, shabbier. Candy was still a wonderful girl to dance with, to hold hands with across the table, but to tell you the honest truth, I was bored.

"Tired?"

"You wear me out."

She laughed long and low. "We'd better get back to the room. I don't want you to fall asleep on me the last night."

"Is it the last night?"

"It feels like it."

"I've been putting off telling you," I lied. "They told me I had to come back to work tomorrow. One of the other kids has the same thing that they think I have. That means three of us are out —"

"I've really liked being with you and want to have this last night very much, but I understand it's enough."

What a strange girl. Flashes of kindness and intuition, then that awful stifling need of hers, stored up year to year. "And you? Will you go home now?" I asked.

She held a cigarette for me to light and I admired those gentle hands, insistent hands that even now made me throb. "Not yet," she said, and I knew she'd be at a bar again tomorrow, ready for one more girl before she went back to sit in the dentist's chair.

"Listen," I said, "you ought to think about leaving him. You ought to find a girl you can get the same kind of setup with as you have with him. They're around, you know, girls who want to settle down, support their lovers."

The look of fear in her eyes shocked me. "No," she said harshly, "I'm okay the way I am. Why rock the boat?"

But I knew I had to take my own advice. Even when I'd gone out with more than one girl at a time, I *knew* them, was friends before and after. "Let's go back to the room," I said, taking hold of her wrist, wanting to start the long night so that I could get some sleep and spend Wednesday alone.

She stood, in her graceful way, and took my arm. We played at love as we walked back to the hotel and played at love into the night. Then she let me sleep and in the morning she slept on. I kissed her goodbye. She didn't wake. Or didn't want to say goodbye. I took one last look at the disheveled room, at her lovely face, liking the new way I'd found of going crazy. Even though I had no regrets, it had all been kind of sordid. I had to do better for myself.

Chapter 9

Frenchy Goes to Florida
Late Spring, 1967

For the first time in her life Frenchy was on a plane. Excited and scared, she sat with legs spread, feet planted firmly before her, hands gripping her thighs. If she was going to die it would be now, on takeoff, over Flushing Bay. She just knew it.

"People live through airplane flights every day, Genvieve." Her brother was flying high too, high and mighty with the money he was earning to be making long distance calls to New York and paying for her to fly down to see Maman in Tarpon Springs. "Gen," Serge had said, "Maman misses you. It's either this or she says she's moving back home. You want to live with her again?" It sounded like a threat. Did he know what kind of life she was leading in the City now, by herself? Did he suspect?

Another engine roared and the cabin of the plane vibrated. Frenchy let go of her legs long enough to triple-check her seat belt. A stewardess hung over her, asking if everything was all right. "Sure thing," Frenchy said, flashing her most charming smile.

Then the stewardess stood talking into a microphone, explaining how to escape a plane which had crashed. Holy Christmas, thought Frenchy, trying valiantly to pay attention.

"It's safer than driving a car," Pam had claimed. Did the driver of a car go through this every time she started the motor? Hell, no. Still, the stewardess treated it all casually. And she sure was cute.

The stewardess sat facing the passengers and strapped herself in. She was no fool either. The man on the aisle seat next to Frenchy scratched his leg and Frenchy eyed him suspiciously. Better not be next to any damn pervert, she told herself. Suddenly, the terminal began to slide away from Frenchy. Holy Christmas, she thought, it's like the ferry only without the safe feeling of water under you. She began to pray, not knowing exactly who to pray to. "If anybody's up there, I forgive all the crap I been through and all the rotten things that happen in the world, just let me live through this, please, let me get home safe to my little apartment in New York. I swear I'll go to Fire Island with Lydia. I swear, I swear." Satisfied she'd traded one large fear for another, she dared to open her eyes. The plane hadn't moved any further. How long would this go on?

Now she *had* to go to Fire Island, she thought. No getting out of it. Maybe it would rain. Maybe Mercedes wouldn't go. That damn kid was a troublemaker. Frenchy bit her tongue. I'm sorry, she prayed again. I didn't mean that for real. I like the kid. I like everybody.

They were taxiing now, gaining speed. She held her breath, feeling as if she were in the elevator going up to the top of the Empire State Building. Her stomach turned over as they left the ground. She considered the throwup bag in the seat pocket, looked appraisingly at the stewardess, swallowed hard. The plane leveled out. Piece of cake, she said, smiling in the general direction of the stewardess, hoping the sweat on her forehead didn't show. She was glad her hair fell over her forehead today — the first time she'd worn it like this since she'd transferred down to the Village. While there wasn't anyone to pretend for in New York anymore, she would spend four days doing nothing but pretending. Perhaps she could slip away from Maman now and then . . .

"You may now unfasten your seatbelts. Please note the non-smoking sign is still lit." The man beside her took a briefcase out from underneath the seat. Frenchy left her seatbelt on, but slumped a little. She turned toward the window and looked out on huge white clouds. Holy shit, she breathed, shrinking back into her seat. She was on *top* of the clouds.

A few hours later, Frenchy arrived, shakily at the airport. She was alive. She was exhilarated. And proud of herself for surviving the first half of the trip. The stewardess' warm smile had said goodbye. Was it especially warm toward her? She had read a gay novel about a stewardess. Then she saw her mother and brother and sister-in-law. She stood taller, and feeling like a visiting dignitary, checked her stride and walked for Maman. What would Maman think if she reappeared walking like a Mack truck!

"Hello, hello, hello," everyone was saying at once and kissing her. Her mother, tears in her eyes, was babbling in French.

Outside the terminal it was hot. Frenchy wished her brother could have arranged this trip for winter, when the New York streets were turning gray with snow and beginning to look like dog kennels. But still, she thought, trying to look everywhere at once out of the windows of Serge's car, it was nice to get away for a few days.

She wasn't exactly lonely in her small apartment. She saw Pam now and then, had been back out to Jessie and Mary's, had seen Lydia once more. There was always the bar. And Marian from the Bronx A&P had been down to visit a couple of times. Still, at night, when she turned out the light, there was never anyone beside her.

Why she had no longer had any desire to sleep with girls, she didn't know, but there it was. It was kind of nice in a way. Like she was waiting for the right one. Or the right time. Drifting.

Her brother's kids were pointing out palm trees, the water that seemed to be everywhere, strange buildings. Frenchy had pictured Serge in a big old brownstone, or at the least, a three-story house like Jessie's or Edie's. But this house was weird — low and a pink color. Small from the outside, but huge inside.

What a new world — surrounded by strange trees and flowers, insects that seemed a foot long, and lizards. Frenchy wished she were here with someone, someone who counted, to share it all. She decided to write a letter, tell someone about it. But who?"

"Dear Lydia," she wrote that night, sitting alone in the kitchen. The kid would get a kick out of a letter, hearing about strange places.

"It must be nice," she wrote, "to live with people who know who you are. I mean, my family loves me, or they think they love me, but I know they're loving a me they want me to be. In your house you know your mother is gay and you love her anyway. You can all be yourselves.

I guess I wanted you to know how good that is in case you never thought about it.

"I'm thinking," she went on, "of telling my family I'm gay. At least my brother. So let them kick me out if they can't take it. I got my ticket back to New York. I don't need a family. I think it's nice to have one, but only if they're really your family.

"It's real pretty down here with a lot of sunshine and bright colors. Not so much like New York. It's summer here. And hot. Like our summer. I'm real tired now, but will tell you more tomorrow."

The next night after the household had settled, she sat in the kitchen again. "It's funny how kids grow up different," she continued. "Here you are playing drums because you have a mother who thinks it's cool, while my two nieces take piano lessons they hate. When I ask the older one if she ever thought to take up drums she says no, that's for boys. I told her about you, kid, and she says you must be a tomboy. I wanted to smack her one for thinking that is a bad thing to be.

"There's a lot of what my mother calls foreigners around Tarpon Springs, but I laugh when she says that because she talks French and calls other people foreigners! They're Greeks. We had lunch at this Greek place. Let's you and me find a Greek restaurant in New York next time you visit me. OK Kid?

"So we walked around the docks, not big ones like in the City, but more like Fire Island. I guess I'll see you there next. I'll tell you a secret, I'm nervous about going there because I haven't seen your mother in so long.

"There are so many boats it feels like I'm on the Staten Island Ferry, being downtown here. Maybe I'll go fishing with the kids the last day. Only the boys fish but maybe if the little girls see me doing it they'll do it too. Boy would I like to go out in a boat myself. Someday we'll all be rich and have one of those fancy yachts I see around here right?"

Frenchy's brother came into the kitchen as she was finishing the letter. He didn't look like the father of five kids, only like her brother: small and dark-haired, heavily muscled and with a dark beard. Serge had worked over-time because a machine at the plant had broken down. Greasy and tired, he sat down across from Frenchy and began wearily to shovel into his mouth the supper his wife had left in the oven, alternately swigging from a beer bottle.

This was the moment, Frenchy thought, to tell him. She thought about Serge's beautiful new home, with its swimming pool and carport, his big important job, his very normal, well-brought-up kids, his nice, but kind of washed-out wife. Only a couple of years older than Frenchy, his wife dragged around half-dead all the time. Why would any woman want to be straight?

Serge finished his meal, wiped his mouth on the back of his hand. He smiled at her, "So, Gen, you having a good time? You glad you came? You're making Maman very happy. Five grandchildren aren't enough for her, she wants you too."

"Yeah," said Frenchy slowly. "It's nice to be down here. Must get boring, though."

"Why?"

"It's not New York."

"You're right there. But with a houseful of kids, a wife, a mother, overtime and keeping up the pool and yard — who needs New York?"

"I guess you don't."

"So where do you want to have the wedding? Here or up north? It would be cheaper down here." He grinned. "Just kidding, Gen. Don't look at me like you want to kill me. You're pushing thirty. Ain't you never going to do it?"

"No," said Frenchy firmly. She opened her mouth to tell him why.

"Well, I guess I done enough work for two, eh?" He laughed, lifting his beer. "You want to be a spinster, be one. Maman worries, is all."

Frenchy could see a queer sister was the farthest thing from Serge's mind. What good would it do to tell him? Besides, wasn't this terribly personal? Would *he* ever tell *her* anything about his life beyond what she could see? She got up in disgust. "Thanks, Serge. I won't need a place to go. I can take care of myself."

"Can you?" He smiled, obviously not believing her. "Good."

If only she were in her butch clothes, she thought. Maybe he'd believe her then. She stalked off as if she were wearing them, but by the time she'd settled in the living room she'd calmed down. He meant well. He just didn't understand that there were women who didn't need men. If she told him she was gay he'd feel really bad. So far as he knew he really was important, essential in the world. After all, he owned his wife, his kids, didn't he? He was certain he was indispensible — that was why he took on so much responsibility, to prove it. She got under the covers of the sofabed and stared into the darkness, hearing the steady whirr of the air conditioner. It makes him feel important, like a man. She shrugged. He could have it, he could have it all. After two more days she could go home.

"Hi, Lyd," she wrote the next night. "I decided not to tell my brother last night. I can't see telling him anything I don't have to. There's something about telling it to a man, even my brother — he might never forgive me because it would hurt his pride, me not wanting a man. Maybe I shouldn't even say that. Maybe you'll want a man someday yourself. I would still like you.

"We went to Spring Bayou today which is part of Tarpon Springs and a beautiful part. I can't get used to all the palm trees. How can America be so different in so many places? We are real lucky to be Americans where it's easier than some places to be queer and it's so beautiful.

"What I like best is walking downtown in Tarpon Springs past all the markets. It reminds me of New York. Yes I am homesick already. Families run the stores and everybody works in the store from mother to father to kids. Wouldn't I like a business like that. Funny, about America, you learn the only way is up and then you get there and it's too high, you don't want it. Let me be one of the little people. It helps too having good friends like you kid. Tomorrow's the last day and then I can come home. It's kind of nice, living in a family like this. Don't get me wrong, I can handle living alone okay. I don't even get lonesome, but I can see what's good about having people around you who care. And like I say, it's important they know who you really are. What you want out of life. How you understand things because of the way you are.

I'm going to sign off now and get some shuteye.

Love ya kid,
Frenchy Tonneau

By the next evening Frenchy felt drained. They had driven up the coast for a picnic. It had been a long, confusing day full of kids, a tiring irritable grandmother, and the empty chatter of Frenchy's sister-in-law. All Frenchy wanted to do was go to bed and stay there until she had to go to the airport. Then her mother cornered her in the kitchen.

"Genvieve, you are taking care of yourself, no?"

"Yes, Maman," she said, her defenses down. She had not been as careful as she once was with her mother, now that her tolerance for hiding herself had disappeared. Alone with her mother for the first time, she felt as if once more she were wearing too-tight patent leather shoes and a starched crinoline.

"Why, then, are you so thin?" Her mother pinched her arm.

"Ouch!"

"There should be enough there so that doesn't hurt! No, Genvieve?"

"Yes, Maman."

"What do you eat?"

Frenchy rolled her eyes at this impossible question. "Whatever I want."

"Three meals a day?"

"*Oui.*" Damn. She would not talk French to her.

"And the girls? You still play cards with them?"

"Yes, Maman."

"Any boyfriends?"

"No."

"You are smart, *mon petit chou.* They are no good. Give you babies, then run away, die."

Frenchy sat down at the kitchen table. She did not meet her mother's eyes, but listened more intently.

"Except Serge. A good man. Stays with her. He will live to enjoy grandchildren . . . to take care of you."

So this was where she was leading. The poor woman, so tired out from her day, yet forcing herself to stay up and assign care of the daughter she could no longer care for.

"I don't need nobody taking care of me," Frenchy mumbled.

"You say that now. When you are old, what then?"

"I'm putting money away."

"Money! Always money. What good is money when you are alone? An old lady alone in New York City? Not for my child."

"I won't be alone."

"Who then? Who will care for you?"

How difficult it was, sometimes, to keep this from her. How happy her mother would be if she knew there would be someone, that she may even have found her. That she might even have a daughter of her own soon. Her mother would like the laughing, outgoing Lydia. "Maman, it's okay. I will not be alone," she reassured her.

"So I thought when I was young. He died."

Frenchy did not point out that even if she married, there was still no guarantee that anyone would take care of her, no guarantee her own man wouldn't die, too.

Maman said with a bit of contempt, "I don't know why you live in Greenwich Village."

She felt a flash of the old fear. Did her mother suspect? She watched her, but the aging woman across from her was slowly shaking her head in the dim light from the stove, staring sadly at the table.

Her resentment grew. She wouldn't ever again live away from her real life to please anyone.

Frenchy asked herself, what can I do? She'll worry if I tell her I'm gay, she'll worry if I hide it from her. Her fists were so tight her nails began to cut into her palms.

"It's the children, Genvieve. It's making children who fill your world." Her mother looked up at her. Her glasses glittered with reflected light. "No one is as important as your own blood. Once there are people in this world of your own blood, you have ties no one can cut."

It was Frencny's turn to stare at the table. Oh, yeah? she thought. How much would common blood mean, Maman, if you knew I was queer? How much would you love me then, Maman? Maybe she could love her queer-child, still, or love the shadow of that child she could salvage from the truth. But could it ever be the same as a mother's love for a child who embraced her own ways? There would be hurt — Frenchy had not chosen her way to live. There would be fear — Frenchy would be punished for being herself by the god her mother believed in. Wouldn't there be a thousand subtle rejections of the queer-child's ways? Assuming people were straight was a habit to straights. Maman was a straight like any other. Even should she open those arms wide to Frenchy, wouldn't there be a shudder deep inside at the touch of the queer-child?

She needed to be welcomed for who she was. Yes, she needed someone, she needed people. What had she been learning all these years but who her own were, how to touch them, how to let them touch her and how to let them bind themselves to her?

No, Frenchy decided, she didn't need this old woman and her blood-brood, this worried, needy old woman who claimed her for her own, who had only what she had created: an illusion of her daughter. She would not dispel that illusion by giving her her real self.

But oh, she longed to cry in her mother's arms. Frenchy's fists loosened as she strove to control her breathing, to keep from crying. She longed to hear Maman say, "Ah, I knew all along and it is fine, my daughter. Difference — I welcome it. I cherish you for it. I am proud of you."

Gently, Frenchy walked the sighing woman to her bed, and left the room so that her mother could change into her nightclothes without her daughter watching.

She felt weighed down by rage and frustration. Her mother was confused, hurt by Frenchy's silence. And even knowing how much she had spared her, Frenchy would always bear this guilt. And how tempted she was to blurt it all out. Wouldn't the unburdening be worth the pain? The whole world believed it was wrong to be what Frenchy was. Couldn't she at least tell her mother the world was wrong? But how hard this had been for her, herself, how long it had taken her to learn it.

"Genvieve!" her mother's loud whisper came, just as it had in the Bronx for so many Saturday nights. Frenchy had hurried, then, to change quickly into the person her mother expected. Genvieve had never existed. Even the illusion of her was gone, burnt up in a few short months of freedom. She lived nowhere but in Maman's mind. And heart.

Let her dream of a daughter to kiss goodnight, Frenchy thought, striding into the living room. Frenchy Tonneau is alive and well and sleeping on the couch. She lit a cigarette, something she'd never done in the same house with her mother before. Staring through the picture window at the dark night sky that curved over Florida, and over New York City too, she thought of the women she would be returning to in New York the next day and how bound she was to them.

* * * * *

The reds and yellows of her embroidered jacket the only brightness under the dull, rain-laden sky, Frenchy lounged against the railing by the ticket booth at the Bronx Zoo, one foot behind her on the bottom rail. It was all she could do to keep from pacing. Instead, she lit cigarette after cigarette, experimenting with different poses and ways of holding the cigarettes. If Marian didn't get there soon, she feared they would have to talk in a doorway to escape the rain — and things would to be too close for comfort.

She had decided, on her return flight from Florida, to tell Marian she was gay. Maybe because she'd never told this to anyone straight before. Maybe because she hadn't told her mother. Was she somehow seeking her own mother's acceptance by telling another straight mother? Maybe she was just plain sick of hiding it.

Finally her friend came in from the street. Frenchy

remained where she was, giving Marian the full effect of who she was. Nothing would be hidden today.

"Hi, Genie," Marian called.

Frenchy lifted one hand in greeting, still carefully casual.

"What's all the excitement about? Sorry I'm late." Eagerly smiling, Marian stood before Frenchy, her face innocent, and open. She was still youthful, but her figure was starting to go. Unlike Mercedes with whom she found herself comparing almost every girl she saw these days, motherhood had stretched and thickened Marian.

"Needed to talk to you, Mar," Frenchy answered, pushing off the railing and leading Marian to the walkway. "Want to look at some animals?"

"We really *are* going to the zoo!"

Frenchy smiled at this despite her tension. "You like the zoo?"

"I like the idea of going with you." Her smile warmed Frenchy who suddenly felt Marian's reaction would be positive. "Instead of the kids, that is," Marian finished quickly.

Turning away from her as they began walking, Frenchy tested her own reaction to the idea that Marian was giving her signals that she wanted to come out. Once she would not have doubted that she was in love with Marian and would gladly have complied. Now, she wasn't so sure. Marian was pretty, and only a couple of inches taller than Frenchy, but her looks did not make Frenchy long for her. It would be pleasant to make love to her, but Frenchy doubted she would let Marian be *her* lover. They had good times together but, though Frenchy had learned passion was not the heart of a relationship, she sought a spark, something more than a comfortable feeling.

Marian was studying her face as they walked. Frenchy looked at her and smiled nervously.

"What is it, Genvieve?" Marian asked encouragingly,

slipping a hand under Frenchy's arm.

Poised on the edge of saying it, Frenchy allowed herself another moment of indecision, trying to predict Marian's reaction and trying, too, to prepare herself for it.

"Marian, I'm gay," she said, exhaling, filled with relief. For the first time in her life she'd said it, let it out, refused to hide, had escaped her own silence — but she felt as if she had jumped off a cliff and now hung suspended.

Marian stopped, her smile still in place. Frenchy grew even more hopeful. Marian's hand slipped from her arm and Frenchy now began to feel as though she were falling.

A hand raised to touch her mouth — as if to stifle a scream — her eyes not surprised but filling with horror, Marian stepped away from her. Stepped away, turned, and began to walk hurriedly down the path.

Her first impulse was to stamp out her cigarette, whirl around and leave in disgust. But she couldn't. Marian had been her friend until a moment ago.

She began to follow Marian, feeling little now but determination. Marian had to understand. It was so simple, Did she think Frenchy was trying to seduce her? Marian had disappeared from sight, but as Frenchy rounded a bend she saw her far ahead, running. Why was she heading further into the park if she wanted to get away? Frenchy had a quick, intuitive thought that Marian was running, not from her, but from herself.

She cut across the grass. Marian, in her panic, didn't see her until Frenchy had almost reached her. Then Frenchy caught up with her, got in front of her, blocking her.

"Get out of my way. You — you —" Marian's face was ugly with hatred. "Hypocrite!"

"Hypocrite?" Frenchy was astonished at the word.

"Pretending to be my friend!"

"I wasn't pretending, Marian, honest. I wanted to be your friend. That's all. I didn't want to do anything to you."

Marian was crying now, her shoulders heaving. Frenchy longed to comfort her, but didn't dare touch her.

"You're a fraud."

"Why am I a fraud when I just told you exactly who I am so we could be better friends?"

"I don't want to be *any* kind of friend with a queer."

Frenchy was disgusted, but determination won out. "Why not? You were friends with me before you knew."

"I know. I even let my *children* near you."

"Listen, Marian," Frenchy said, planting her small body, hands on her hips. "I never touched you, never came on to you. I don't molest kids. I don't give a good goddamn what you do and with who — tell me what difference it makes who I do it with?"

"You're sick."

"No way. I'd be sick if I tried to be something I'm not. I'm tired of that kind of living."

"You're unnatural. God will punish you."

"Seems like somebody *is* punishing me, making me talk to such a dumb chick."

They walked in silence for a while, Frenchy kicking roughly at some stones while Marian averted her tear-stained face. Maybe it would pour rain, thought Frenchy, and they could part. She could give up. She glared quickly at her friend and saw she'd at least stopped crying.

"Marian, if I wasn't gay I wouldn't be me. And you liked *me.*"

"You tricked me."

"I never pretended to be straight. You knew I didn't go out with boys. You knew I moved to Greenwich Village."

Marian began to cry again and pushed Frenchy away. It did begin to rain and Frenchy stood under the downpour. She followed as Marian began to walk.

"I never said I wanted you to go to bed with me," she called, "I just wanted you to understand."

Marian's blonde hair was soaked and hung limply toward her shoulders, the curl stretched out of it. The colors in Frenchy's jacket grew even brighter in the darkness. Frenchy was surprised at her own patience, her fortitude. They had walked in a circle that brought them back to the animals. Marian stopped in the sheltering overhang of a cage. Frenchy stood outside in the rain.

"You'd think I was one of them — those tigers," Frenchy said, throwing a wet hand in their direction. "You'd think if they let me out I'd devour you. You'd think you wanted me in there."

Head lowered, Marian stood quietly. Frenchy felt that a struggle was being fought in Marian, and hoped some part of Marian wanted to listen to her. She stared at the woman she once found so attractive who now stood there, her charm washed away as if by the rain.

Suddenly Marian shrugged. Frenchy's heart leapt with hope.

"It's where you and your kind belong," spat Marian, and turned and walked toward the exit from the park.

Frenchy felt beaten. She walked to the rail outside a cage and gazed at the splendid animal inside. Who judged that either of them should belong in a cage, she wondered. The tiger certainly disagreed about her fate, and dreamed of escape. But here, in the world of the judges, she was safer in a cage. They would kill her uncaged. From indoors came another tiger, another brightly colored, stubbornly warring beast who paced briefly, then growled menacingly at Frenchy before collapsing heavily against her companion. Frenchy was glad, if they had to live caged, that they at least had each other.

* * * * *

It was still pouring rain when she left the subway and she arrived at Pam's place drenched and sneezing, near tears. Pam took her in and wrapped her in a huge pink towel, gently taking her clothes off under it. Too dulled by emotional and physical fatigue to care about anything but warmth and comfort, she gladly gave up her key so that Dorene could get her some dry clothes, nor did she mind when it was bathrobe and pajamas. But after a bowl of soup, some coffee and a piece of homemade cake, and one too many isn't-she-adorables, she shrugged Pam off.

"She's feeling better now," Pam teased, and Frenchy had to smile.

Pam picked up her latest drawing. "What do you think of this, Frenchy?"

She looked silently at the two women in the drawing, one dressed in jeans and T-shirt, the other naked in her arms. Both had short hair, but the one in clothing was slightly more dominant. Frenchy smiled. "It's sexy," she admitted, glancing shyly at Pam.

Pam looked very pleased. "Now," she said, "are you going to tell us what happened? Or are we just a repair shop, here to put Frenchy Tonneau together again?"

Frenchy looked at her old lover and at Dorene, who had been working with two pieces of clay, and held both up to show her: halves of an egg.

"I told Marian I'm gay. She ran from me." Frenchy began to pace as she spoke, wrapping her robe more tightly around her, feeling silly marching around in pajamas, yet comfortable. "I felt like it was hanging over my head with enough people. Like my family. At least I could tell *her*. Shit," Frenchy said, whirling on them in disgust, "at least my family wouldn't of run away. I don't think."

"It happened to me once like that, too," said Dorene, "and it may not be over for you." Dorene put the clay egg down, now intact, but with the shadow of a crack showing. "Mine wasn't. It was my sister, Vera. I was seventeen, she was eighteen. I'd just come out and I was all excited, here I'd found the love of my life. We were going to live together in Greenwich Village and be rich and famous and live happily ever after. I was so full of it all, I was busting to tell someone. Vera got it. She was engaged and as sure and full of her life as I was. After I told her she stopped talking to me just like that." She picked up her egg and crushed it with her hand. "Nobody noticed, though. We weren't home much, either of us, and they were all excited about her wedding. I went to the damn wedding."

The clay began to resemble a tiered wedding cake. "Then it was just me at home. Vera moved off Long Island." She crushed the cake as she had the egg and began again. "Till she came home with a broken nose. She needed to talk to someone then. Do-rene understood. Sistah Do-rene was all sympathy. I helped her get her straight self together again, get her divorce and, finally, get her married again. This time to a better guy. So far." Her hands were still. "But she never ran from me again, Frenchy. We're better sisters now than we ever were. She learned it wasn't so important what I was as what I had inside me. She came back."

"So you think I ought to just sit on it?" Frenchy asked.

"It worked for me," Dorene advised.

"Why don't you stay with us? I'll make you dinner," Pam said.

"No, I'm tired. I got to go upstairs. Thanks," she said, rising and gathering her clothes. "Thanks for everything. I feel better. You're right, Dorene. I should just sit on the Marian thing. If she gets over it she'll call. Otherwise I don't have time for her."

"You stay warm," said Pam, straightening the collar on Frenchy's robe.

Chapter 10

Fire Island
Summer, 1967

Summer came, dripping moist heat. Instead of being anxious about going to Fire Island Frenchy looked forward to getting away from the heat for a day.

Her life seemed to hang as heavily about her as the still air. She was very aware of her age, and felt as if her life was standing still and would do so until she died. Her days were a comfortable round of work and the bars, broken by frequent explorations of the City from the base of her tiny perch in Greenwich Village. Girls didn't interest her except as friends: she still wanted none in her bed. Yet she was bothered by desire; her dreams were filled with the pleasures Pam had shown her. She knew she could go to Pam and Dorene for sex. But even if she could over-come her aversion to a threesome, she knew that wasn't what she wanted. Nor did she want just Pam. She would hate herself, even if Dorene said she didn't mind. They might *think* it was okay with them, but she knew better. It had to bother anyone deep down inside.

A few days before the picnic Lydia called.

"I'm calling about Saturday. Are you still coming?"

"Sure thing, kid," Frenchy assured her, reaching for a cigarette, but deciding she was too hot to smoke. "I got the day off and everything."

"Great. Listen, Esther will be there! Remember I told you she ran away? She's coming back tonight!"

"That was some long vacation."

"Remember how nobody knew where she was and we were scared she ran off with someone else? It turned out she left a note for Edie on her bed! Edie couldn't bear to go in Esther's room, but *I* finally went in there," Lydia said proudly, "and there was the note."

"So where did she go?"

"Home to North Carolina. She stayed with her mother and father, saw her old friends and stuff. She's all fired up about civil rights down there and might go back to work on it."

"And leave Edie again?"

"They don't know how to work it out yet, but boy is Edie glad to know Esther still wants to be with her. And so am I."

Frenchy realized her depression had lifted. Maybe this was what she needed, to see people she cared about. Her solitude might have some purpose if she came out of it appreciating her friends more. "So who else will be there?"

"Um. Me. Edie and Esther. Jessie, Mary, Beebo. She

came over here once. She's a lot of fun too. Did you know she used to play drums?"

"Beebo? Can she see to play them through the dark shades?" Frenchy laughed. It would be good to see old Beebo again.

Lydia giggled with her. "I guess so. She plays a good drum. Besides, I asked her." She dropped her voice almost to a whisper. "You can't tell this to anybody, okay? She doesn't want anybody to know, even my mother. But you're different."

Frenchy felt greatly complimented. "What?"

"Beebo wears the shades because something's wrong with her eyes. She might go blind, she thinks."

Oh, Beebo, Frenchy groaned inwardly. "Why doesn't she want us to know?"

"I guess she thinks you won't like her."

All alone with *that*, Frenchy thought. We're so alone inside ourselves. "Okay. I won't say nothing, but you tell her to *tell* her friends."

Lydia continued with her list of who was going. She paused, briefly, then added, "And of course, my mother."

Frenchy stubbed out her cigarette. It was for sure then. She'd thought Mercedes might chicken out. Half-hoped she would. "What are you guys bringing?" she asked, steadying her voice.

"Edie said to tell you to just bring you."

"Some prize," muttered Frenchy. "How about beer or something?"

"I don't know, wait." Lydia covered the phone. "You can bring some if you want, but we're going by car, we can carry more. Ma says we'll get there around ten." Lydia laughed into the phone. "Edie said we'll hang my teddy bear from the beach umbrella so you can find us!"

As she finished dressing, Frenchy pushed Saturday to

the back of her mind. She knew Beebo was at the bar, getting quietly high, as she did every night. As long as she had to pretend to know nothing about Beebo's problem, she couldn't do much, but she could at least be something more than a drinking partner. She could be a better friend. Maybe Beebo would like to come over to her place and listen to old records some night.

It was still hot when she reached the street, but night had come. Why hadn't she ever thought of asking the gang up to her place? The bars were a habit she might want to cut down on. But she couldn't worry about that now; her mind was on getting to Beebo.

* * * * *

Saturday came, sunny and clear. Jessie had parked the car by the ferry dock and the group spilled out of it like so many clowns at a circus, arms full of supplies. They walked to the ferry overladen and laughing and glad to be among so many other gay people. They staked a corner of the boat for themselves and piled up their goods like immigrants from a straight city.

Only Mercedes moved away from the group. She found a sheltered spot toward the front of the boat, stretched out her legs in the sun and half-dozed, her mind caught in anticipation of seeing Frenchy again. Fantasies took her over.

A moment before the ferry departed, a small figure in jeans and a brightly colored embroidered jacket ran on, clutching a cooler and gym bag. She found a seat in the back of the boat between a gay male couple and some straights who were looking around the boat with excited curiosity. Frenchy half-dozed beside them, hardly aware of anything but the warming sun and the sea-scent enveloping her. It occurred to her that Edie's crowd might be on this boat, but she wasn't yet ready to see them.

She allowed a sense of Mercedes' nearness to grow in her, as if the voyage out were a voyage to her. She relaxed, and indulged herself in daydreams of Mercedes.

* * * * *

We're sitting across from each other in the living room at Edie's. Edie and Esther are in the kitchen making dinner. We're making the kind of talk you can when your mind isn't on it. I try not to look at Frenchy too much 'cause I can't hide how turned on I am. She doesn't look at me either. My voice is getting gravelly like it does when I make love. Maybe she remembers this from the bar where she tried to make me. Whatever the reason, she looks up full at me. The stereo's on; but I don't care what's playing. I can't look away from Frenchy anymore. We stand up and move together somehow. We're facing each other, so close I can smell the scotch she's been drinking, so much more appealing than Candy's sweet rum. It's intoxicating.

We touch lips, almost not touching. Move away, back quick. The feel of the soft special flesh of her lips melts me. My knees are weak, I reach out for her, I'm afraid to touch her. We catch hands, begin to move our fingers. I slide mine up the outside edges of her hands. She curls her fingers against my palms and moves them back and forth. I feel myself dripping. We stand like this, kissing lightly, a long, long time, knowing Edie and Esther were standing in the kitchen doorway a couple of times, then seeing them make out in the doorway until we smelled food burning. A cry, giggles, noise and pots and pans.

We break away, smiling, still touching hands. Frenchy's eyes are shining, glazed with passion and happiness. My high cheekbones feel like they're even higher in my face and my eyes are little slits, closed by our slow burning. We sit together on the couch, not touching at all, staring at each other. It's going to be okay, I think, and feel my face re-arrange itself back to normal.

* * * * *

Birds flying. Their wings, thousands of them, beating, flapping, making a scary noise. The ground rumbling. Mercedes' lips like a flower opening under mine.

I stand taller, wanting to take charge. Remember she doesn't like that and relax into myself again. Funny, when I do that I get lost in her lips. Smooth, velvet, full, then suddenly wet, searching for me, wetting me. I open mine just a little. We balance our whole lives against each others' lips, she leaning on me, me on her, both away, both to-gether. I feel Edie in the doorway behind us. I should stop, she'll see me, short and helpless against how I feel about Mercedes. I hear kissing sounds and know Edie's not interested.

Hands like baby birds in a nest, moving against each other. Her little hands around mine. Moving up and down till I can't keep mine still. Touching her palms like they're someplace else, like I'm making love to her. Ooh, I can't stop and her lips want more and more. I move my lips side to side, against hers.

Flaming lips, eyes, hands. Her breath hot, hot, hot in my mouth. The light bright, so bright through my closed lids I'll never be able to see the same again. The smell of burning all around us. I don't care if we turn to cinders that blow away together. Mercedes.

She pulls back, smiling. I realize Edie burnt something making out with Esther. The house is filled with all our heat. I smile back at Mercedes, almost not able to see her, *she's such a dark, blurred shape in the brightness that fills my eyes.*

* * * * *

Frenchy, naked, unbuttons my shirt slowly. My breasts feel all of a sudden important, swollen out of their own size. I want to be crazy sexy. I want to shimmy them against Frenchy's hands. When we get my pants off I want her to pick me up so I can wind my legs around her hips and press myself, all open, against her. I wish our two wet parts could meet fully, rub against each other. She makes me feel the way the books say: abandoned.

I reach between her legs. She jumps when I touch her. Okay, Mercedes, I tell myself, cool off. This girl needs help. Her eyes are closed, her face looks like she's in pain. "Frenchy, you want me to stop?" "No," she says. "If this is what I got to do to get you, I'll do it."

I feel so guilty, making her do it. It's for her own good, goddamnit. But how am I going to turn her on when she doesn't want me to? I rub my breasts against her and her face relaxes a little. "Frenchy, Frenchy, I want you," I groan.

She asks, her eyes wide open, "You do?" "Don't you believe me?" "It's hard to." "Oh, I do, I do, baby," I say and reach down to stroke her again. She's damp. I feel like I just came. A little bit of dampness on this girl is more exciting than anything I've ever had done to me. I would do anything, I thought, to make her wetter. I could give her the wetness of my mouth. The thought turns me on even more. How I want her to touch me. But no, I was going to lick this. I giggle to myself, thinking I really am. I feel terribly nervous, kissing all down her flat little body, afraid she'll stop me. She has a ridge of black curly hair from her belly button down, and I get this warm thrill all through me to know something so intimate about her. I love her, love her, love her, and here I am, my lips kissing her, my tongue wetting her, my hand fighting to get in on the action too. She's wet and slippery and I can tell she's liking it because there's more moisture than just from my mouth and it's all Frenchy and me mixed up together. I'm dizzy moving my mouth around on her.

Her hips move. I feel like singing the national anthem. I lift my face to see her face and I can't because she follows me up, seeking my mouth with her body. Dear Frenchy, I thought. You're a woman, all woman and, after this, all mine.

* * * * *

I lie on the bed thinking, Okay, I'm scared. I admit it.

I feel like Mercedes is going to torture me, not make love to me. She can do anything she wants to me now with my clothes off. It's like that first scary time with Pam. I take a deep breath, wanting a cigarette.

I picture the beach at the Cape. The water is clear and endless. All around me are beautiful girls in bikinis, their bodies glowing in the sun, shiny with suntan lotion, their breasts pushing out of their halters, their hips curved inside their brief pants like a smooth mystery I want to touch.

Mercedes touches between my legs and I snap out of it. Did I want to stop, she says. No, I thought, but I don't say that. I have my butch pride. She gets busy with her mouth, then rubbing those round breasts all over me. Some muscles in my thigh begin to tighten, like they did when Pam used to do this to me — like bits of fire darting in my thighs.

The ocean swells and falls in front of me. So blue, so big. All on top of it the curves of water roll and bounce *and run in and out. The sunlight is like a yellow see-through dress on top of it.*

I look down on Mercedes who's moving like I'm making love to her. She's really into it. I guess I must be doing okay. Not being too clutzy, as Pam would say. But me naked under a woman who isn't Pam? I'm embarrassed. Ashamed, for a minute. Then the bits of fire in my thighs reach up and come together in one burning spot. Then streak up further, until they reach my heart. My whole chest feels full of flames, my head a place groans come out of.

The water rolls toward me. All the little waves come one on top of the next. Break on the shore, wash back, join the sea. The little waves get bigger. They blend into each other, more and more and more of them. They look beautiful, make me feel beautiful. I feel my chest lift, my head fall back. The one big wave they make gets bigger, bigger, till I'm scared it'll be a tidal wave. It stands over me, ready to break, and the fear drains out of me as the wave turns into a world full of blue soft water with sun shining through it.

And it rolls down over me, warm, loosening, lifts me to float in it. I'm happy, so happy and warm and safe; it takes me out of myself. I'm in it with Mercedes, but I am it. Our hearts melt inside it. Our spirits touch, I swear, I can feel it happen. And I feel such love for the woman whose mouth lifts, wet and glistening from me, whose eyes are full of love and gladness for me, whose brown body lies all warm against me while I return to my own body and use it to lift my head toward Mercedes.

* * * * *

The air was cooler on the dock than in the City. Frenchy dawdled, feeling languorous after her spate of fantasies and still nervous about meeting Mercedes before she was ready. For the first time she looked in the direction her friends were supposed to be. Could they be that small group struggling over the sands overburdened with beach supplies? She ought to go help. But she had her own to carry, she couldn't help much. Or did her hesitation have more to do with Mercedes? . . .

When she reached the dock, she saw no one she knew. These days she didn't know nearly as many kids as she once had. She thought back to her days of table hopping as if she'd been a movie star in some bygone era. Everybody had known Frenchy Tonneau. She'd been with half the girls in any bar at any one time. All those girls had settled down now, except for a few who were still looking, still eyeing Frenchy, but probably had her pegged as no good. Probably never figured her for the type to be mooning over some girl she couldn't have.

A girl she couldn't have. The sun beat down on Frenchy's head and she curiously lifted her hand to feel the heat in her hair. Once the thought of not having any girl she wanted had been inconceivable. There was no such creature. Like in the love stories, mused Frenchy, you always want what you can't have. So look at me now, seven years later. I'm not the same person. Maybe the new Frenchy could have exactly what she wants. But how am I going to tell Mercedes? How can I show her I've changed without acting like an ass?

She lit a cigarette and settled in to wait until the next ferry came. She'd make her way down the beach with a crowd, be invisible as long as she could. Besides, the hot sun felt good with ocean breeze laced through it. A gust of wind left her hair disheveled and she patted it back in place. But it didn't seem worth it to rebuild her pompadour;

the wind would just knock the starch out of it again.

* * * * *

Finally the blankets were spread, the coolers arranged, the beachballs blown up, and last but not least, the teddy bear hung from the umbrella, dangling from a piece of rope Jessie had lassoed under its arms when Lydia objected to hanging it by the neck or leg.

That kid, Mercedes thought affectionately. She won't kill a spider, an ant, and she's even kind to stuffed animals.

Mercedes looked down toward the water where everyone else had gone for a first dip. When Frenchy came, she wanted to be dressed and protected, not in a dripping, uncomfortable bathing suit with sand all over her legs. Besides, she'd just gotten her hair the perfect length for this cut and, despite the wind, she knew it looked great.

The waiting had begun; she hardly knew whether she wanted Frenchy to come sooner or later — whether it would be better to be alone or in the group when she arrived.

And then she saw she had no choice at all. In the distance an embroidered jacket was bobbing from side to side through the crowds and blankets.

How in the world do you carry all that stuff and still diddybop, she asked silently, admiringly. Her heart hurt at the sight of the small butch, her hair blowing in the breeze, her head turning this way and that looking for the teddy bear. Mercedes remembered her fantasies on the boat and lost her breath a little. Would — could — any come true? Maybe Frenchy hadn't changed. Maybe nothing, still, was possible for them. *I won't turn femme*, Mercedes pledged again, feeling a little crazy at the thought, feeling threatened and vulnerable.

Slowly, keeping her eyes on Frenchy, Mercedes slipped the teddy bear out of its rope. She could still hide it, she thought, and immediately dismissed the idea. Frenchy would inevitably find her. If only because Mercedes was going to make damn sure she did. She raised the bear in her hands over her head, swinging it from side to side until the motion drew Frenchy's eyes and she started toward Mercedes.

* * * * *

Frenchy was remembering her walk through the sand the day she'd met Mercedes long ago. How her feet had burned, how stubborn she'd been about the pain. She glanced down at the sandals Pam had finally persuaded her to buy. Why hadn't she owned a pair long before? Because they didn't fit her image, that was why. Butches didn't wear sandals. . . . When she looked up a teddy bear was swaying in the air, a pair of light brown hands wrapped around its stout body. She kept walking toward the bear casually, as if she saw Mercedes every day of her life. For real. Not just in dreams.

* * * * *

Frenchy and Mercedes stood face to face, inches away from each other, looking into one another's eyes. Frenchy was remembering that Provincetown night when she first fell in love with this face. There was still something wild about it, but it was softer, as were the eyes. Their light was different, not so distracted, pained. Had Mercedes found the peace she was looking for, without Frenchy? At the same time Mercedes was aware of a great gladness welling up inside her as she noticed a new confidence in Frenchy:

her eyes were more clear, she seemed no longer to be hiding her self. Had Frenchy gotten stronger and braver without Mercedes?

"How've you been?" asked Frenchy in that way she had of talking out of the side of her mouth.

Mercedes fought with her fear, shrugged casually and talked from the side of her mouth too. "Not bad at all. How about you?"

I've missed you, Frenchy wanted to say. "I'm doing okay," she said instead. "We got a lot of catching up to do."

"Yes. We have," said Mercedes slowly. She knew it was up to her to take the next step. Frenchy had risked last time, and lost. "I'd like to. Catch up, that is."

"Frenchy!" cried Lydia, throwing herself, cold and wet, against Frenchy. Hugging her, Frenchy looked past her at Mercedes.

"Some kid you've got here," she said, smiling and rubbing Lydia's dripping hair.

"I know. Though I don't know how, with all her Ma put her through."

"I'm sure it was worth it," Frenchy said, her arms around Lydia, still smiling.

Still clinging to Frenchy, Lydia looked from one to the other of them. "Hey, you two want to swim?"

They answered with nervous laughs.

"I just got here," objected Frenchy.

"I'm going to wait till I'm so hot I need to," said Mercedes, quickly regretting how she'd said it, not looking at Frenchy.

For the first time hope soared in Frenchy as she realized that Mercedes was embarrassed and why. So she thought of her that way too . . .

"Isn't it great here?" asked Lydia.

"Not so pretty as Florida," said Frenchy.

"You liked it down there?" asked Mercedes.

Frenchy wondered, for the thousandth time, if Mercedes had read her letter to Lydia. "It's okay. But it's not New York City."

"You're damn straight," agreed Mercedes.

They smiled at the bar phrase. "Maybe we won't have much to catch up on," said Frenchy, then worried she was assuming too much. Maybe people hadn't told Mercedes everything about her. "News travels fast in our club. Like about my trip to Florida," she explained.

Jessie, Edie, Mary and Esther had come up from the water, and all grabbed for their towels at once. "How you doing, old pal?" asked Jessie, snapping her towel toward Frenchy.

Suddenly everyone was greeting her, like the old days down at the bar. Edie hugged her. Small, burly Esther shook her hand and Mary stood in the background looking from Mercedes to Frenchy and clapping her hands excitedly.

"I'm starved," said Jessie.

"It figures!" Frenchy teased, and they all laughed and began to rummage for food and drinks.

Beebo found them and called over to the crowd from the bar, to Hermine and the two girls they were with. Frenchy's group decided to move to the larger group's site and that caused a half hour's confusion. Frenchy helped, glancing now and then at Mercedes who was in the thick of the move, and managed to avoid her eyes.

Frenchy was very glad she had come. Not only for the hope she felt about Mercedes, but also the great feeling she had seeing all her friends together.

In the midst of carrying a heavy cooler, Mercedes stopped and looked at Frenchy smiling at all the activity. Frenchy Tonneau, she said to herself, her tongue feeling the name.

Frenchy was not looking cool, even with a beer can in her hand. Her hair was a mess and she stood in such a relaxed way you couldn't tell if she was butch or not. Mercedes picked up the cooler again.

Frenchy saw her struggle with the cooler and started toward her. No. She stopped herself. No gentleman stuff. She turned away. Mercedes wouldn't do it if she couldn't handle it herself.

Noon came and with it a huge feast. Other groups had arrived, the barbeque provided by the bar was going, everyone was drunk on beer and sunshine. All the depression and heartache from nights at the bar seemed to have dissipated. Friendships were renewed, old lovers hugged one another, no one wanted the day ever to end.

Except Frenchy. There was no way to be alone with Mercedes. Both were surrounded by the crowd, and no one had seen Mercedes for so long that she had considerable catching up to do. Frenchy remembered back to the days when she'd stand outside the House of Detention with a girl, arguing that she couldn't go home with her. Now she had a home of her own — how could she get Mercedes to it?

But Frenchy too, despite the changes in her life, seemed to know everyone on the beach whether from her bar or not. Once she walked to the water's edge and hoped Mercedes would come to her. By the time Mercedes was able to break away, Frenchy had been joined by someone else.

Their energy slowly disappeared. The sun had burnt their bodies and their faces to discomfort. They had stopped drinking; Mercedes especially did not want to get drunk. Women from the bar were firing up the charcoal again for supper when quiet finally descended.

"Are we staying for supper or what?" Jessie asked her group.

"I want to stay!" cried Lydia.

"So do I," said Jessie.

Mary looked at her very red face disapprovingly. "I think you've had enough."

Mercedes said to Lydia, "You want to stay, little one?"

Lydia hung her head. "I met this kid," she admitted shyly. "She's from Jersey. I'll probably never see her again after today."

Mercedes was amused and concerned. "Can I meet her?"

"Sure! Her mother's gay too! She's fourteen," Lydia added, obviously impressed a fourteen year old would be interested in her.

Hermine shouted over from her blanket, "Let's all take a nap. If we feel like it when we wake up, we'll stay for supper!"

Activity began again, but more quietly. Mercedes got up to go meet Lydia's friend. "Can I come?" asked Frenchy, a tremor in her voice Mercedes had never heard before.

Lydia took her mother and Frenchy by the hand and led them up the beach. A tall young girl ran swiftly between the blankets to meet them.

"There she is!" cried Lydia.

She and Lydia hugged as if they hadn't seen one another for years. Frenchy looked at Mercedes. Both smiled. Both envied the spontaneity of children. Both were aware of the emptiness of their hands now that Lydia had flown from between them.

Doreatha gravely shook their hands and invited them to meet her mother. Frenchy worried briefly that Mercedes would have all too much in common with another gay mother, but the meeting was polite. Frenchy saw that the mother, also tall, was well into her forties and not Mercedes' type at all. They exchanged invitations and phone numbers and by then the girls had wandered off. Unbelievably, suddenly, Frenchy found herself alone with Mercedes.

"I'm bushed," said Mercedes. "We got up at five this morning."

"Me too."

"Want to find a place to sit for a while before we start back?"

"Suits me fine," Frenchy said coolly. Mercedes looked at her with a little of the amused love she felt for Lydia, but with a breathlessness her daughter did not inspire.

They wandered to a slightly more secluded spot and sat together looking out toward the water.

"I remember walking on the beach outside the Ace of Spades at P-town," said Mercedes.

"Do you?" asked Frenchy. "I think of it all the time."

A while later Mercedes, unable to stand the heavy silence, the promise of touch, asked, "Ever been back there?"

"No. I don't know if I want to now."

Mercedes heard her say "without you" in her mind. "I guess it wouldn't be the same." She paused, deciding what to say next, then spoke almost despite herself. "Lydia said you thought that weekend changed your life."

Frenchy went red, but Mercedes was looking away from her. Gulls cried above them. The crowds seemed far away. Frenchy began to play with the sand between them. "It did. I found out I have the ocean in my blood." She looked up at Mercedes. "My family lived by, worked on, the sea. Being up there I felt — at home. I never wanted to leave. It made me see everything different, made me feel like I was living my life in a little shell. I don't mean I figured that out right away. It took a long time." She was silent, scooping up sand and letting it fall from her hand. She said, "And of course I met you."

Mercedes knew she would hear the small whispered choking sound of those words in her mind over and over the rest of her life. She picked up some sand in the spot where Frenchy was digging and let it fall over Frenchy's hand. Frenchy stopped digging. She slowly turned her hand until she could catch the fine sand that fell on her sensitive palm. When Mercedes' hand was empty she lay it flat, palm up. Frenchy spilled the same sand back onto it, leaving her hand in the air. Like a quick bird, Mercedes' hand came up to touch Frenchy's, to brush it and fall down again. Swooping after it, Frenchy's hand fell also. The two hands lay there. The women watched them, as if they had a life of their own, as if their hands would play out their fate.

More? thought Mercedes. *Must I do more?* If only she were femme, and didn't have to initiate again. She could let her fate rest in Frenchy's next move. But she had taught Frenchy well and now it seemed she needed a new way to do things with her, a new language to speak in, to show desire. "Frenchy," she said, in her own choked whisper, "Frenchy help me."

Frenchy looked at her, at her strained eyes, her chest rising and falling as if she were out of breath. And she understood. Mercedes didn't want to be butch, she didn't want Frenchy to be butch. Like Lydia and Doreatha, Mercedes wanted them to come together equally, somehow.

Frenchy smiled. She felt light and free and wise. No longer did she dread being passive, nor did she need to restrain her desire to act.

She leaned toward Mercedes, her arms coming up as Mercedes leaned toward her, her arms rising also. They touched lips, then each other. They lay back together, relaxing into one another. How familiar it felt, how comfortable, home-like. How they fit. They lay there, melded together, their hands still, breathing together. They held together tightly. Suddenly, Frenchy began to tremble, then cry. Mercedes held her, nearly crying herself to see Frenchy let go like this before her. She stroked Frenchy, soothed her. "It's okay," she said, over and over as Frenchy murmured, "I'm sorry, I'm sorry," in her arms.

Frenchy wiped her face, moving away. They smiled, shyly, and Frenchy leaned to kiss Mercedes, used her body, her hands in ways she was used to, while Mercedes drew her down, held her close again, stroked her back. Moving against one another like the night they danced, their passion built. When they could stand it no longer they relaxed again, kissed long, gently, touched and exulted in one another until they could laugh delightedly each time they touched something new: an earlobe, an eyelid, a wrist. They had, after all, a lifetime ahead.

They sat up finally. "Hey," Frenchy said, winking, "we had such a long engagement, wouldn't you feel better waiting for the wedding night?"

Mercedes laughed and jumped up, pulling Frenchy with her. Alight with happiness, they ran toward Lydia, who was playing a giggling, clumsy game of catch with Doreatha. The three caught one another in embrace. Lydia motioned Doreatha to join them.

Aware of how they must look: the tall, dark Doreatha, the shorter, lighter Lydia, the even lighter and shorter Mercedes, and then herself, smallest, palest, Frenchy told them what she saw and they laughed.

Lydia beat a tattoo on her thighs and the three formed a line behind her as she began to snake her way through the crowd. They whooped and laughed, sang snatches of songs. A few small children joined the line, several drunken adults. They went snaking back to their blankets where Esther rose and began to sing *Oh Happy Day*. Soon a whole crowd was singing. Beebo inverted an empty cooler and began to drum loudly, while Doreatha grabbed Lydia and began to dance.

On the edge of the group stood Frenchy and Mercedes. Both cried now, gently, embracing. What long, impossible years they had lived through. How useless all their fears seemed now.

Mercedes whispered, under the noise of the crowd, "What a wonderful wedding."

The singing went on, blended with what seemed like a hundred transistor radios, while Frenchy squeezed her tightly and asked, "Can you come home with me tonight?"

"Can you stop me?" replied Mercedes.

* * * * *

After the packing up, the trek to the dock, after the long ride home, after, finally, their half-asleep bumbling toward the Morton Street apartment, their groaning climb up the stairs, Frenchy and Mercedes reached home. Sore, sunburnt, dry-eyed from the sun and wind, they simply smiled wearily like two old friends, and took separate showers. Frenchy gave Mercedes a pair of pajamas and made coffee hoping it would wake them up. They sat nodding at the kitchen table.

"Some honeymoon," Frenchy managed to say.

Mercedes yawned. "Listen, I don't mind. Really I don't." She yawned again. "We've got all our lives ahead of us. To me it'll be a pleasure just sleeping with you."

Frenchy reached across the table. "Yeah. Me too."

"What do you think, Frenchy, you think we can work it out?"

Frenchy could see Mercedes' need for reassurance under the exhaustion. "I'll stake my life on it," she said strongly. "As a matter of fact, I'll *give* my life to it."

"You don't know me very well."

"I know you have a kid and I know you been in

hospitals. So I like crazy dyke mothers. So arrest me."

"I'm just saying it won't be easy."

"Like living with me will be? You know how long it took me to be with you this afternoon?"

They nodded over the last of their coffee. Frenchy was pleased to see Mercedes carry her cup to the sink. She wouldn't be another Pam — they would have a whole set of their own problems. They walked to the bedroom.

Lying side by side, they were suddenly wide awake with the coffee and the newness of being together. Mercedes took Frenchy's hand in hers. Frenchy felt her strengthening desire for Mercedes, its heat like another blanket over her. Mercedes turned on her side, facing Frenchy. She slipped a hand under Frenchy's pajama top.

"I just want to feel you," she whispered. "To make sure you're real and here with me." Frenchy's skin was so smooth, her ribs felt so frail — as Mercedes always thought she would.

With minimal movement, burrowed into a circle of rising warmth which slowly closed around them, they began. Tentative with each other, they slipped the pajamas off their slight trembling bodies. Then they were overwhelmed by a desire that cared nothing of exhaustion, or of fears, or of endings.

Soon Mercedes leaned back. Those dark eyes beneath her, that thick black hair, the fine small body under her hands — She felt like an artist drawing a woman. Each part of Frenchy she touched came alive.

At the same time, Frenchy shivered as the cool night breeze touched her sweat. The smell of Cape Cod was in her nostrils. The sound of the sea in her ears. The motion of the waves moved through her body. Mercedes was as deeply part of her as all this.

Then Mercedes touched Frenchy very gently with one finger. Frenchy did the same for Mercedes. They brought their lips together barely touching, and kept circling with their fingers. Frenchy thought she couldn't. Mercedes pulled away a couple of times so she would not. Frenchy's lips jerked away from Mercedes'. Mercedes felt this and heard the sharp intake of Frenchy's breath. She brought herself back to that lovely little finger and pressed against it, as it once more began to rotate. She felt her own breath become uneven, her face flush, Frenchy's breath on her cheek, heard the moan, whose moan? heard the two cries together, felt a breeze come in through the window and lift them away, away, away beyond themselves.

Then shyly, her voice thick and needy, Frenchy said, "Do it again."

Chapter 11

Home Free
Summer, 1972

Frenchy left work a half hour early. She paused outside the doors of the A&P, lit a cigarette with her battered Zippo, and went off toward 8th Street, hands in her pockets. She walked head-down, partly out of habit, partly in fascination of her desert boots. These new boots had the disadvantage of not making her as tall as the old black ones, but she'd been head cashier a few years now, so her authority was recognized. And standing on her feet all day hurt less in these.

She loved her job now. Her days were not nearly so grueling as when she'd first started, when she'd expected one catastrophe after another. She called the cashiers "my girls," and she thought, protected, guided and helped them all. Her store had the lowest turnover of cashiers in Manhattan and she was damn proud of that. Some were even gay, now that she did the hiring. One of the gay cashiers, in fact, had suggested the anniversary present. As she walked, she watched the bright flash of her desert boots. She didn't need the old boots ouside work, either.

Five years today. Who would have thought it? Frenchy made her way past the shabby little shops, mourning the loss of the old neighborhood. She had joined a community association working to keep the Village as it had been. The Sea Colony and the rest of the old places were gone, but no more of this tawdry 42nd Street facade, this cheapening influence, if she could help it. She puffed up her chest as she inhaled her cigarette. She coughed. Smoking wasn't the joy it used to be. She was thirty-three, but damn if she didn't still feel like twenty-one.

Except, of course, she was calmer, and happy. Much of her old walk remained despite the new boots; she still somewhat resembled a 1950s teenaged punk, a tiny Elvis Presley. But no one on 8th Street laughed or made comments about her anymore. Was this because she was older and had therefore taken on some degree of respectability? Or did she simply come across as less brash, less challenging toward the world, having found her place in it? She dropped her cigarette and checked her hair briefly in a window. Now that she didn't train it into unnatural heights and dips, it looked pretty good all the time. She had, as of this morning, twenty-eight grey hairs. Loving the way older dykes looked, she'd tried to comb her hair so the grey would be obvious against its black background. She would have to be patient, she'd have a shock of grey soon enough.

A willowy, long-haired faggot was leafletting. "How beautiful!" he said as she passed. She raised one eyebrow and looked quizzically at him. "Your jacket," he explained. "I adore it! Did you decorate it?"

Frenchy chuckled, "No, my ex did," she said. That jean jacket Pam had embroidered so many years ago still excited comment everywhere she went.

"You ought to march in it," he said, pushing one of the leaflets on her.

"March?"

"On Christopher Street Day. To show gay strength and solidarity."

She glanced at the paper skeptically. She remembered the riots a few years back, and she'd watched the parade a couple of times. But it had nothing to do with her, a bunch of hysterical drag queens getting excited.

"Watch for the posters. This year we hope every gay in the city will march!"

She walked on. Weren't things better without drawing attention to themselves more? Gay people were exposed enough. Maybe it was okay for men who could defend themselves against cops or angry straights; maybe it was okay for gays who didn't have to worry about losing their jobs if they went to jail; but she would play it safe. If the way she lived and walked and looked wasn't enough to tell the world she was proud of who she was, then the hell with it. She'd been marching all her life.

She reached the store that sold Indian jewelry Mercedes liked. Frenchy wanted something spectacular for their fifth anniversary. They had made reservations at a gay woman's restaurant — vegetarian dishes. The cutesy little bar they had downstairs, with tiny stools and bright colors, didn't look like a gay bar as far as she was concerned, but Lydia had recommended it. When she stayed with Frenchy and Mercedes, usually a couple of times a month now that she was a freshman at Queens College, living with Edie, she'd cook vegetarian dishes to tempt them to give up meat. Frenchy insistently called herself a "meat and potatoes man."

"Woman!" Lydia would protest, but Frenchy didn't believe in these women's lib ideas Lydia was always spouting. But at least it was a lesbian restaurant.

Frenchy took her glasses from her breast pocket to see the cases and cases of Indian jewelry. Glasses! Mercedes had sent her to the eye doctor, wanting to know why Frenchy was squinting so much. She'd come home to Mercedes sheepishly, but her eyes weren't too bad. She gotten aviator-style glasses with photogrey lenses, so half the time she fancied she looked like a Florida-bound pilot in sunglasses.

There, she said to herself. That piece, a mottled brown stone like an eye, in the middle of a silver sunburst. It looked like Mercedes. Like those warm brown eyes and the light she'd brought into her life.

She watched the saleslady giftwrap it, thinking of the miracle of Mercedes. Sure, she got kind of weird now and then. Sure, sometimes her moods were erratic. It used to scare Frenchy because she hadn't understood. Frenchy had grown up gay in a straight world — but Mercedes had been gay *and* poor, a teenaged mother, *and* Spanish. All that had made her crazy. Now, like Frenchy, she fit somewhere, and had relaxed more; and she'd started talking to a woman Lydia had heard about in college, a lesbian who counseled lesbians.

She was passing the vacant lot where the Women's House of Detention once stood when she remembered to pick up cat food for Chiquita and Banana. How horrified Lydia had been at the names they'd chosen for the two kittens they found in a box in the hallway last year. She'd said they were racist and sexist! Mercedes had laughed and said, "You want us to call them that, instead? Racist and Sexist?" The sheltie was named Ace of Spades. Frenchy's life wouldn't have been complete without Sunday mornings with Ace and Mercedes, walking to get the papers and baked goods.

Drooping under the two bags of canned food she now carried, Frenchy made her way slowly toward W. 12th Street. The apartment had been a find, but Frenchy had missed her shabby little place on Morton Street, had missed Pam and Dorene. But soon afterwards, Pam had moved to California and Dorene had been with her new lover almost as long as Frenchy with Mercedes. Pam had had a couple of shows out in California. She'd wanted Frenchy to fly out there to see her. But five hours of hanging over America? Pam had to be nuts. It was bad enough she had to go trooping down to Florida once a year.

Frenchy struggled up to the second floor and fumbled for her key. Mercedes opened the door. "I thought you'd never get here!"

Mercedes was glowing. She wore jeans and a white shirt, with a red corduroy vest. Her ears were pierced and a few attractive lines had grown along her face, crazy lines, she called them, but her face with its high cheekbones had the same taut surface. She took a bag from Frenchy.

They put groceries away, laughing together, and pulled each other close. "Happy anniversary, babe."

"Happy anniversary to you, Mer."

Ace gently pushed her nose between them and they patted her as they hugged. A cat jumped to the countertop, landed with one foot on a can, half lost her balance and sent the can spinning to the floor. "Banana!" yelled Frenchy, startled. The cat leapt off the counter and ran to the next room. Ace skittered out of the way. Chiquita sat calmly on the sunny windowsill cleaning a paw.

As Frenchy dressed, Mercedes stocked the cat food shelf. At this milestone in her life, she reflected, she and Frenchy had been happy for five years, sex was getting even better, she'd had her job even longer than her relationship, she'd lived in the same place almost five years, and Lydia was doing well in college, even if she did have some strange ideas.

She looked around the kitchen. Frenchy did most of the cooking, even when Jessie came to dinner and teased her about doing a femme's job. Mercedes felt at home in the unusually large, well-lighted room. Whenever their friends came over, the kitchen was where they settled. She'd put up orange curtains, the tablecloth was yellow, they'd laid their own orange and brown linoleum. That was the great thing about living with Frenchy, who wasn't afraid to fix things around the house any more than Mercedes. They shared their tasks and kept house together in a way Mercedes never imagined two butches could.

She relished her happiness. Sometimes she still felt crazy, but now she had the counselor to explain, very simply, without a lot of bullshit about her early childhood, how and why she reacted the way she did. She was beginning to wonder if she shouldn't take the counselor's advice and get involved with one of the groups Lydia belonged to, a group of Puerto Rican and black and Asian women who talked about their common experience.

"How do I look?" asked Frenchy, parading in her jeans and shirt.

Mercedes tried to figure out what she was supposed to be noticing. "Handsome, as usual," she finally said.

"You didn't notice my new T-shirt!" Frenchy complained.

"Of course!" said Mercedes. Frenchy had taken to wearing different colored T-shirts under her shirts instead of a bra, like the longhairs. How much more daring new young lesbians were about how they dressed, with their long hair and buttons everywhere. In earlier days, Mercedes and Frenchy had to wear at least three items of apparel of their own sex in New York or risk getting busted for cross-dressing.

"You look great," Mercedes said, shepherding Frenchy

out the door. They ran down the stairs and walked arm in arm, grinning.

Later, through the twilight streets of New York, Mercedes and Frenchy walked home. Full of food and wine, they walked slowly. Mercedes kissed Frenchy beside the fountain at Washington Square. "Just look at that lavender sky!" she said, remembering another time, under another lavender sky, with another woman who helped her on her way to health and to Frenchy.

"What are you thinking about, Mer?"

"Just remembering before you. How bad it was, how slowly I came back alive."

Frenchy, too, had her memories. She was thinking of the day Pam had spotted her on the bench they'd just passed.

Frenchy opened the apartment door and reached for the light.

"Happy anniversary!"

Their shock lasted only a second, but in that second Frenchy had time to fear: had the police come to round up all the queers at last? But then she saw Lydia, their friends, the cake, the gifts. In joyous surprise they turned to one another, eyes wet. Before they were swept up in their friends' attentions, Frenchy looked meaningfully toward their bedroom with its large soft bed, and Mercedes smiled at her. "Later," she whispered, squeezing Frenchy's hand.

Lydia, a few inches taller, stooped to her mother, and Frenchy saw them as they would look in another thirty or forty years: Mercedes white-haired and wrinkled, her body perhaps slightly bent from lifting heavy patients, even smaller than she was now, again in the embrace of this tall, healthy-looking daughter who had nothing to hide from them as they had nothing to hide from her. She sighed, shrugging off her embroidered jacket. From behind her, someone took it, and she turned.

"Pam!" she shouted. "How in hell did you get here?"

"I was coming to New York anyway, so I came early for your celebration!"

Frenchy laughed, and surprised Pam by taking her arm and leading her to the bedroom. "Look," she said. "I wanted you to see this." The framed drawing of the woman in jeans and T-shirt making love to her naked partner hung over the bed.

Pam gave a joyous little cry and hugged Frenchy.

"We thought about hanging up work by some famous artist, but yours is still my favorite."

"Far out! I'll send you more."

"Hey, Frenchy!" called Jessie from the living room. Frenchy excused herself.

Lydia was leading her mother into a dance. Mercedes looked sheepishly up at her browner, longer-limbed daughter until the song was over.

"Happy fifth!" cried Jessie, applauding.

Frenchy found herself next to Edie. They hugged. "It seems like such a short time since Lydia would use my basement to practice drums," said Edie. "What a short five years! Happy anniversary." Edie kissed Frenchy's cheek.

"How's it going with you two?"

"We still have our ups and downs. I'm finally learning not to be hurt by what Esther needs to do. I know she loves me, but she's got other fish to fry. Did she tell you she's starting a lesbian chorus? There are five of them already."

"What about that civil rights stuff? Her spending every summer down there just to register voters?"

"This is what she believes in. Now Lydia has her going to this women's group at the college. They talk about women and racism. Lydia wants me to start a group of white women who want to do something about racism, but I'm not really a group person." Edie laughed. "I'd rather have dinner on the table when Esther comes home tired from her groups."

Frenchy said, "I sure wouldn't mind talking to somebody else with the kinds of problems we have — a white girl with a Puerto Rican."

Edie shook her head, looking amused. "I've lived such a sheltered quiet life. Now, little by little, the world is gathering in my living room. All these women Lydia brings to me, Esther brings home . . ."

Lydia was dancing again, with Beebo, leading her carefully. Beebo had finally admitted her failing sight. Several months ago, all of a sudden, Hermine and Beebo had announced they were in love after years of being friends. Beebo had wanted her all along, but hadn't wished to tie any girl to her blindness. The first thing Herm had done was steer Beebo to an uptown specialist, and new hope through a surgical technique.

Hermine was setting up a table of food with Mary. Completely in her element, Mary dished and ladled. She still wore too much makeup for Frenchy's taste.

Frenchy scooped up the excited Banana, who'd been streaking through the room, and asked Esther, "Going south again this summer?"

"I'm not sure. Some people down south think when they get north they're going to be home free. But there's a lot of work I could be doing here. Maybe I should stay."

"That would make Edie happy."

Esther looked at Frenchy, amused. "You can stop taking care of her, you know. I'm not going to run away from her. I feel like for our relationship to fail now, everything I believe in would go down the drain. Everything from how I love to how I want to live."

Frenchy was studying her red pinky ring. "I guess I didn't think about it like that, exactly, but maybe I have been worrying about her."

"I *know* you have. For years. I worry about *Mercedes*, too. She may not have been my lover, but she *is* my sister."

"I wouldn't hurt Mercedes for anything in the world!"

Esther turned to Frenchy, hand extended. Frenchy took it and shook it solemnly. "That's just how I feel about Edie," Esther said. "A woman like that, who can understand me needing to leave for a while so I can come back to stay. Not that they *need* us to take care of them," Esther said, looking at Mercedes and Edie dancing together.

"Well, they might of once," concluded Frenchy, "but I guess they do okay for themselves now."

Their friends began to leave. Frenchy thought: if they come for us tomorrow, we've had this, and we'll be stronger for it.

She remembered being afraid to touch in the streets. Getting kicked out of PamPams for greeting friends. Being herded into bars or having nowhere at all to go. How it felt not ever being able to tell your family who you were. Playing guessing games with straight friends. Marian's face when Frenchy had told her. The catcalls in the street. Hiding her clothes. Being afraid.

It all added up, she thought. It's all made life damn hard. And it's all still out there.

Lydia and one friend were left. "I think you're great," said Lydia, bending to kiss them. "Congratulations."

"Thanks for making us such a nice party," said Mercedes.

"Yeah, well, we have to make our own celebrations, you know," said Lydia. "Nobody else will." She stopped halfway to the door. "By your twenty-fifth anniversary, if everybody helps, stops hiding in their closets and gets out and works or marches or tells their stories, we'll be able to have your party — in Times Square if we want!" Everyone laughed but Frenchy.

"I don't think I'd want a party in Times Square..." Frenchy faltered. "I don't know exactly how to say this, what I want to say —"

"Go ahead, Frenchy, I want to hear," said Lydia. "I think you've always had a lot of courage, living like you did when it was so much harder to be a lesbian."

"Courage?" mused Frenchy. "I guess so. If courage is being scared and going ahead anyway." She laughed. "If that's courage, then I'm courageous every day of my life, being afraid to be gay and doing it anyways."

She struggled for more words. "I'd settle for being able to get off the subway at Times Square instead of Fourteenth, for walking like a dyke, like myself, from Forty-second Street to Eighth Street, and not being afraid of a thing. Is that too much to ask?" She took Mercedes' hand. "Maybe by our twenty-fifth it won't be." Her voice shook, but she stood tall in her low boots, she stood proudly in her home next to her lover, like a swashbuckler in the prow of her ship, going out to sea.

A few of the publications of
THE NAIAD PRESS, INC.
P.O. Box 10543 ● Tallahassee, Florida 32302
Phone (904) 539-9322
Mail orders welcome. Please include 15% postage.

BEFORE STONEWALL: THE MAKING OF A GAY AND
LESBIAN COMMUNITY by Andrea Weiss & Greta Schiller.
96 pp., 25 illus.   ISBN 0-941483-20-7 $7.95

WE WALK THE BACK OF THE TIGER by Patricia A. Murphy.
192 pp. Romantic Lesbian novel/beginning women's movement.
                                      ISBN 0-941483-13-4   8.95

SUNDAY'S CHILD by Joyce Bright. 216 pp. Lesbian athletics, at
last the novel about sports.   ISBN 0-941483-12-6   8.95

OSTEN'S BAY by Zenobia N. Vole. 204 pp. Sizzling adventure
romance set on Bonaire.   ISBN 0-941483-15-0   8.95

LESSONS IN MURDER by Claire McNab. 216 pp. 1st in a stylish
mystery series.   ISBN 0-941483-14-2   8.95

YELLOWTHROAT by Penny Hayes. 240 pp. Margarita, bandit,
kidnaps Julia.   ISBN 0-941483-10-X   8.95

SAPPHISTRY: THE BOOK OF LESBIAN SEXUALITY by
Pat Califia. 3d edition, revised. 208 pp.   ISBN 0-941483-24-X   8.95

CHERISHED LOVE by Evelyn Kennedy. 192 pp. Erotic
Lesbian love story.   ISBN 0-941483-08-8   8.95

LAST SEPTEMBER by Helen R. Hull. 208 pp. Six stories & a
glorious novella.   ISBN 0-941483-09-6   8.95

THE SECRET IN THE BIRD by Camarin Grae. 312 pp. Striking,
psychological suspense novel.   ISBN 0-941483-05-3   8.95

TO THE LIGHTNING by Catherine Ennis. 208 pp. Romantic
Lesbian 'Robinson Crusoe' adventure. ISBN 0-941483-06-1   8.95

THE OTHER SIDE OF VENUS by Shirley Verel. 224 pp.
Luminous, romantic love story.   ISBN 0-941483-07-X   8.95

DREAMS AND SWORDS by Katherine V. Forrest. 192 pp.
Romantic, erotic, imaginative stories. ISBN 0-941483-03-7   8.95

MEMORY BOARD by Jane Rule. 336 pp. Memorable novel
about an aging Lesbian couple.   ISBN 0-941483-02-9   8.95

THE ALWAYS ANONYMOUS BEAST by Lauren Wright
Douglas. 224 pp. A Caitlin Reese mystery. First in a series.
                                      ISBN 0-941483-04-5   8.95

SEARCHING FOR SPRING by Patricia A. Murphy. 224 pp.
Novel about the recovery of love.   ISBN 0-941483-00-2   8.95

DUSTY'S QUEEN OF HEARTS DINER by Lee Lynch. 240 pp.
Romantic blue-collar novel.   ISBN 0-941483-01-0   8.95

PARENTS MATTER by Ann Muller. 240 pp. Parents'
relationships with Lesbian daughters and gay sons.
                                               ISBN 0-930044-91-6   9.95

THE PEARLS by Shelley Smith. 176 pp. Passion and fun in
the Caribbean sun.   ISBN 0-930044-93-2   7.95

MAGDALENA by Sarah Aldridge. 352 pp. Epic Lesbian novel
set on three continents.   ISBN 0-930044-99-1   8.95

THE BLACK AND WHITE OF IT by Ann Allen Shockley.
144 pp. Short stories.   ISBN 0-930044-96-7   7.95

SAY JESUS AND COME TO ME by Ann Allen Shockley. 288
pp. Contemporary romance.   ISBN 0-930044-98-3   8.95

LOVING HER by Ann Allen Shockley. 192 pp. Romantic love
story.   ISBN 0-930044-97-5   7.95

MURDER AT THE NIGHTWOOD BAR by Katherine V.
Forrest. 240 pp. A Kate Delafield mystery. Second in a series.
                                               ISBN 0-930044-92-4   8.95

ZOE'S BOOK by Gail Pass. 224 pp. Passionate, obsessive love
story.   ISBN 0-930044-95-9   7.95

WINGED DANCER by Camarin Grae. 228 pp. Erotic Lesbian
adventure story.   ISBN 0-930044-88-6   8.95

PAZ by Camarin Grae. 336 pp. Romantic Lesbian adventurer
with the power to change the world.   ISBN 0-930044-89-4   8.95

SOUL SNATCHER by Camarin Grae. 224 pp. A puzzle, an
adventure, a mystery — Lesbian romance.   ISBN 0-930044-90-8   8.95

THE LOVE OF GOOD WOMEN by Isabel Miller. 224 pp.
Long-awaited new novel by the author of the beloved *Patience
and Sarah*.   ISBN 0-930044-81-9   8.95

THE HOUSE AT PELHAM FALLS by Brenda Weathers. 240
pp. Suspenseful Lesbian ghost story.   ISBN 0-930044-79-7   7.95

HOME IN YOUR HANDS by Lee Lynch. 240 pp. More stories
from the author of *Old Dyke Tales*.   ISBN 0-930044-80-0   7.95

EACH HAND A MAP by Anita Skeen. 112 pp. Real-life poems
that touch us all.   ISBN 0-930044-82-7   6.95

SURPLUS by Sylvia Stevenson. 342 pp. A classic early Lesbian
novel.   ISBN 0-930044-78-9   6.95

PEMBROKE PARK by Michelle Martin. 256 pp. Derring-do
and daring romance in Regency England.   ISBN 0-930044-77-0   7.95

THE LONG TRAIL by Penny Hayes. 248 pp. Vivid adventures
of two women in love in the old west.   ISBN 0-930044-76-2   8.95

HORIZON OF THE HEART by Shelley Smith. 192 pp. Hot
romance in summertime New England.   ISBN 0-930044-75-4   7.95

AN EMERGENCE OF GREEN by Katherine V. Forrest. 288 pp. Powerful novel of sexual discovery.   ISBN 0-930044-69-X   8.95

THE LESBIAN PERIODICALS INDEX edited by Claire Potter. 432 pp. Author & subject index.   ISBN 0-930044-74-6   29.95

DESERT OF THE HEART by Jane Rule. 224 pp. A classic; basis for the movie *Desert Hearts*.   ISBN 0-930044-73-8   7.95

SPRING FORWARD/FALL BACK by Sheila Ortiz Taylor. 288 pp. Literary novel of timeless love.   ISBN 0-930044-70-3   7.95

FOR KEEPS by Elisabeth Nonas. 144 pp. Contemporary novel about losing and finding love.   ISBN 0-930044-71-1   7.95

TORCHLIGHT TO VALHALLA by Gale Wilhelm. 128 pp. Classic novel by a great Lesbian writer.   ISBN 0-930044-68-1   7.95

LESBIAN NUNS: BREAKING SILENCE edited by Rosemary Curb and Nancy Manahan. 432 pp. Unprecedented autobiographies of religious life.   ISBN 0-930044-62-2   9.95

THE SWASHBUCKLER by Lee Lynch. 288 pp. Colorful novel set in Greenwich Village in the sixties.   ISBN 0-930044-66-5   8.95

MISFORTUNE'S FRIEND by Sarah Aldridge. 320 pp. Historical Lesbian novel set on two continents.   ISBN 0-930044-67-3   7.95

A STUDIO OF ONE'S OWN by Ann Stokes. Edited by Dolores Klaich. 128 pp. Autobiography.   ISBN 0-930044-64-9   7.95

SEX VARIANT WOMEN IN LITERATURE by Jeannette Howard Foster. 448 pp. Literary history.   ISBN 0-930044-65-7   8.95

A HOT-EYED MODERATE by Jane Rule. 252 pp. Hard-hitting essays on gay life; writing; art.   ISBN 0-930044-57-6   7.95

INLAND PASSAGE AND OTHER STORIES by Jane Rule. 288 pp. Wide-ranging new collection.   ISBN 0-930044-56-8   7.95

WE TOO ARE DRIFTING by Gale Wilhelm. 128 pp. Timeless Lesbian novel, a masterpiece.   ISBN 0-930044-61-4   6.95

AMATEUR CITY by Katherine V. Forrest. 224 pp. A Kate Delafield mystery. First in a series.   ISBN 0-930044-55-X   7.95

THE SOPHIE HOROWITZ STORY by Sarah Schulman. 176 pp. Engaging novel of madcap intrigue.   ISBN 0-930044-54-1   7.95

THE BURNTON WIDOWS by Vickie P. McConnell. 272 pp. A Nyla Wade mystery, second in the series.   ISBN 0-930044-52-5   7.95

These are just a few of the many Naiad Press titles — we are the oldest and largest lesbian/feminist publishing company in the world. Please request a complete catalog. We offer personal service; we encourage and welcome direct mail orders from individuals who have limited access to bookstores carrying our publications.